Unexpected Metamorphosis

Alissia Roswell: Book One

Tianna Holley

Unexpected Metamorphosis

Copyright © 2013 by Tianna Holley

ISBN 978-0-9894908-0-1

Published by:
Canton Walk Publishing

Other Books in the Alissia Roswell Series

Unexpected Metamorphosis (2013)
Unexpected Entrapment (2014)
Unexpected Peril (2015)
Unexpected Beginning (2016)
Unexpected Legends (2017)

Chapter 1

Alissia Roswell pulled the key from the ignition, filling the air with silence. There, in front of her, stood the aged oak tree near the pond on her family's property. Her gaze went to the base of the tree, where a deep hollow concealed her teenage diary.

She suffered many things during those years and often sought refuge beneath the winding branches of the great tree, crying herself to sleep in her frayed and faded sleeping bag.

Within days of her high school graduation, Alissia left her childhood home in Jesup, Georgia, vowing she would never return. On her drive out of town, she visited the tree and wrote her last diary entry. She then placed the journal back in its secret location, thinking she would never see it again.

Although usually not an emotional person, she suddenly found herself fighting back tears. She let out a small, sarcastic laugh as she reminded herself she had not cried once since returning to town—not even at her father's funeral.

It had been less than a week since her older sister called with the unexpected news. While sobbing uncontrollably, Janet told Alissia that a man fell asleep at the wheel of his SUV. He swerved into their father's lane, killing them both instantly from the impact. Alissia could only imagine her father's eagerness on the first day of deer season, as he drove toward the hunting club in the early morning hours.

Though she loved him dearly and was very close to her father as a young child, all that changed after an accident at work left him on disability and without a job at the pulp mill. Within a few months, he began to drink, and her loving father suddenly turned into a stranger she greatly feared.

He often searched for her while in one of his drunken rages, and at the age of twelve, Alissia quickly learned how to hide the bruises he left behind. His love turned to hate, and the father she knew died that year.

Before the accident, he taught her to ride a horse, hunt, fish, and so much more. One of her favorite memories consisted of her sitting quietly next to him in a tree stand, eagerly awaiting a deer to step into the clearing. Her father, full of pride the day she killed her first deer, bragged about it to everyone he knew.

Alissia let out a heavy sigh as her thoughts turned to the events of the past few days. Although she occasionally talked on the phone to her mother and sister, she had not seen them in over ten years. After seeing her mother's tears, Alissia now felt somewhat guilty for abandoning her. Maybe she should have flown her mother in for a visit, and maybe she had been wrong for turning her back on her mother and sister.

Her parents divorced shortly after Alissia left town, and her father moved into a mobile home on another area of their property. Neither of them ever remarried, and although they no longer lived together, her mother often cooked and cleaned for him. Even after all he did to the family, she continued to love him.

Alissia left her SUV and walked to the tree, where she gently stroked her fingertips along the bark. She learned early in life not to trust anyone, and during her teenage years, she pulled away from everyone to become a loner. Struggling to make sense of her life, this tree soon became her only friend.

"I missed you," she said softly, pulling her hand away. Looking down at the hollow, her desire for the diary grew strong. She scanned the area for a stick to help drag it out, and shortly thereafter, she sat at the base of the tree holding a dirty, old ammunition box.

A mix of emotions flooded through Alissia as her mind took her to places she had not been in many years. This time she did not fight the tears, and it took a moment before she wiped the last one from her face. She then took a deep breath and pried opened the box.

Suddenly, a strong force propelled Alissia into a rapid spin, as if being sucked into a tornado. White lights spiraled around her, and her stomach lurched as a sharp pain rose up within her body. A roaring, train-like sound drowned out her screams. Becoming lightheaded, she closed her eyes, just as her body slammed into an unyielding, rock-solid surface.

*****

Barely conscious and in severe pain, Alissia tried to focus on the distant sound of dripping water. She noticed an earthy scent coming from the rough surface beneath the side of her face. Opening her eyes, she scarcely made out a cavernous wall in the dimly lit surroundings. With her pain too great to move, she soon lost consciousness again.

Alissia's eyes shot open, as her back arched in pain from a raging fire coming from within her body. She tried to scream before her mind shut down, pulling her back into darkness.

The next time she regained her awareness, a strong, throbbing pain filled her body. The sound of voices in a foreign language spoke over her, as if in a heated discussion. With blurry vision, she vaguely saw the outline of two small faces staring down at her.

Suddenly, they stopped talking and spun around. One of them whispered something before they scurried away.

Shortly thereafter, dirt and rubble flew up in front of Alissia, as a man abruptly stopped a few feet away.

"Alexandra?" he asked, panting heavily.

Not waiting for an answer, he rushed to her side and fell to his knees. He scanned the full length of her body. Then he gently turned her over and gasped.

"I'll get you out of here," he said, his voice trembling. As he gently scooped her body into his arms, her weary eyes closed, and darkness consumed her.

Chapter 2

Alissia awoke to a strange, blue glow surrounding her. With squinting eyes, she stared at a group of blue, glowing ivy flowers that climbed up the poles of the four-poster bed she rested in. Looking up, she saw the stars of the night sky shining through a tinted, clear ceiling.

The sound of two men talking outside the room caught her attention, and her brows furrowed in concentration as she tried to make out their unfamiliar, thick accents.

"What are you going to do?"

The other man let out a long breath before answering, "I really don't know."

"Are you going to tell the Eldership?"

"I don't think that's such a good idea. What I did was illegal, and it wouldn't solve anything. They'd be more focused on what I did than on trying to help her. You know how strict the laws are."

"What are you going to do about work?"

"I told Darius I had a private matter I needed to take care of. I didn't tell him anything else, so I'm sure he'll be checking on me."

"Oh, you're awake," said a cheery, female voice.

The room suddenly brightened by glowing, white ivy plants growing along the stone walls. The unfamiliar woman walked to the door and knocked lightly before stopping at the side of the bed to smile down at Alissia.

She appeared to be in her late twenties, with some freckles decorating her pale face. Small, blue flowers adorned her long, auburn brown braid, matching her simple, ankle-length dress.

The two men entered the room, and Alissia immediately noticed their strange clothing and knives strapped to their leather belts, reminding her of a Renaissance festival she once visited.

Tall and rugged, with unruly, light brown hair, the first man looked as though he spent most of his time working outside. His weathered face welcomed Alissia with soft and kind eyes.

The second man wore much finer clothing, with his thin, white poet's shirt tucked inside his dark pants. Short, chestnut brown hair topped his head. He joined the woman at the side of the bed and asked, "How are you feeling?"

Alissia eyed each person in the room. "Where am I? And what happened?"

The man at her side gave a reassuring smile. "My name's Grady." Motioning to the others, he added, "This is my cousin, Anika, and her husband, Langley. This is their home. You appeared to be hurt badly when I found you, so I brought you here for help."

The woman joined her husband at the foot of the bed, and they both gave a warm smile as Alissia looked their way. Turning her attention back to Grady, she asked, "Why didn't you take me to a hospital, and how long have I been here?"

She looked down at the unfamiliar, oversized shirt she wore.

"Oh, I did that," Anika quickly assured. "You were completely covered in blood and dirt, so I had to remove most of your clothing before washing you. I promise the men weren't in the room, and the lights were low." With a confused look, she added, "You don't seem to have any bruises or wounds from your fall, so I'm a little confused as to why your clothes were covered in blood. Can you tell us what you remember?"

Alissia looked up at the stars, and her forehead wrinkled in thought. "I was at the pond when something happened. It felt like I was being pulled and ripped apart while being flung through the air." She closed her eyes and winced as foggy memories filled her mind. Opening her eyes, she turned to Anika. "I don't remember much after that, but I remember the pain. It was as if I was being burned from the inside. Like my blood was on fire."

With a worried look, Anika asked, "That's all you remember? Do you remember when Grady found you?"

Looking up at the man standing next to her, another memory flashed through her mind. "I remember voices in a foreign language."

Anika turned to Grady with a puzzled look. "I have no answer."

"What's going on? How did I get here?" Alissia asked, a bit harshly, trying to mask her fear.

"You need to explain everything," Anika said, looking at Grady. She walked out of the room, and her husband gave a reassuring smile to Grady before following, shutting the door behind him.

Looking uncomfortable, Grady carefully sat down beside Alissia, but when she began to sit up, he quickly stood.

"Let me help you," he said, grabbing another pillow.

She let him place the pillow behind her back, and he sat down on the bed again. Her stomach felt somewhat itchy, and she lightly scratched at it.

"I really don't know how to tell you this, Alexandra—"

"Alissia," she interrupted. "My name used to be Alexandra, but I changed it years ago." Concealing her fear, she asked cautiously, "How do you know my old name?"

He nodded. "I promise I'll tell you everything." After a thoughtful pause, he continued, "Think of one earth, yet two very different realities. You were brought here by something similar to an invisible rope. Do you remember opening the box holding your journal?"

"Yes."

"Well, someone from our reality set up a connection to it. It was triggered once you opened the box, and you were pulled here. This has never happened before, and it appears as if it wasn't easy for you."

His words only added to her confusion, and she frowned skeptically. "Why would someone bring me here, and who did it?"

His body shifted, either for extra comfort or from tension. She could not tell.

"Some people in our reality study your reality in hopes of learning more about it," he said calmly. "We call them Watchers, and they can get small glimpses of where you're from. It's our belief that our Creator formed our realities from the same world, and there're a lot of similarities between them. Our people even seem to speak some of the same common languages. If I recall, you call your language English; whereas, I speak Norian. Although it's similar, you don't know many of our words, and I'm sure I don't know a lot of yours. And, obviously, our accents are very different."

He paused, searching her eyes for understanding, and she nodded for him to continue.

"I'm not a Watcher, but I took some classes many years ago. In a watching class, we learn how to open something resembling a window looking into your reality. Since our power source is from the gift of nature, we can only open windows in natural settings in your reality. It seems our most prestigious school is located in a place that's very natural on your side, because it's a lot easier here to open a window than it is in some areas. There are some places we can't seem to open a window, no matter how hard we try, and we believe this means there isn't enough nature on your side. Maybe that's where your side has a city. Does this make sense?"

Not really believing him, she decided to go with it and answered, "Kind of."

"Once a Watcher opens a window, it records what's on the other side. We can pick up traces of emotions, and that gives us a hint of where to set up a new window. There has to be nature on your side, but we also don't want to open a window where there aren't any people."

He stared at the door for a moment. When he turned back to Alissia, she thought she noticed a troubled look on his face. He gave a slight smile before continuing, "During my training many years ago, I was partnered with Agro. When we were given our assignment to open a window, we opened one near the tree you often went to."

He looked back at the door and said, "The window recorded, and we were to give a written report on our observations. However, after watching the first few recordings, Agro and I agreed we didn't want to share anything about you with our class. It seemed too personal, so we agreed to open another window for the school and close our connections to yours.

"During this time, Agro's life was filled with trouble," he continued, turning back to face her. "Things had never been that good for him. His mother was sick for many years, and his father started doing experiments, hoping to save her. He was desperate, and he began to do illegal things and was eventually arrested. During the trial, Agro's mother died. He blamed the elders for her death and believed she would have gotten better if his father had never been arrested and taken away. He thought the elders should have had mercy and released his father so he could continue to work on a cure. Instead, they decided his father was guilty and sentenced him to life in prison."

He paused, and a look of sadness came over his face. "Agro soon withdrew from everyone at school. I thought he was depressed from all that was happening, and I worried for him. I would go out of my way to find him and talk to him, and I often visited him in his room."

Grady let out a sigh and gave a weak smile before continuing, "He managed to finish his training and moved to another city on the other side of the mountains, and I was chosen for a position within the Eldership here in Allure." Meeting her gaze, he explained, "Allure's one of our biggest cities, and it's where the main offices are located."

Alissia nodded, and he looked down and began to fiddle with a button on the sleeve of his shirt. "Seven years passed, and I lost all contact with him. Then, one day I received an unmarked package at my home."

Dropping his hands into his lap, he looked back at Alissia. "I was shocked to find it was a stack of notes and recordings from your window, and it contained a jade, which is very rare and expensive. It's also illegal to have."

Looking intently into her eyes, he said, "Although I closed my connection to your window, Agro continued to record the window and experimented with it."

He paused for emphasis before dropping his gaze, and Alissia felt herself swallow apprehensively.

"He tried to open it so he could enter your reality," Grady continued. "His notes indicated he found a way to get a slight tear into the window. He couldn't send anything physical through it, but with the help of the jade, he was able to send out a surge of power and link it to your journal.

"He decided if he couldn't send anything through the window, maybe he could *pull* something through it. The link was sort of like a rope that could pull you through the opening, and he hoped your body would make the hole bigger."

Grady's eyes scanned her covered frame, and he shook his head. "I could only imagine what something like that would do to you, and I realized after watching the recordings that he did this after you left home. I feared you'd return one day, so I tried to find a way to break the link."

He frowned, turning his gaze back to the door. "All my attempts were unsuccessful, and all I was able to do was attach a power surge to a ring so that I would know when you were pulled through." Turning back to her, he added, "By this time, it had been several years since you left, so I hoped it would never be triggered."

He held up his right hand to show a fresh burn mark around his ring finger. "This morning, the ring sent a surge of power, and that's when I went to find you."

"And how am I going to get home?" she asked, still not ready to believe him.

With a troubled look, he answered, "I don't know. The jade's low on power, and even if it weren't, I don't know how to send you back. I have to study the window first. I also don't know how safe it would be for you to go back through. When I found you, you were covered in blood. You looked as if you were on the verge of death, and I didn't think you were going to survive. We still don't understand what really happened to you and why you don't seem to be physically hurt now."

She closed her eyes and let his words sink in, trying to think of who would go through the trouble of playing such a cruel joke on her. Her eyes went to the glowing flowers in the room and the handcrafted furnishings, and she wondered how much money they cost. The peculiar flowers looked real, not plastic.

"What do you mean by recordings?" she asked, testing him. "What exactly did you see?"

He looked down at his hands in his lap. "I closed my side of the window after the first two times of seeing you; however, I watched all of his recordings when I received the package."

"And what exactly did you see?"

Not looking up, he answered, "The recordings were of you at the tree."

"How long? A few months? A year? And could you see and hear me?"

He cleared his throat uncomfortably and turned to meet her gaze. "I could see and hear you, and the recordings were for a little more than two years. They stopped the day you said you were never coming back." He looked down at his hands again and said softly, "I know about all the things your father did to you. I saw your tears, and I heard everything you said, even the whispers."

Alissia closed her eyes and turned away, wishing she could disappear.

In the beginning of her father's abuse, she often cried in front of others, but after a couple of years, she realized her tears only showed a weakness that never got her anywhere. Already an expert at hiding bruises, it only took a little more effort to conceal her true emotions, and Alissia soon learned how to look completely unaffected as she took each of her father's blows.

To everyone around her, she suddenly appeared cold and unemotional, and she took great satisfaction in their confusion. She vowed to herself long ago that no one would ever have enough control over her to cause her pain or see her weak, and she had kept that vow ever since.

The angst inside Alissia grew even stronger as a certain private memory came to mind. Wrapped in her sleeping bag under the tree, she had cried for what seemed like hours. As she prayed out loud, the reality of her weakness began to seep in, and her prayers soon turned into self-condemnation.

She had been on a date earlier that night, and although she continuously said no to his advances, he did not listen. In the end, he got what he wanted, and she blamed herself for allowing it to happen. She went to her diary that night full of guilt and shame, hating herself.

Alissia did not know how she would ever be able to face the man sitting next to her. Even if she did regain control of her emotions, he would be able to see right through them. No matter how unemotional she appeared, he knew the truth. She was capable of being hurt, and she hurt deeply.

After a while, she opened her eyes and turned to face him. He still sat next to her, staring down at his hands.

"That was over ten years ago," she said flatly. "I was a different person back then. I also thought I was alone during those moments, so don't expect me to act like that now."

He turned his head to look at her. "I don't expect you to act in any way, and I don't expect anything from you. I only want to help you with this situation. I destroyed the recordings and will never mention anything on them to anyone." After a short pause, he added, "I am curious about one thing, though. Why'd you come back?"

"My father died," she answered unemotionally.

"I'm sorry to hear that." He stood. "Would you like to try to get up now, or would you rather I leave you here to rest some more?"

"I want to get up," she said, feeling the need to go to the bathroom.

He nodded. "Then I'll have Anika help you."

Not long after he left, Anika came in and provided a robe. "I'll go to Allure tomorrow to buy you some new clothes, but considering how small you are, I may have a challenge."

Alissia followed the woman into a small sitting room with a fireplace and cozy furnishings. A beautiful, stone wall divided the room from the kitchen, and a pleasant, floral scent filled the air. Strategically-placed stones, glowing from within, brightened the room, along with glowing blue and white ivy that grew along the walls, stopping at the polished wood floor.

Anika chuckled. "I don't know anything about your reality, but from the look on your face, I'm starting to believe there's a big difference."

Alissia nodded and looked up at the night sky through the tinted, clear ceiling. Then she followed Anika to an exotic bathroom with water flowing down a stone wall, landing in a small, in-ground pool. A blue glow came from the bottom of the pool, lighting the water. Non-glowing flowers of various colors surrounded the stone pool, and at one end, something resembling a large lily pad with a pink flower floated on top of the water.

As Alissia stood at the edge of the pool looking down, Anika pointed to the floating flower. "That's a purifying flower. It absorbs all the impurities and dirt, so the water stays clean at all times—no matter how dirty my husband gets from the horses."

Alissia looked up in confusion. "This is where you bathe? You use the same water?"

"This is where we bathe," Anika answered, grinning. "The purifying flower keeps the water clean, so we don't have to change it." She pointed to the glowing ivy on the wall. "Those are called bellas. If you place their roots in water, they glow. We keep these lit at all times, but we'll pull the ones from your room out of the water during the night so you can sleep."

She pointed to a clear, gallon-sized container at the edge of the pool and a small bottle beside it, each half filled with grey powder. "If the water isn't hot enough for you, sprinkle a little of that over the rock in the bottom of the corner."

Anika picked up a few bottles from beside the pool. "You can choose one of these to wash your hair and body. They're made from a variety of scented and purifying flowers." She pointed to another bottle near the edge of the pool. "That one's for hair removal, so you *don't* want to use it."

She set the bottles back down and walked over to a small table beside a sink and mirror. Picking up another container, she said, "This is what you put on afterward to moisturize your skin." She opened the cabinet beneath the small table and pulled out another bottle. "You can have this. It's new. We use it to clean our mouth. You swish it around your mouth for a bit before spitting it out."

Once Anika finished explaining how to use the plumbing, she gave Alissia another large shirt before leaving the room.

The sound of water trickling down the wall, as well as the sight and smell of the flowers, soothed Alissia. She walked to a mirror in the corner of the room and stared at her reflection, frowning at the dried blood in her long, dark hair.

After removing what little clothing she wore, she dipped her foot into the warm water and smiled. She slowly stepped into the pool and squatted, fully immersing her body. When she came up, she noticed some blood floating to the roots of the large flower, as if being sucked into them.

Out of curiosity, she went to the corner of the pool and looked down to find a stone surrounded by a pile of other stones. She felt heat coming from the one in the center, and she guessed the wall around it kept people from accidentally stepping on it.

Alissia picked up the small bottle and opened it before pouring some of the powder over the center stone. She set the bottle back down and watched as the water bubbled around the stone, sending heat into the pool.

She smelled the scented soaps, and after making a selection, she scrubbed her hair and body with the help of the washcloth. Then she sat on a ledge in the water and leaned back into a relaxing position, where she closed her eyes and considered the events of the day.

After drying off, she wrapped the towel around her body and walked to the mirror, where she brushed her hair. When she realized she did not have a blow dryer or straightening iron to tame her wild, natural curls, she frowned and set the brush back down.

She cleaned her teeth, and then she removed the towel and hastily began to apply scented lotion to her body. As her hand rubbed across her stomach, she felt something strange and looked down to find two small handprints branded into each side of her abdomen, directly beneath each rib cage.

Staring into the mirror, Alissia placed her hands over the child-sized prints. Her butterfly tattoo on the upper, right side of her navel and the new handprints nearly covered her entire stomach. Although she did not feel any pain as she pressed down on them, they slightly itched. Her brows furrowed in worry, as an uneasy suspicion grew within her.

She quickly dressed in the shirt and robe Anika left, making sure to tie the robe securely. Even then, she felt uncomfortable over her lack of clothing in front of strangers. Her Aunt Marge often told her as a child, "Girl, whatever bait you use will determine the type of fish you catch." After being raped, she knew what type of man she did *not* want to catch.

As soon as she stepped out of the bathroom, her stomach growled from the smell of food, and she made her way to the kitchen to find the men sitting at the table. As Anika poured their drinks, she noticed Alissia and said, in her thick accent, "I timed it just right. Everything's ready, and you must be starving. Eat as much as you like, and make yourself at home."

Grady got up from his seat and pulled out a chair next to him, and Alissia sat down. Anika brought steaming bowls of soup and fresh bread to the table before joining them.

Alissia smiled politely and listened as they told her about the ranch Langley and his father managed and lived on. She learned that people traveled from far distances to buy horses from them. Anika went to school to become a teacher but left her career two years ago when she married Langley, and she now contributed to the family ranch.

After two bowls of soup and some bread, Alissia's hunger no longer distracted her, and she abruptly interrupted the conversation. "How did I get the handprints on my stomach?"

An uncomfortable silence filled the room as the others looked at each other in confusion.

"I have two handprints branded on me," explained Alissia, "and since they're completely healed, I'm wondering how long I've really been here, who did it, and why."

"Can you show them to us?" asked Anika.

Alissia glanced at Langley and Grady before turning back to Anika. "I'll show them to you."

They left the confused men at the table and walked back into the bedroom. In an attempt to be modest, Alissia got back into the bed and pulled the covers up to her stomach. She then opened the robe and lifted the shirt she wore. Anika ran her fingers along each handprint.

"I noticed these earlier but thought they were something you did before coming here. They appear to be severe burn wounds, but they're completely healed, as if they've been on your body for a while. Are you saying they're new?"

"I've never seen these in my entire life," Alissia stressed. "You didn't do them?"

Anika shook her head. "No. How about the butterfly? Is it new, too?"

"No, I've had that," Alissia responded.

With a worried look, Anika said, "I really think the men should see this. I've never seen or heard of anything like this before. Is it possible for them to look at it?"

Alissia nodded before Anika left the room, and she soon returned with both men following. They all stared down at the handprints in confusion, and Grady began to rub his fingers along them. Pressing down, he asked, "Does it hurt?"

"No, it's just a little itchy."

His fingers traveled to her tattoo. "How about the butterfly? Was it there before?"

Her body stiffened as he touched her hidden scar, and she quickly pulled the blankets up to cover herself.

"It was already there," she snapped, knowing he knew the reason for the scar, yet the person that had given it to her never even knew about it.

She and her father had been alone one night when he grabbed a small knife during one of his drunken rages. He managed to stab her with the tip of it before she took it from him, and the next morning, the only evidence left of the night before was her father's black eye and swollen lip.

She was certain he did not remember what happened, and by then, her mother was used to not asking questions. Alissia kept the wound tightly bandaged until it healed, and she never told anyone about it. It happened a year before she left town, and years later, she covered the scar with the small, butterfly tattoo to symbolize the change it represented in her life.

After being cut by her own father, Alissia swore she would never allow herself to be a victim again, and she never gave him an opportunity to strike her after that night. If he even came close to her while drunk, she attacked first—her fierce punches fueled by an intense rage and hatred.

A look of regret instantly appeared across Grady's face, but he quickly recovered when Langley said, "It looks as though it was done with severe heat. Did you notice how small the hands are?"

Alissia told them about the searing pain she felt in the tunnel, along with the foreign voices she heard.

"Maybe this explains why she didn't have any bruises or cuts, yet she was covered in blood," Anika said. "Could someone have healed her before you got to her? I've never heard of such a thing, but with the amount of blood on her clothing, I think she was severely hurt."

"Who could have done it?" Grady asked.

The three of them looked at each other, shaking their heads.

"Where did you say you found her?" Langley asked.

"She was in a hidden cave on the edge of the mountains." After a pause, Grady added, "I can do some research at the Eldership. I also need to figure out what happened to the window she came through."

They all agreed that Grady needed to do some research, and then the men left the room, closing the door behind them. Anika sat down on the bed next to Alissia. In a gentle voice, she said, "I know this is hard for you. I can only imagine what I'd do if I were thrown into a different reality. Are you married, and do you have children where you're from?"

Alissia stared at a group of glowing flowers across the room. "No, but I had a great job and friends. What am I supposed to do here?"

"Don't worry about that. We aren't going to throw you out on your own, and Grady will find answers. Who knows? Maybe you can go back home one day, and this will just be an adventure."

"Yeah, but when? If I don't get home soon, I'll lose everything. What will I tell people when they ask where I've been?"

"We'll think of something," replied Anika, with a reassuring smile. She stood. "Would you like to join us or stay in here for the night?"

"I'll stay in. Thank you."

"Then I'll pull the lights for you."

Anika walked to the corner of the room and pulled the ivy's roots from a container. Within seconds, the bright, white flowers stopped glowing, leaving the only light in the room coming from the blue ivy spiraling up the bedposts.

"Do you want me to pull the other lights also, or do you want them to stay in?"

"They're fine. I like them."

Anika left the room and shut the door, and Alissia rolled onto her side. Anika's question about marriage and children came to mind, and she let out a long sigh.

"And who's going to miss me?" she whispered to herself.

Although her friends would wonder what happened to her, she doubted any of them would cry over her disappearance. She was always the fun one that loved being around lots of people, and she rarely ever spent time alone with any of her girlfriends. Allowing anyone to get that close and private always scared her, and she believed it was much safer to socialize in a group.

What about her family in Georgia? She knew her mother and sister would be extremely upset and confused by her disappearance, and she hated to cause them pain. Her SUV at the pond, with her purse and cellphone in the front seat, would be their only clue in her disappearance.

A sudden knot filled her stomach as a thought entered her mind. Did her diary follow her into this reality, or did it stay behind for her mother to find?

It took a long time for Alissia's thoughts to settle down, but she eventually drifted into a restless sleep. When she awoke the next morning, she experienced an eerie feeling of being watched, only to find no one else in the room.

Chapter 3

While dressing, Alissia decided not to allow herself to dwell on her bad situation. Allowing herself to get depressed would not get her anywhere, and she told herself she needed to accept things and move on.

When she sat down for a warm bowl of oats, Anika told her that Langley went to work on the ranch, while Grady decided to take a look at the window that pulled her into this reality.

Anika seemed eager to go clothes shopping, and she checked Alissia's measurements and asked what colors she liked best. Alissia got the impression that the woman loved to shop and would greatly enjoy her day.

She told Alissia she would try to hurry so there would be something for her to wear before the men returned, and while she was gone, Alissia could relax in the pool or go outside. She showed her where to find food, and then she left, leaving Alissia alone for the day.

Alissia walked outside and sat on a group of large stones arranged into a bench. Massive shade trees surrounded the stone cottage, and flowers and ivy seemed to be everywhere. Plants grew abundantly, and birds and scurrying animals filled the trees. It reminded her of pictures she often saw on greeting cards and paintings, and everything about the place soothed her.

As a child, she spent much of her time outdoors, even having a pet horse named Savannah that she loved to ride. Her father taught her how to shoot a gun and how to fish, and beach seining on Jekyll Island with friends and family still brought a smile to her face.

All through the night, the men would drag a large net on the bottom of the ocean floor, while others would haul coolers along the beach. Each time the loaded net would come ashore, young Alissia would run to it, wondering what strange creatures she would find. With a flashlight in hand, she would grab the shrimp and fish, throwing them into the coolers. She would always squeal in fright if she got too close to a pinching crab or a stingray.

She remembered fishing for catfish and frog gigging with her father. She would shine the light into the frogs' eyes, paralyzing them in place, and her father would stab them with a little pitchfork. Sometimes he would hold the light and allow her to shoot the frogs with a pellet gun. Sounds of owls, crickets, and bullfrogs always filled the night air, along with a slight breeze.

During those early years, Alissia loved being outside under the stars, where she often encountered snakes and alligators—their eyes glowing slightly above the water.

The happiest moments of her life ended too soon, and she sometimes wondered what life would be like if her father never started drinking. She most likely would never have left Jesup.

Instead, she moved far away from her hometown, and things changed drastically for her. School and work consumed her life during the first years after her move, and she did not have much time for anything else. After finishing school, most of her outdoor life consisted of walks on park trails and visits to a few beaches near her home in New Jersey.

Alissia sat outside for most of the morning, and after a small lunch, she took a nap. She spent the rest of the afternoon sitting on the stone bench, and although she told herself not to worry, she feared she would never be able to return home. She thought about her mother and sister's reaction to her disappearance, and it troubled her.

She eventually went inside and found a snack, and Anika soon entered the kitchen.

"You're going to love what I picked out for you!" she shrieked. "I got the smallest size I could find in everything." She set the packages on the table and began to pull out a variety of clothing, along with hairpins to match the new outfits.

"Oh, wow!" Alissia said, holding up a shirt. She tried to hide her discomfort with a smile. "You really shouldn't have bought this much for me. It's a lot."

Anika grinned. "I didn't buy it. Grady did. I got to spend my day shopping for new clothes with someone else's money." She pointed into the air for emphasis. "And don't feel bad about that, either. He works for the Eldership and can afford it." In a serious tone, she added, "Besides, I can only imagine what it's like for you to be here, and Grady told me to spend whatever I thought would take your mind off things. I didn't fail, did I?"

Alissia shook her head, and Anika said, "Will you try them on for me? Grady said women wear pants a lot where you're from, so I only got you a few dresses."

Alissia tried on the clothes and was surprised at how well everything fit. She loved the way the soft material felt against her skin. Although pleased with everything, her favorite piece of clothing was a brown pair of riding boots.

She decided on a leggings outfit and went into the kitchen to help with dinner. Anika's pleasant mood, along with the new clothing, made her feel better, and she noticed herself laughing more than once.

Just as they finished preparing the food, the men came into the kitchen, and since Alissia did not eat a big lunch, she was extremely hungry when they all sat down to eat. She ate her vegetables without any trouble, but when she brought the meat to her mouth, she involuntarily gagged without anyone noticing. She ate everything else on her plate, but not wanting to be impolite, she tried to eat the meat again. This time, she gagged louder, and everyone stopped talking and looked her way.

"Oh, no. You don't like chicken," said Anika. "Do you even eat chicken where you're from?"

Still nauseous, Alissia answered, "Oh, yes. I eat chicken all the time. I don't know what's wrong with me. I think I'm just sick on my stomach tonight."

"How have you been feeling today?" Grady asked.

Uncomfortable by everyone's attention, she tried to give a reassuring smile. "Fine. I've had a good day, and I don't know why I feel sick right now. It'll go away." Thinking of a distraction, she asked, "So, what did you find out about the window?"

His face took on a troubled expression. "From what I can see, I don't think it changed much. It looks somewhat larger, but the gap's still small. You definitely didn't bust through the window. I think you squeezed through instead."

"If I had broken through the window or made a larger gap in it, could you get me home?"

"I don't know," he answered, shaking his head. "The jade's too low on power, and I don't know how I can get another one. I don't know a lot about this. What Agro did is extremely illegal. I'm beginning to think we really need to find him. He may know more than what's in his notes. He also may have a way to get another jade."

"Where do you think you're going to find him?" Langley asked. He wiped his mouth with a cloth napkin.

"I know he lived in Pallen, so I'm going to begin there. I plan to start preparing for the journey tomorrow. The biggest challenge is going to be taking unexpected time from the Eldership. I don't know what explanation I'm going to give."

"Can't you just tell them you're going to Pallen to help a friend?" asked Anika. "I mean, how much time have you taken off in all these years? I'm sure they'll understand you need some time away. I know of others within the Eldership that have done it."

"She's right," Langley added. "Since most of your family lives in Allure, you haven't taken as much time off as a lot of the others."

Grady nodded. "The other problem is finding an escort for Alissia."

"Why do I need an escort?" Alissia asked, not hiding her confusion.

The others looked at each other before Anika answered, "In our reality, a lady doesn't travel alone with a man unless they're married or relatives. If you and Grady travel alone, it would draw a lot of unwanted attention to you."

Alissia nodded in understanding, and she wondered what other differences she would find in this new reality she now seemed to be stuck in.

Anika turned her attention back to Grady. "Who do you trust enough to ask? Your sister could probably help."

"I think she's the only person I *can* ask."

"Why can't we go with them?" Langley asked Anika. "We've never been there together." A smile crept to his face. "We could spend our winter in Pallen, and it would be the perfect vacation."

Anika's eyes widened with surprise. "What about the ranch?"

"You know winter's our slow season. Father and the others can manage everything as long as I'm back by early spring. It'll be close, but I think we can get back in time."

"We can spend our winter in Pallen?" Anika asked. Langley nodded, and she let out an excited squeal.

"Where's Pallen, and what exactly are we doing?" Alissia asked.

"It's a city on the other side of the mountains," Grady answered. "We're going to have to leave as soon as possible before it gets cold. Once we get there, we can't cross the mountains again until after winter."

"It's a beautiful city," added Anika, with a distant look in her eyes, "and it's going to be like a vacation." She cocked her head, eyeing Alissia. "Well, it'll be once we cross the mountains. Can you ride a horse?"

"It's been a long time, but I had one as a child," Alissia answered.

Although the thought of seeing Grady every day made her feel uncomfortable, the idea of riding a horse along mountain trails sounded somewhat appealing.

"You know what this means?" Anika asked, giving Grady a sly grin. He shook his head, and she rolled her eyes. "We need to go shopping for traveling clothes. She'll need warm clothing for the mountains."

Grady laughed, nodding his head in agreement. "You two need to go shopping tomorrow." Becoming serious, he added, "But Alissia doesn't need to talk out loud in front of anyone. I don't know of anyone that talks like she does, not even from overseas. It's too noticeable and will cause too many questions. We need to decide where we can tell people she's from, and we're going to have to teach her how to speak using our enunciations."

Although Alissia's strong, South Georgia accent had lessened somewhat over the past ten years, it always got noticed while living in the North, and she could only imagine how bad it would be in this reality.

After dinner, she followed Anika to a cozy chair in the couple's bedroom, where she listened as Anika excitedly described the city of Pallen while going through her clothing.

When Alissia went to bed that night, she had a hard time falling asleep. Although she enjoyed Anika's company and the coming journey intrigued her, she could not put aside how much she would have to depend on others to survive in this reality. The fear of losing her independence greatly outweighed everything else, and she made a vow to find a way to take care of herself.

She awoke the following morning with a strong and eerie sense of being watched during the night. After putting on her new robe and opening the bedroom door, she immediately smelled something similar to bacon, and she gagged.

Covering her mouth with her hand, she ran to the bathroom. After emptying the contents of her stomach, she rinsed her mouth and washed her hands. She then tried to walk to the kitchen but got sick again. She ran back to the toilet, where she retched some more before calling out to Anika.

"Are you all right?" Anika asked, entering the room.

"It's the smell of the food. It's making me sick on my stomach."

"I have something that'll help with that. I'll be back."

Anika left the room and soon returned with a small vial of green liquid. Although it tasted foul, Alissia desperately wanted to settle her stomach, and she quickly forced it down.

"Wait here while I get the smell out of the house," Anika said, walking out of the room.

Once the scent cleared and she no longer felt sick, Alissia washed her hands and face. She slowly made her way out of the bathroom to find Anika in the kitchen scooping warm oats into a bowl. Eyeing Alissia with concern, she set the bowl on the table.

"I made you something else. Do you think you can eat this?"

Alissia nodded and sat down. Anika set a cup of juice beside the bowl before taking the opposite seat. "Do you want to stay here today and rest while I do the shopping?"

Alissia shook her head. "No, I feel a lot better. I'm fine now that the smell's gone."

No longer feeling sick and in an attempt to appease Anika, she ate all the oats in the bowl. She looked forward to seeing more of her new surroundings and did not want to be left behind again.

After getting dressed, the two women walked along a shady path leading to the stables, where they found four horses tied to a post under a tree. Langley had already saddled two of them, and Anika explained that the other two would carry back their purchases.

As a child, Alissia told everyone she would live on a ranch one day, and that desire came back as she neared the horses.

While rubbing Celia's neck, her horse for the day, a strange sensation filled her, as though she felt what the animal felt. She suddenly knew that the horse greatly enjoyed her life on the ranch, and images began to flash through her mind of what Celia had seen and experienced that morning.

"Alissia!"

Pulled back into reality, she stepped away from the horse and Anika's hand on her shoulder.

"Are you all right?" asked Anika, staring at her in concern.

Alissia nodded and smiled, forcing herself to regain her composure. "Yeah, I'm good. Are you ready?"

"Only if you're all right. I brought some mild medicine in case you start to feel sick again, and you look like you already need it. Are you sure you don't want to stay?"

Alissia swiftly climbed into the saddle and smiled as she looked down at her new friend. "I'm fine. I promise I don't feel sick."

As they rode in silence, she pondered what happened between her and the horse. It was a bright and sunny morning, and her eyes soon began to burn. When she closed them, she found relief, but the pain resumed when she opened them again.

"Is something wrong, Alissia?"

With her eyes still closed, she stopped the horse. "Something's wrong with my eyes. They burn every time I open them." By now, her head throbbed, also.

Anika stopped her horse beside Alissia and leaned toward her. "Let me see if something's in them. Can you open them?"

Alissia forced her eyes open for a short moment before the pain caused her to close them again.

"I couldn't see anything. Let me take off my sunglasses and try one more time."

Through clenched teeth, Alissia responded, "One more time." After taking a deep breath, she opened her eyes, only to close them again at the sound of Anika's gasp.

"What's wrong?"

"What color are your eyes?" Anika asked.

"Green. Why?"

"Well," Anika said slowly, "your eyes are now light purple. I mean, *really* light purple."

Alissia frowned in disbelief. "How can my eyes be purple?"

"Here," said Anika, placing her sunglasses in Alissia's hand. "Put my glasses on and see if they help. I've never seen eyes that color."

Alissia accepted the strange sunglasses, hand carved from bone and tortoise shell. She put them on and waited a moment before opening her eyes.

"A lot better." She smiled. "The sun was burning my eyes, and my head still hurts." Not wanting to drink another unpleasant vial of medicine, she added, "This'll probably clear my headache. Is the sun different here than where I come from?"

Anika shook her head. "I don't think it's our sun. I think it's your eyes. They've turned purple."

Although confused, Alissia did not want to discuss the strange events until after she thought about them for herself. Ignoring her headache, she nudged her horse forward.

"You ready? We'll figure this out later."

Anika gave an uncertain look. "Yes, but I need you to keep the glasses on while we're in town. Don't take them off under any circumstance. Will you agree?"

"I won't speak, and I won't take off the glasses. I'll even act mute and blind if you want me to."

Anika reluctantly nudged her horse, and the two of them soon stopped outside the elaborate city gates of Allure. A large stone wall covered in bella ivy surrounded the city, with the ivy getting its water from a moat at the base of the wall. A stone bridge crossed over the moat, and detailed carvings adorned the massive, open doors of the gate.

Alissia stared in awe. "Are y'all expecting a war?"

"We haven't been at war in many years," Anika said, amused by Alissia's reaction. "But these walls were built at a time when war was a common thing. That was before the Eldership was in charge, and different kings ruled over the land. The kings were always at war with each other, and when the Eldership was formed, it brought peace by uniting everyone. Now, Allure is the head government city. It's been that way for years."

As they rode over the bridge, Alissia thought of fairytales filled with knights and castles. She looked around in wonder as they passed through the daunting entrance, and her curiosity grew even stronger as she stared at the stone buildings covered in flowers and ivy. She had never seen a city filled with so much nature.

Instead of using cars, people walked or rode in rickshaws, and many of them made eye contact and smiled at each other. Most of the women wore long, comfortable dresses with sandals on their feet, and they all had long hair.

They left their horses at a nearby stable, and as they began to walk through the city, Anika asked discreetly, "Does this look anything like where you're from?"

Still in shock and full of wonder, Alissia shook her head. "Nothing at all."

Anika nodded in understanding. "From what little Grady has told me about where you're from, I believe we're a lot more natural than what you're accustomed to. We rely on the gift of nature for everything. The bella ivy is all throughout the city to provide light during the night, and it's a beautiful sight. All the reservoirs of water are kept clean by the purifying flowers, and there are many other uses for plants."

Alissia no longer had a headache, and she enjoyed shopping during the next two hours. Anika did all the talking, and the only problem Alissia experienced happened while passing a man cooking meat outside a restaurant. The strong odor made her nauseous, and she quickly scurried away.

Everything intrigued her, even her new traveling clothes made from a strange and comfortable material. As they entered a shop filled with bottles lining the shelves, Anika said, "We need to get some traveling soaps and hair washes from here."

They made their way to the back of the store, where Anika chose a bottle from one of the shelves and removed the lid. She lifted it to her nose and took a whiff before turning to Alissia.

"Since we won't be around water much, we'll need to use this to wash. It's made from a mixture of purifying flowers, along with other cleansing substances and scented flowers. You should pick out the ones you like."

The two women continued searching for their personal hygiene items, and after they purchased everything they needed and had the packages delivered to their horses, Anika said, "The men are in town gathering supplies, and we're supposed to meet them for lunch." She smiled and added, "We're a little late, though."

They found the men already seated at a table in the courtyard of the restaurant. Alissia went to the bathroom before joining them, hoping to finally have a chance to see her eyes in private. However, the mirrors positioned over the sinks, located in the tight space between the men and women's bathrooms, bustled with activity.

At the table, Grady stood and pulled out a chair, next to him and across from Anika. She sat down and soon noticed an uncomfortable silence. Grady finally turned to her and asked, "Do you mind lifting your glasses so I can look at your eyes?"

Alissia chided herself for leaving Anika alone to explain things without her. Scanning her surroundings, she noticed they had a little privacy from where they sat, and she lifted the dark glasses.

"Let me see," Anika said, leaning across the table. Still holding up the glasses, Alissia turned toward Anika and Langley. Her friend shook her head, staring hard into Alissia's eyes. "They looked a lot different earlier. They were a very pale shade."

Alissia turned back to Grady, and he leaned in closer. As he studied her eyes, she felt his warm breath on her face and noticed his fresh, woodsy scent. Her pulse quickened from the unwanted attention, and she cringed as she felt herself swallow nervously.

"Have you noticed her hair?" Asked Anika. "It's even more noticeable in the sunlight."

Alissia immediately lowered her glasses and stared back at the others with wide eyes, her hand instinctively going to her hair. "What's wrong with my hair?"

Grady picked up a cluster of curls and began to examine it. Once satisfied, he leaned back in his chair and said, "Right now, the irises of your eyes are purple, and your hair also has a deep purple hue to it that I didn't notice before. Is that your normal hair color?"

She shook her head. "No."

More than anything, she wanted to find a mirror. Lines of worry creased her forehead as she turned to Anika. "How bad does it look? Honestly."

Anika laughed. "That's the first thing that comes to your mind?"

"Let's see," Alissia answered. She lifted her hands to count on her fingers. "In the past few days, I've been squeezed into another reality, found a set of handprints branded onto my body, had a weird incident with a horse, and now, I have purple hair and eyes. I think I'm beyond confused at this point. The only straight answer I know I can get is whether my hair and eyes look freaky or nice."

They all paused as the waitress came to take their order, and since Alissia had not even looked at the menu, they needed a little more time. After she walked away, Grady picked up the menu and began to explain it to Alissia.

Anika silently watched for a moment before interrupting. "Maybe you shouldn't order anything with meat in it."

She explained to the men how Alissia had gotten sick that morning from the smell of cooked meat and then again, when she smelled the meat cooking outside. She also reminded them how Alissia had reacted to the meat the night before.

Alissia smiled and reassured them that she felt fine. Secretly though, she felt even more anxious than the night before. She told herself that her body was only trying to adjust to this reality. Nobody knew what to expect, since she was the first to be pulled through a window.

Turning her attention back to the menu, she found she really did not want to eat anything with meat in it. Since most of her diet usually consisted of fruits, vegetables, whole grains, and nuts, she did not become too concerned. She decided to try a vegetable plate, and the waitress soon came back to take their order.

As soon as the waitress walked away, Langley turned to Alissia. "What did you mean when you said you had a weird incident with a horse? Anika didn't mention that."

"Because I don't know anything about that," Anika announced.

Although she tried to appear unaffected by Langley's question, Alissia knew her eyes gave away her displeasure when she looked at him. He had been sitting quietly during their entire conversation, and when he finally decided to open his mouth, it had to be that question. How could she explain what happened that morning when she did not even understand it herself?

Thinking about the horse, she stared down absently at the table with her eyebrows furrowed and chewed on her bottom lip. After a while, she let out a sigh and looked up.

"This morning, when I began to pet Celia, I had a weird experience. I really don't know how to explain it. It was . . . kind of like we bonded."

Looking at Langley, she said, "I can tell you that she loves her life on your ranch. She loves the people around her and the horses, also. It was a strong feeling that went through my mind, and for a moment, I felt as though I *was* her. Everything was very clear, and I even experienced what she saw, smelled, and tasted this morning."

After a thoughtful silence among the group, Langley turned to Grady. "Have you ever heard or read about anything like this in any of your studies at the Eldership?"

Grady shook his head. "Never, and now I'm trying to decide what we should do about going to Pallen. I really need to do a lot of research at the Eldership's library about this. At the same time, we've got to leave soon if we're going to cross the mountains, and I'm also wondering if any more changes are going to happen to her." Glancing at Alissia, he added, "Last night, her eyes were green."

"What exactly is the Eldership? How does it rule?" Alissia asked.

"The Eldership is our form of government," Grady answered. "The training begins during our middle school years, as they choose children with the highest academic performances and offer them the best training in their school. Then they choose the best graduates for jobs within the Eldership. The highest position is an elder. I'm a member, but I'm not an elder. You have to be a lot older for that."

"But at the rate you're going, you'll be one," Langley said. He turned to Alissia. "The best way to get promoted within the Eldership is to continue training during your adult years, and I think Grady here is always registered for some type of training. He's also luckier than a lot of the others, because most of his family lives here. That means he never takes a long leave to visit family in other cities, and he puts in more time."

"Are you supposed to be at training now?" Alissia asked, looking at Grady.

"I was registered for some classes, but I've already taken care of things at the Eldership. I told them I have to take a leave."

They stopped talking as the waitress brought their food and re-filled their drinks. As soon as she walked away, Anika asked, "What if you see someone from the Eldership today?"

Grady gave a half shrug. "I've already told them I'm going to be traveling. That means I have to make preparations, and that's exactly what I'm doing today."

"What are our plans now?" asked Langley.

Grady thought for a moment before answering, "I think I should go to the Eldership library for one or two days to see if I can find anything about Alissia's changes. Then we can continue with our plan to go to Pallen. I need to find out what Agro knows about the window and if there's a possibility for her to return home. Pallen has an extensive library, and I can do more research there."

Alissia forced her voice to sound calm as she asked, "What do you mean *other changes*? Am I not going to be a human anymore? How bad can these changes be?"

"I don't see anything that's too worrisome," Grady said reassuringly. "However, I do think you should experiment with other animals to see what happens and find out how this bonding works. It sounds like a gift, not a curse." He smiled at Alissia. "And as far as your hair and eyes, you still look beautiful."

"Thank you, but I would still like to see myself in a mirror right now." She took a sip of her drink, not wanting to meet his eyes.

He cut off a small portion of his steak before holding his fork out to her with the meat attached to it. "Can you see what happens if you try to eat this?"

She took the piece of steak from his fork and held it to her mouth. The smell, along with the thought of it, made her feel nauseous, and she quickly set it down on the edge of her plate and shook her head.

"She can't eat meat," Anika said flatly. She turned to Alissia. "Do you normally eat meat?"

"Usually about once a day, if that. I've never been a big meat eater, but it never made me sick."

As they ate the rest of their meal, Langley agreed to finish shopping without Grady so that Grady could begin his research at the Eldership. The women soon said goodbye to the men and went back to their shopping.

Alissia still felt uncomfortable about spending so much of Grady's money, and she mentioned it to Anika more than once. Anika continuously laughed and reminded her that he was a single man that worked for the Eldership. He could easily afford their shopping spree. However, her husband had set a limit, and after reaching that limit, she focused on shopping for Alissia.

Eventually, Alissia noticed that her clothing costed more than Anika's. When she voiced her concern, Anika stopped walking and turned to her with a serious expression.

"Alissia, Grady is a member of the Eldership, and that's a very prestigious position within our society. It means that he dresses in finer clothing than most people, even Langley and me. Some people will ask innocent questions about our group. Langley and I are married. Grady and you are not. We could say that you're my sister, but it won't work if we see anyone we know. Langley's family has been in business for many years, and people travel from far distances to buy horses from them. They have a reputation throughout the land, and since a lot of people know my family, we have to be very cautious.

"We talked things over last night and decided to make it appear as though you and Grady are courting, and it's our custom that he begin to provide for you during the courting process."

Alissia's eyes narrowed. "And what exactly do you mean by the word 'courting?' You mean dating?"

"No, it's the next step after dating. It means you're engaged."

As Alissia opened her mouth to object, Anika quickly interjected, "It doesn't mean you have to marry Grady. A courtship can easily be broken."

Alissia crossed her arms and frowned. "Why can't we just say we're dating?"

"That wouldn't be right. You don't travel with someone you're dating unless you want to draw attention to yourselves. This way, there won't be any questions. Langley and I are your escorts, so nothing is inappropriate. We'll easily blend in with others, and it goes along with our customs."

"Why didn't y'all tell me?"

"Grady thought you might get upset, so he was going to tell you himself tonight. He didn't want you to hear of your engagement from someone else. He wanted to be the one to tell you."

Alissia's face softened as she uncrossed her arms. "Is there anything else I should know about this trip?"

Anika thought for a moment. "Well, when we're in the mountains, we won't be around people, but once we're in Pallen, we will. You may, at times, have to actually act as though you're engaged to Grady."

Alissia's frown returned. "What are you trying to say?"

"It shouldn't be anything big," Anika reassured, "but if he sees someone he knows, there might be questions about how the two of you met, among other things. The main secret we have to guard is where you're from. That's more important than ruining reputations." Looking hard into Alissia's eyes, she stressed, "That'll ruin both of your lives."

On their way back to the stables, the two women stopped at a bakery, where everything looked and smelled delicious. Instead of the processed white flour and sugar so often seen in her reality, the golden loaves smelled of fresh spices and honey.

She and Anika bought a variety of bread and sweet rolls, and once outside the shop, Alissia began to eat one of the freshly baked treats. She savored every bite, and without guilt, she indulged in another one before arriving at the stables.

With their horses already loaded and waiting for them, Anika paid the stable fee, and they began their short ride home.

At the ranch, a hired hand took away their horses, while another one helped the women to the cottage with their packages.

Alissia went straight to the bathroom, where she stared at her violet eyes in wonder before inspecting her dark brown hair, which now had a purple tint to it. When she washed her hands, she noticed her fingernails seemed longer and healthier, with a glittery, light purple tint to them.

With trembling hands, she pulled back her hair and trailed her fingers along her ears, checking for pointy elf ears. She opened her mouth and searched for fangs, and then she let out a sigh of relief when she found nothing new.

At dinner that night, she forced herself to smile and act natural in front of the others. Shortly thereafter, she stepped into the bathing pool and felt a warm, tingly sensation in her feet. The glowing blue light beneath her began to shine brighter, and without even thinking about modesty, she called out to Anika.

"What is it?" Anika asked, running into the room.

"The light got brighter when I stepped into the water, and it hasn't done that before. Is that normal?"

Anika's eyes widened, and she shut the door and walked over to the pool. Except for her head, Alissia stood completely submerged in the water, her arms hugging her chest.

"The light comes from a glow rock at the bottom of the pool," Anika explained. "It's solar powered. That's one of the reasons most buildings have clear roofs. If the –"

A knock came from the door and Grady called out, "Is everything all right in there?"

"Everything's fine. I'll be out in a moment!" Anika yelled over her shoulder. She turned back to Alissia. "If you're making the rock glow brighter, you're giving it more power somehow. After you get out, we can do a few experiments."

Alissia nodded, and Anika left the room.

"I make things glow now," Alissia whispered in disbelief. "I'm like a flashlight. No, I'm one of those little glow worms. I'm a glow girl."

She quickly bathed, and afterwards, she paid close attention to her skin as she rubbed floral-scented lotion onto her body. She got dressed and ran a brush through her long, curly hair before gathering her dirty clothes and opening the door.

"We'd like to do a few experiments," said Grady. He and the others appeared to be waiting for her in the sitting room.

Alissia nodded and tossed her dirty clothing onto the floor of her borrowed bedroom. Then she sat down beside him on the sofa. He bent down to retrieve one of the stones piled at his feet. It glowed and was about the size of a baseball.

"This is the same type of stone at the bottom of the bath," he said, holding it out. "It's already been powered by the sun, but I want to see what happens when I give it to you."

She felt a slight tingling sensation in her hand as soon as she picked up the smoothly carved rock, and it immediately began to glow brighter.

Grady held out his hand. "Let's see what happens when you give it back to me." She placed it back in his hand, and it continued to glow brightly.

"It's fully charged," said Langley, shaking his head in disbelief.

Grady reached down and selected a perfectly round and flat stone, about the size of a small, thick pizza. He stood and said, "We'll need to go outside for this."

Stepping onto the porch, the various-colored, shimmering flowers growing along the cottage and the edge of the stone bench momentarily distracted Alissia.

Anika laughed. "I forgot. They don't have bella ivy where you're from, and this is new for you."

Alissia shook her head, her eyes never leaving the natural art surrounding her. "It's so beautiful—serene and peaceful. We don't have anything like this."

Her sense of wonder must have spread to the others, as they all seemed to stare around with a renewed sense of appreciation. After a while, Grady left the porch and placed the rock on the stone bench.

"This is a heating stone," he explained, as Alissia and the others joined him. "We use these to keep our homes warm in the winter. They come in all shapes and sizes, depending on what they're used for. The sun also charges them. This one hasn't been charged, because it's been in storage. I want to see what happens when you touch it, but you have to be careful, as it's extremely hot when charged."

Alissia nodded and tentatively reached out to touch the rock with her fingertips. The same tingling sensation she felt earlier went through her fingers, and she watched as the stone began to smoke and glow brightly from within.

"Is it burning you?" asked Anika, her dumbfounded expression matching those around her.

Alissia pulled her hand away. "No, I just felt a tingling sensation in my fingertips when I first touched it."

"Let's try more of them," Langley said eagerly.

The group continued to experiment with various types of solar-powered stones, and they soon learned she could charge all of them. She had no effect on the type of stone that heated the bath, but a chemical reaction with the powder heated it, not the sun.

As Alissia lay in bed that night with the blue bella flowers glowing on each of the bedposts, she stared up at the stars and worried what she would look like in the morning. She imagined herself with purple skin and pointy ears, and those thoughts soon led to a tail and fangs.

She awoke in the morning with the same feeling of being watched, and she jumped out of bed and rushed to the standing mirror in the bedroom. After searching her body for more changes and not finding anything new, she smiled in relief.

She joined Anika in the kitchen to learn that Grady left for the Eldership early in the morning, while Langley went to work on the ranch.

After Alissia ate breakfast and dressed for the day, she and Anika walked toward the stables. Unlike the plastic sunglasses from her reality, she now wore a new and expensive pair, hand carved and made from the shell of an animal she knew nothing about.

Not wanting anyone around during their experiments, they found a secluded tree resembling a pink weeping willow, and they placed a blanket beneath it.

Anika left Alissia under the canopy of the tree as she went to find some animals. Moments later, she returned carrying a sleek, black cat. A brown, shorthaired dog followed them, and as she sat down on the blanket, the medium-sized dog strolled over to Alissia and plopped down in front of her.

"That's different," Anika said. "Mosh doesn't usually like strangers very much."

Wagging his tail excitedly, he pawed Alissia, and she noticed a fresh, small wound on the outside of his front leg. She chuckled at his playful demand for attention and began to pet him behind the ears.

Within seconds, Mosh's memories and feelings of the past couple of days took control of her. She even experienced the same annoying ache he felt in his wound. She learned he got it from a recent fight with another dog as she relived the battle from his memories. Eventually, she was able to think for herself again, and she pulled her hand away.

"Well," Anika shrilled, causing the feline in her lap to flinch, "what happened?"

Alissia inspected her fingers but found nothing out of the ordinary. She then looked up with a bemused expression. "He expects me to heal him."

"How do you know that?"

"I relived his most recent memories and felt the pain from his leg, but . . . then I sensed his excitement over me healing him. He *really* believes I'm going to heal him."

Anika absentmindedly stroked the cat as she thought for a moment. "Do it again, but try to heal him this time."

"And just how am I supposed to do that?" Alissia challenged.

"I don't know," Anika countered, giving a shrug. "You charged all our solar rocks. How did you do that?"

Alissia shook her head. "I just touched them, and it happened."

"Well . . . just try something."

She turned her attention back to the dog sitting expectantly in front of her and slowly reached out with her hand. There was no scab, and she frowned as the tips of her fingers touched the moist body fluids. Almost immediately, she pulled her hand away.

"Nothing happened."

"Maybe you have to think about it and give it a little more time," Anika coaxed. "What were you thinking?"

Alissia frowned at the goo on her fingertips. "How gross it is."

"What does gross mean?"

"I didn't want to touch it," Alissia answered, wiping her fingers on the blanket. "It looks yuck. You know. Not sanitary. Not clean. What would you think if you had to dig your fingers into it?"

"Oh," said Anika, waving her hand dismissively. "Try to think healing thoughts. Try to comfort him."

Alissia turned her attention back to the mutt in front of her. He cocked his head, and she laughed at the adorable look he gave.

"I'll do it, but I'm going to try it with my hand on his fur first."

She began to pet the dog's back and immediately felt the bond again. This time, she quickly took control of her thoughts. Instead of allowing his memories to consume her, she focused on his pain, and a warm sensation flowed through her arm and out of her hand.

She continued to comfort the dog until the sensation ended. Then she pulled her hand away. Looking down at his leg, she found the wound completely healed, with fresh fur where it had been.

"You did it!" Anika shrieked, grabbing the cat as it tried to jump out of her lap. "How'd you do it?"

In a daze, Alissia studied her unchanged hand and arm as she answered, "I focused on his pain. Then I felt something warm in my arm flowing out of my hand."

Anika eagerly held up the cat. "See what happens with this one. His name is Lou."

Alissia took the cat and set him in her lap. As she pet him, the bond took control, and she relived his most recent memories before pulling out of it. With Lou purring loudly, she said, "Someone loves to play with mice. I don't like mice, but it's sort of cruel how much joy this cat gets from torturing them before eating them."

Anika laughed as she gave Lou a quick pet behind the ear. "I wonder if you can talk to them. You know what they feel, and you share their memories. What if you can talk to them as well?"

Alissia curiously looked at Mosh and gave the command for him to bark. The dog complied, and she turned back to Anika in surprise.

"Try something else," Anika said excitedly.

She looked down at the cat and said firmly, "Go back to Anika's lap." She then watched in disbelief as Lou obeyed.

The previous night her new abilities and appearance scared her because she had no control over them, but her experiments with the animals proved that she could control some things.

Beaming at Anika, she said, "Let's go find some more animals!"

Chapter 4

Over the next three days, Alissia did not see the men very often. Langley stayed busy packing necessities for their journey and getting some last minute things done on the ranch, and he came home late each night.

Grady spent his days at the Eldership library, and he spent his evenings preparing for the trip. He did not come back to the ranch at all one night, because he stayed at his home in Allure to pack. Another night, he ate dinner at his parents' house and asked them to watch his place while he was away.

Although Alissia and Anika spent most of their time packing and preparing food for their journey, they continued with their experiments. Animals—even wild ones—came to Alissia naturally, and they desired her touch. They followed every command she gave, and she continued to heal those that needed healing.

When she held an insect, she did not see anything. If she concentrated, she could faintly feel what it desired at that time. Some focused on searching for food, while others seemed to be seeking a place to hide eggs. Although it took more concentration, she could tell them where to go.

Her hair continued to change. On her head and eyebrows, it was now a deep shade of purple, resembling the color of dark grapes or plums. The hair on her arms was much lighter and only noticeable in the sun.

The purple tone of her irises depended on the amount of light they received, and they continued to be sensitive to bright light. With a faint glow to them, they reminded Alissia of cats' eyes, and she spent a lot of time staring at them in the mirror. Although they matched perfectly with her new hair color, they did not look human anymore, and she knew she would need to hide them behind dark glasses.

Her shimmery, light purple nails gave the appearance of a fresh manicure. Her skin looked as though she applied shimmery body lotion, and her hair seemed much softer and shinier than normal.

In her reality, she would have had to spend a lot of money on lotions, contacts, hair dyes, and treatments to look this way. She would have stood out in a crowd and got noticed everywhere she went.

However, contacts did not exist in this reality, and people did not dye their hair purple—especially their eyebrows. Although her old reality would accept her and consider her beautiful, in a rebellious way, this natural reality would not.

The handprints no longer itched, and Alissia awoke each morning with the same strong feeling, as though someone watched her. She enjoyed Anika's pleasant personality, and they spent a lot of time discussing the differences in their homes and lifestyles.

Her new reality revolved around nature, and the beauty of the place continuously astounded her. Anika loved to talk about their Creator and His gifts to them.

Grady's absence over the last few days relieved some of her stress, as she still did not want to be alone with him. She did not like how vulnerable his deep knowledge of her past made her feel. On their last night at the ranch, he entered the kitchen as everyone else finished dinner.

"I think I found something in the library this morning," he said eagerly, sitting down beside her. "It's not much, but I found a book that mentioned an ancient race of people that were small. They were called Lamians and were rarely seen but greatly feared. I only found one reference to them and couldn't find anything else. Since they're an old race, I checked the translation for the meaning of their name." He gave an uncertain look. "I doubt it means anything, but the word 'lamia' translates as witch and velder."

Alissia's brows furrowed in confusion when she realized she knew the meaning of the word 'lamia' before he even told them. She even knew velder meant vampire.

Grady must have misunderstood her reaction, and he said reassuringly, "They may not even be the ones responsible. The only reason I think they could be involved is because of the size of the handprints. The fact that people thought of them as witches means they could have practiced unknown magic." He smiled encouragingly. "I've never even heard of them before today, and we may find something different in Pallen's extensive library."

Alissia took a deep breath, taking comfort in her beating heart and need for air. Later that night, she endured an extremely restless sleep, and the next morning the feeling of someone's presence in her head grew even stronger. As she got out of bed, she determinedly told herself not to worry about something she could not fix, and she dressed for the day.

Langley and Grady took the lead as they traveled that morning. A group of packhorses followed, while the women rode a short distance behind them. Alissia distracted herself from her worries by talking to Anika, but after they stopped for lunch, her friend decided to ride with her husband.

Alissia was grateful that Grady did not try to ride next to her or pursue a conversation. Instead, he quietly followed her from a short distance.

Her mind soon began to wonder, and she decided to do some experiments for a distraction. Noticing a bird in a tree ahead of her, she mentally willed the animal to her. She had never attempted anything like that before, and she doubted it would even work.

When the bird left the branch, Alissia quickly held out her finger, and once he landed, she petted him and allowed the bond to take control.

Moments later, she silently willed the bird to leave, and she laughed to herself as he took flight. Wanting to try again, she willed Celia to stop, and the horse followed her silent command. She willed her to go again, and she obeyed.

"Having fun?"

Even her fear of being alone with Grady could not take her excitement away. As his horse strolled up to hers, she gave a mysterious smile. "What do you mean?"

"You know what I'm talking about," he said playfully. "How long have you known you could mind speak with animals?"

"I just found out, and you're the first to know."

"What else have you learned this week?"

She told him about her experiments, and then she listened as he shared what he had been doing over the past few days. He also talked about his family, and she learned he and Anika came from a large, well-known family, with most of them living in Allure.

They continued with their conversation until they stopped for the night, and she found herself surprised at how easy he was to talk to. If he never mentioned anything about her past, maybe she would not feel so uncomfortable around him.

They set up camp and settled down for dinner, and as everyone ate, she told them of her experiment with the bird.

Langley immediately offered her a job on his ranch. He said if he had that much power with animals, things would be a lot easier for him.

After cleaning the dishes and securing their food for the night, everyone began to get ready for bed. Alissia used the floral cleansing gel for the first time and was highly surprised by its effectiveness. She felt fresh and clean, and she began to think of the purifying flower as a miracle plant.

Once inside the women's tent, she crawled under her blanket, and Anika covered the small glow stone.

Alissia immediately sat up and looked around. She blinked a few times before looking down at her hands.

"Um . . . Anika?"

"Yes?"

"I can see in the dark."

Anika sat up. "What do you mean, you can see in the dark?"

"I *mean*, I can see clearly in the dark," answered Alissia, staring at her friend. "I can't see in color, but I can see everything around us. I've been sleeping with the bella flowers, and this is the first time I've been in the dark since I've been here."

Anika went back to her spot beneath her blanket. Her eyebrows furrowed in thought as she stared into the darkness above her. "I wonder what else you can do that we don't know of yet." She rolled onto her side, leaving Alissia to stare at her back. "We'll tell the men in the morning. I think they're already asleep."

Hearing the sound of mild snoring coming from the other tent, Alissia silently agreed and lay back down. About an hour later, she rolled over and gave a frustrated sigh, too restless for sleep.

The sound of movement among the leaves caught her attention, and she guessed it to be from a small animal. Listening closely, she focused on the creature and soon felt the presence of his mind. She willed him to her.

As he walked toward her, she sat up and carefully unbuttoned the flap of the tent, making sure not to wake Anika. A short moment later, she could barely contain her excitement as he entered.

About the size of a cantaloupe and with long and floppy ears, his nose looked pointy. Except for his long, thin tail, fur covered his body.

Alissia picked him up, letting the bond take control. Shortly thereafter, she petted him for the last time and mentally told him to leave. She then listened for the sounds of another animal. When she did not hear anything, she reached out with her mind and felt the presence of a variety of creatures within the surrounding area. Focusing on one in particular, she willed him to her, and within minutes, something similar to a mouse entered the tent.

After bonding with him and sending him away, she forced herself back to her blanket. Although filled with excitement, she knew she would be getting up early in the morning and needed to sleep.

"Alissia, time to get up." Anika shook her again. "Come on. Don't you want to tell the men what you learned last night?"

She slowly opened her eyes and gave Anika a dirty look.

Her friend grinned. "You really don't like mornings, do you?"

Alissia sat up and tried to force herself awake. She smacked her lips a few times before accepting the dark glasses Anika held out.

"Why do you have to sound so happy first thing in the morning?"

Anika laughed. "Because we're on our way to Pallen, and I know what's there. You'd be excited, too, if you knew how beautiful the city is."

Alissia did not have time to reflect on her vivid dream filled with mountain landscaping. She quickly dressed and helped Anika prepare breakfast while the men packed the tents and saddled the horses.

As they ate, she told them of her night vision and how she called the two animals to her, and everyone agreed she should continue with her experiments.

Just as the day before, Anika rode beside her in the morning, while Grady stayed with her that afternoon. Both of them gave her language lessons, and although she learned new words, she greatly struggled with imitating their accent.

That evening, they set up camp near a stream, and the men caught fish for dinner. Since she could not be near the smell of cooking meat, she and Grady took a walk along the edge of the water while Anika and Langley prepared the food.

The water attracted wild bella flowers, and they filled the landscaping with a beautiful display of various glowing colors. As she and Grady sat on a large rock, the magnificent beauty, along with the sound of the stream, soothed her. After a long, contented silence between them, he turned and smiled.

"You love the outdoors, don't you?"

Alissia nodded as she tucked a strand of curls behind her ear. "I haven't spent much time outside in the past ten years, and it's been a long time since I've immersed myself in nature like this." Motioning to a cluster of bella flowers winding around a tree, she added, "And my reality doesn't look anything like this. It's beyond beautiful."

"What was your life like?" he asked, lightly swiping at an unseen piece of lint or dirt on his lap. "Are you missing anyone right now?"

She turned and stared out at the water in front of her. "After I left Georgia, I moved far away and got another waitressing job and started school. Between school and work, I didn't have time for anything else. Once I graduated, I found a job as a legal assistant at a law firm, and after a year of working there, I talked my employers into paying for more school. That's how I became a paralegal." She turned to him with a questioning look. "I don't know if y'all have those here, but they help lawyers."

He nodded, as if he understood.

She let out a sigh and frowned, turning her gaze back to the running water. "I was just getting to the point where I could actually have a life. I was finished with school. Had a great job and condo. Loved my church. And I loved my friends."

"Do you miss it now?" he asked softly.

She thought for a moment. "I had friends, but none of them were close. I'm not missing anyone." She gave a half shrug and turned to look at him. "Anika's fun, and I've got these new powers. This trip through the mountains is the most beautiful landscaping I've seen in my entire life." She smiled. "I actually like it here."

He returned her smile, and after a pause, she began hesitantly, "But . . ."

"But what?" he asked, his eyes searching her face.

Lines of worry filled her forehead as she looked down. "But how am I going to get a job and support myself here?" She shook her head and looked back up. "I've been *very* independent all my life, and suddenly, I can't do anything for myself. I don't think I'll ever be truly happy until I find my place here. I can't depend on you for the rest of my life."

"I have *plenty* to share, and I don't want you to worry about that," he assured. "But I do understand what you're saying. You want your independence back."

"Exactly!"

"You heard Langley. He could use you on his ranch, but you'd have to hide your abilities from others."

"I only want a job where I'm needed," she said, looking hard into his eyes. "I don't want one out of pity."

Grady smiled. "None of us pity you, Alissia. I think Anika even admires you."

"And why would Anika admire me?" she asked skeptically.

He leaned toward, his face suddenly serious. "You've been through some amazing things this past week. Just being squeezed into another reality would be enough to break most people—but not you. She sees your determination and admires that in you."

Suddenly uncomfortable by his attention, Alissia turned her gaze back to the water. "What's Pallen going to be like?"

He hopped to his feet and held out his hand. "Why don't I tell you as we walk back to camp?"

Later that night, she and Anika talked and laughed in their tent until they fell asleep. Mountains and tunnels filled Alissia's dreams, and she remembered them clearly when she woke.

The men packed the tents as she and Anika prepared breakfast, and while slicing some fruit, she accidently cut herself with the knife. Staring down at her finger with wide eyes, she watched as purple blood oozed from the cut.

With a shaky hand, she set the knife down and glanced around. Relieved to find everyone still busy with their chores, she grabbed her finger and forced a smile onto her face.

"I'll be back," she said to Anika.

Not waiting for a response, she scrambled away from the camp, stopping behind a group of trees. She examined her finger to find the cut completely healed, the purple blood the only evidence left behind.

She slowly sat down on the grass, her mind in a frenzy. "I'm no longer human," she moaned. She shook her head. "What am I? And what else is going to turn purple?"

"Alissia?"

Grady's gentle voice came from behind, startling her. She instinctively forced a smile onto her face and tried to sound natural as she answered, "Yeah?"

He sat down beside her. "Are you all right? Anika's worried about you."

"I'm fine," she reassured. "I was just surprised. That's all. I found something new. Wanna see?" He nodded, and she held out her hand. "I need your knife." Noticing the hesitant look on his face, she laughed. "I'm not going to do anything bad with it."

He gave her the knife, and she quickly ran it across one of her fingers, causing the purple blood to flow.

"That's not all," she said, wiping at the blood. "Watch."

The two of them silently stared in disbelief as the cut miraculously healed.

"I'm not a human anymore."

He gave a weak smile. "This doesn't mean you're not a human. It just means you're different."

"*Really*?" she asked sarcastically.

He nodded. "We'll find out what's happening to you. Pallen has a large library, and we'll search the historical records until we find something about the Lamians."

"I'm not a human anymore," she stated, holding out the knife. "In fact, I won't be surprised if my skin turns purple, too."

He took the knife and put it away. Using his fingers for emphasis, he touched each of her body parts as he said, "Your elbows are human. Your legs are human. Your ears. Your nose. Your chin. Your neck. They're all human, Alissia."

She frowned. "I noticed you didn't say my hands and eyes are human."

He laughed as he stood and pulled her up next to him. After kissing the top of her hand, he said, "You're still a human, Alissia."

She smiled and pulled her hand away.

"Now, Anika is worried, so we should go eat breakfast," he said. "But first, I need you to promise me something."

"What?"

"Promise me you won't go around cutting yourself anymore."

She grinned. "I promise I'm not going to experiment on myself with your knife. But I wonder how long I can hold my breath and if I can breathe underwater." She laughed at his worried expression. "I'm joking. I've already tried holding my breath, and I learned that I still need air."

Breakfast was waiting for them when they returned, and after they joined Anika and Langley around the small morning fire, Anika cleared her throat. "Everything all right?"

No longer in a panic, Alissia quickly swallowed her food and nodded. With a grin, she announced, "I'm no longer a human. Oh, and I'm going to turn purple." She popped another bite into her mouth, leaving Grady to explain things.

Chapter 5

As they traveled, Alissia kept her mind busy with more language and pronunciation lessons, and she continuously reminded herself that worry would not solve anything. The fall, mountain air chilled, and while putting on her gloves, a comforting thought came to mind. She felt cold, and her heart still beat within her chest—two very human qualities.

She described more of her reality to Anika in their tent that night, and after her friend fell asleep, all of Alissia's unwanted worries filled her mind. It took a long time for her body to give in to a restless slumber.

"Time to get up, Alissia."

Ignoring Anika's cheerful voice, she rolled over. Her friend laughed, ripping the blanket away and giving a few rough shakes to Alissia's shoulder.

She sat up with a scowl. With all the changes in her body, she still hated mornings.

While dressing, Alissia recalled her dreams from the night. At first, she dreamed about herself being purple with pointy ears and fangs, but then her dreams filled with visions of mountains and tunnels again.

Their morning started out as usual, but a light sprinkle began to fall during the afternoon. They prepared camp in the drizzling rain shortly thereafter. Everyone went straight to their tents and put on fresh clothing. She and Anika warmed themselves by a heat rock as they ate an early, modest dinner in their tent.

The sound of rain helped to lull Alissia into sleep, where she dreamed of tunnels and mountain landscaping.

It no longer rained the next morning, and she decided to share her reoccurring dream with the others over breakfast.

"Maybe someone's trying to tell her something," Anika said.

"The Lamians obviously live in these mountains, and they want her to know," replied Langley.

"If they are responsible," said Grady, "we need to try to figure out why they were greatly feared before we go to them. If we can't find answers in Pallen, I can take her back to the tunnels in the spring."

Alissia could not resist. "I'll be purple by then."

That night, they camped by a stream, and as they ate dinner, Anika said, "Langley found a fresh, wild yargon plant." At Alissia's confusion, she added, "Sorry. It's a type of purification flower. When we camp by water, we'll sometimes be able to find them. Since he found one today and we brought a botch stone—that's a heating stone—we can take a hot bath tonight."

The thought of a hot bath brought a smile to Alissia's face, and she wondered how it would be done.

They found a private area near the stream, and Langley pulled out a folded piece of material from one of the packs. It popped open into a sturdy box, and they filled it with water from the stream. Then they tied the yargon plant in place at one of the corners. They positioned a stone in another corner and placed a botch stone on top of it. After pouring the grey powder over the stone, bubbles appeared around it.

After everyone washed, Langley pulled the botch stone from the water, and the men dumped the bath.

Later that night, while trying to sleep, Alissia thought of all the wonders in her new reality. If she did not have so many unanswered questions about her body, she could easily see herself happy in this beautiful and natural place.

When Anika shook her awake the next morning, Alissia gave her usual dirty look before leaving her blanket. As she dressed, memories of tunnels and mountains filled her mind, and she scowled.

If the Lamians lived in the mountains, why didn't they come to her instead of sending her visions? Shaking her head, she forced that thought aside. She painted a smile onto her face and stepped out of the tent.

She continued with her language lessons during the day, and although it did not come natural, she seemed to be getting better at pronouncing some of their words.

That night, Langley and Anika went for a walk after dinner, leaving Alissia and Grady alone by the fire. She no longer felt uncomfortable around him. In fact, she enjoyed his company. He never made the mistake of telling her what to do, and he only gave his opinions when she asked for them. He was a great listener and teacher when they traveled together in the afternoons, and he was always a perfect gentleman around her. She found herself smiling at him often.

"We're traveling at a fast pace," he said, stabbing at the fire with a branch. "The weather's been agreeable."

She nodded, setting her empty mug aside. "I thought it would be somewhat of a rough ride going through the mountains."

"These trails get used often and have been around for over a thousand years." He set the stick down and straightened. "If it weren't for them, it would take months to get through the mountains." He smiled, his eyes scanning the area. "Nobody knows how our ancestors did such an amazing feat of clearing the paths, especially with the dangerous animals in the area."

"What dangerous animals? I haven't seen any."

"It's not a problem if you stay on the trails, but it's greatly known that the animals will attack if you stray. We don't know why," he added, giving a half shrug, "but it's always been that way."

His eyes locked onto hers. "Although, I don't think you'd have a problem with the animals, and I'm beginning to believe the Lamians have something to do with their behavior."

"You think they control the animals around here?"

He nodded. "I also believe they don't want anyone to leave the trails."

Mulling over his words, Alissia gazed at the fire while chewing on her bottom lip. Not wanting the silence to get awkward, she turned and asked, "How long does it usually take to get to Pallen?"

"It depends on who's traveling and when. Winter travel varies each year, and it depends on whether we have a warm winter or a cold one. There've been a few winters in my lifetime these mountains were impossible to cross.

"Each traveling party is also different. If children were with us, things would be a lot slower. We aren't pulling a cart, either. We've had good weather, and we've traveled consistently throughout our days. I'd say we've been very blessed. A few storms could have made this journey long and miserable."

"True," she agreed. "How much longer do we have left?"

"Tomorrow night should be our last night on the mountains."

Her eyes widened in surprise, and he chuckled. Then he began to stare into the fire, his expression abruptly serious. Not wanting to pry, she held out her hands and busied herself with warming them. After a while, he turned and said, "Anika mentioned she told you about how we're traveling as an engaged couple."

Alissia set her hands in her lap, giving Grady her full attention. "She did."

"I know things are different in your reality, but it's very important in our culture. We have strong beliefs that a man and woman are to abstain until after marriage, and traveling together without chaperones would bring a lot of attention to us."

He paused, as if considering his words. "I don't ever want to put you in an uncomfortable situation, and I'm worried about how you feel about doing this. I don't want you to be angry with me."

His eyes locked with hers, searching. "We'll probably see people I know, and there will be times we'll have to put on a show of being a couple. I always want you to tell me if something I do bothers you. What are your thoughts about this?"

An internal war between hurt and anger exploded within Alissia.

"I've said something that bothers you," he said worriedly. "I understand you don't want to do this, but it's all we could think of."

She shook her head. "I'm not upset about pretending to be engaged to you."

"Then what?" When she did not answer, he gently pressed, "Alissia, I want you to always tell me when I've done something to make you uncomfortable."

She stared into the fire, trying to regain control of her emotions.

"What have I said?" he asked, his eyes pleading.

Alissia let out a sigh and turned to face him. "The only reason you're worried about my feelings so much is because you watched the most private moments of my life," she sputtered. "Nobody has witnessed me cry in over thirteen years, and nobody that knows me treats me so delicately. In fact, everyone in my reality believes me to be cold and unemotional. They don't go around worrying about hurting my feelings all the time."

Pointing into the air, she emphasized, "I'm not the weak person you saw under that tree, and I don't go around crying all the time because I can't handle life."

His eyes widened. Shaking his head, he said, "Alissia, I *definitely* don't see you as being so delicate that you can't handle life. If I learned anything from the recordings, it's that you've already handled more than most people ever have to. I don't think a weak person could leave home so young and work so hard to get where you've gotten. I don't even know if I could have done it. I was chosen at a young age to be in the Eldership, and life has been easy for me."

Her eyes went to the fire, and he scooted closer. Putting his hand on her chin, he gently urged her to face him. "The reason I'm so worried about your feelings," he said softly, while staring into her eyes, "is because I never want you to think I'm forcing you to do anything. I was worried that you'd resent me for having to do this, and that's why I said what I said."

He pulled his hand from her face. "Alissia, please don't ever think that I believe you're weak. That's the complete opposite of how I see you."

Alissia's face softened, and she immediately regretted mentioning the recordings. After a moment of silence, he asked, "Do you resent me at all for having to pretend to be engaged?"

She shook her head. "No, I don't resent you at all, and I'm sorry."

"Don't be sorry. I told you I always want you to tell me if I've said or done something to bother you. That's something I never want to do, but I'm sure I'll do it again by accident. Promise me that you'll always tell me."

She smiled and nodded. "I will."

He grinned as he stood and got down on one knee. After pulling out a tiny box from the inside of his cloak, he cleared his throat.

"Alissia," he began, with mock solemnness, "will you pretend to want to marry me?"

She laughed at his sudden change in demeanor. Keeping up with the charade, she put her hands over her heart and looked heavenward, blinking back fake tears. "Oh, Grady," she said dramatically, dropping her hands and looking back at him, "I would love to pretend to marry you."

The gold ring held a square cushion cut blue gem, and as he tenderly placed it on her finger, an unexpected thrill went through her body, causing her pulse to quicken.

He sat back down beside her and grinned. "This is normally where we'd share a big kiss, but I won't push my luck."

The feel of his touch still lingered on her hand, and as she looked back at him in the light of the fire, she noticed his hazel-colored eyes—they always seemed to portray gentleness when looking at her. His intellect and formal training often led Anika and Langley to look to him for leadership within the group—yet he never seemed pompous or arrogant. Although he had a clean-cut appearance, traveling on a horse came natural to him, and he did not appear weak—physically or mentally. He was strong, yet soft.

With her heart pounding fiercely within her chest, Alissia suddenly realized she *did* want to kiss him, and this was the perfect moment for it. Without warning, she leaned toward him and put her hand on the back of his neck, pulling him to her. She then planted her lips onto his.

They shared a long, slow kiss before she pulled away to look into his face. He stared back at her for a moment with a look of surprise. Then he smiled. His hand went to her back, and he pulled her into him.

His lips teased, tenderly and tantalizing, before he went in for another kiss. She felt his other hand on her neck, his thumb caressing the side of her face.

"Well, this is interesting."

In sync, Alissia and Grady tore away from each other at the sound of Anika's voice. Wiping the corners of her mouth with her fingertips, Alissia forced all emotion from her face as she looked at Anika, now staring down at them with her arms crossed. A broad grin filled Langley's face as he hugged his wife from behind.

"I see you're now impersonating an engaged couple," Anika said.

"They both seem to be very good at it too," added Langley. "I don't think we have to worry about others not believing them. In fact, I think we may need to practice our chaperoning skills."

Grady turned to Alissia and winked. "I'd say they're a little too good at their job."

Anika and Langley laughed as they walked to their tents, and Grady stood and pulled Alissia to her feet. As she turned to leave, he pulled her into his arms. "I want you to know how much I enjoyed your kiss," he whispered at her ear.

After giving a short and tender kiss, Grady released her hand. She then walked to her tent in a daze.

"I'm not talking about it," she announced, entering the tent.

Her friend grinned but said nothing as they went through their nightly routine. After crawling into her blanket, Anika propped on her elbows and stared eagerly at Alissia. She responded by covering the glow stone and rolling over.

"Oh, no, you don't!" Anika demanded, in an excited whisper. "You're going tell me about it, and don't think I'm going to let you sleep until you do. I'm not going to leave you alone, so you better start talking."

Alissia laughed as she rolled over. She let out a dramatic sigh before divulging the details, which ended with, "And y'all had to arrive at that exact moment."

Anika squealed, causing Alissia to shush her. The woman stopped abruptly, and her eyes widened. "You grabbed my cousin by the neck and kissed him?" Before Alissia could respond, she added, "He was *definitely* returning your kiss from what I saw."

"Goodnight, Anika," Alissia said, rolling back over.

After a short moment of silence, Anika asked, "Did you plan any of it, or were you suddenly taken in by his natural charm and looks and just couldn't resist?" Not giving Alissia enough time to answer, she added, "I can't believe you attacked my cousin. Is that common in your reality?"

Alissia rolled her eyes in the darkness. "I did not attack your cousin. I gently pulled him to me, and we gently kissed. Now go to sleep."

Chapter 6

The air chilled during the night, and after being forced awake by Anika early in the morning, Alissia dressed in extra layers of clothing. Too busy thinking about the events of the night before, she did not take time to reflect on her latest dream of tunnels and mountainous terrain.

She hesitated at the tent flap, as a fear of awkwardness between her and Grady began to set in. Squaring her shoulders, she decided to act as if nothing had changed between them. She would wait to see how he acted around her.

As she helped Anika prepare breakfast, she noticed Grady looking up at her often while packing. He even smiled a few times. She then realized she was watching him, and she turned away, chiding herself for not acting normal.

Riding beside Anika, she struggled to keep her thoughts on her language lesson, and her friend eventually gave up and began to tease her.

When the time finally came for her to ride beside Grady, she determinedly tried to act natural and appear calm. She did not talk as much, and after a few minutes, he abruptly asked, "You don't regret last night, do you?"

She gave a mysterious smile. "Do you?"

"I should have expected that," he said, chuckling. "I definitely have no regrets about last night. My counterfeit proposal went beyond my expectations." He glanced down at his saddle before turning back to her with questioning eyes. "Do you regret last night?"

"No."

He frowned. "That's all you're going to give me, isn't it?"

"Pretty much," she smirked.

He shook his head with laughter, and she smiled, wondering how she could have ever been so oblivious to his attractiveness—especially his lips.

"We should be in Pallen by tomorrow," he said lightly, "and we'll have the entire winter to find Agro and research the library's historical books. It's a beautiful city—full of art, plays, museums, music, and so much more. I can't wait to show you everything."

Alissia's nerves settled down by the time they stopped that evening, and everyone seemed happy they would soon be in Pallen.

The next morning, they eagerly spoke of the food they would be eating that night and the warm beds they would be sleeping in. As they got on their horses, Grady told her to try to go the entire day speaking with her newly learned accent. He said it needed to become natural for her so that she would not forget to use it.

They arrived in Pallen during her afternoon ride with Grady, and as they passed through a massive set of double doors, she stared around in astonishment. Large statues of men dressed in togas and wearing crowns made of leaves held each door open. With all the tall stone buildings, statues, gardens, and natural paths throughout the city, she could not believe such a place existed. Even the people looked like art—mostly dressed in fine clothing and jewelry that implied wealth.

They stopped at a small, two-story townhouse located in an alley and unloaded their belongings. Anika explained that her and Grady's aunt owned the home. Although the woman usually spent half of each year in Pallen and the other half in Allure, she remained in Allure due to her daughter expecting a baby. This allowed them to stay at the vacation home free of charge.

After they removed everything from the horses, the men took them to a nearby stable within the city, while the women unpacked and put their traveling gear away. Since the home only contained two bedrooms upstairs, Grady would be sleeping on the living room sofa during their stay.

Alissia guessed the small townhouse costed more than Anika's cottage. Beautiful paintings hung on the walls, while formal furniture filled the home. Along with bella flowers, elegant lamps topped with glow stones complimented each of the rooms.

Each room on the lower level contained large windows facing the alley, with stone pedestal tables arranged in front of each window. A medium-sized heat stone adorned each table, and Anika explained that the windows allowed the sunlight to enter the room to charge the stones. As it got colder, they would place additional heat rocks on the pedestals to increase the heat.

Everyone quickly bathed and dressed for a night out, and as they stepped into the alley, Grady took Alissia by the hand.

The glow stones and bella flowers filling the city created a whimsical scene as the sky darkened around them. Grady seemed to enjoy watching Alissia as they followed Langley and Anika along the natural paths.

Anika had told her that many newlyweds spent their honeymoons in Pallen, and Alissia saw them everywhere in the gardens. They sat on the many benches, eyeing the living statues, or they watched the painters while listening to the musicians.

"I told you that you'd find this place mesmerizing," said Grady, giving her hand a light squeeze. "What do you think?"

Remembering to use her fake accent, she answered, "We don't have anything like this where I'm from. It's amazing."

"Will you tell me more about your cities?"

Alissia shared some of the wonders from her reality, and although the idea of subways fascinated him, he said they could never do anything like that in this reality. It would take too much out of the land they highly cherished and needed for survival.

Once they decided upon a place to eat, Grady asked the hostess for a private table for the four of them. Although artistic people surrounded Alissia, none of them had purple hair or wore sunglasses at night, and she continuously noticed people staring at her.

Unlike Allure, most of the women did not wear their hair in natural, long braids filled with flowers. Instead, they pulled their hair elaborately onto their heads, holding it in place with sparkly pins. Some even wore glitter in their hair.

Once seated in a corner with their menus, Grady described her vegetarian meal options. The delicious food, along with the ambiance, greatly soothed Alissia.

He continued to hold her hand while describing the city on their stroll back to the townhouse. Once home, she snuggled up to him on the sofa, and the four of them enjoyed pleasant conversation in the sitting room, where she relaxed and soon fell asleep.

Feeling Grady's lips moving along her forehead, Alissia's eyes fluttered open.

"Did you enjoy your nap?"

She lifted her head from his chest and straightened, looking around the room.

"They just went to bed," he replied, answering her unspoken question.

"How long was I asleep?"

"Not long, and you didn't miss anything." He tucked a mass of curls behind her ear, causing her heart to flutter. "I can tell you've enjoyed tonight. This is the most you've been relaxed since I met you."

She scowled playfully. "Are you saying I'm uptight?" When a look of confusion appeared across his face, she added, "I'm stiff? Not fun?"

He shook his head and laughed. "No, you're not uptight. You've just had a lot on your mind since you've been here. Are you still worried you're going to turn purple and start drinking blood?"

"No," she said, smiling, "but I do wonder what I am."

She glanced down at her hands and began to fidget with the wedding ring on her finger. Her smile faded, and she looked up. "Grady . . . I really can't be considered a human anymore. Do you think I died before you found me?"

He let out a troubled breath. "I don't think you died, but I do think you came very close." His eyes clouded over, and he shook his head, softly adding, "You were covered in so much blood that day."

"Do you really think we'll find answers here?" she questioned, not hiding her worry.

"We have a guess at which people group did this to you," he reassured, tightening his arm around her, "and we have a time period to begin with. We have the entire winter to search for answers, and this city is filled with historical books and records." He nodded. "I believe we'll find something."

She gave a hopeful smile, and he stroked her hair. Closing her eyes, she took comfort in his pleasant, woodsy scent. His touch soothed her, and she relaxed in his arms. When his fingers moved to her cheek, she opened her eyes and looked up at him.

His head lowered, and she readily responded to the tender kiss. After a while, he pulled away and whispered, "I've been wanting to do that all night."

She smiled. "And I've been waiting for you to do that all night."

He kissed her forehead and trailed his fingers along her neck. Then he straightened and took her by the hand. "You should get ready for bed. Your kiss is too tempting tonight."

After a brief kiss, he stood and pulled her up next to him. He brushed his lips against the top of her hand before letting it go.

"Goodnight, Alissia."

She tried to appear calm and graceful as she walked to the stairs, knowing he watched her. Once alone in the bathroom, she leaned against the door and let the façade fall. In a daze, her body trembled with excitement. Her fingers went to her lips, and she grinned.

"I think I like Pallen."

Chapter 7

"Where are Grady and Langley?" Alissia asked, entering the kitchen.

"They already left to begin the search for Agro." Anika pointed to the pot on the counter. "Ready for breakfast?"

Alissia frowned. "Why didn't anyone wake me?"

"Why would someone wake you? We're not traveling anymore."

"Because I'm always the last one up."

Anika chuckled, leaning against the counter. "Alissia, somebody has to be the last person to wake, and you seem to be the best one for that position. I think it comes natural for you."

Alissia stared back at her friend with narrowed eyes, not amused. "But I'm always the last one up."

"You do realize that if I wake you, you'd still be the last person up." Anika crossed her arms, waiting for a response.

"I give up," said Alissia, grabbing a bowl. "What are our plans for today?"

Her friend grinned and uncrossed her arms, pulling away from the counter. "First, we need to go to the market and get some food. Then we can do whatever we want." She grabbed a frilly coin purse from the counter and held it out. "This is yours."

"What is it?"

"It's your money."

Alissia scowled and sat down at the table. After taking a bite of her food, she said, "It's not really my money, and I'm sure it's Grady's."

"We've already had this discussion," replied Anika, sitting down across from her. "If you two are to appear engaged, it has to look as though he's taking care of you. He has one of the most prestigious jobs in the country, and that means you'll be dressed appropriately." She smiled and set the purse down by Alissia's bowl. "That also means we need to go shopping again for you. You'll need some clothes to go to a show, and you'll need something to dance in."

Lines of worry filled Alissia's forehead as she swallowed her bite of food. "Anika, I don't know how y'all dance here."

"Oh . . . I didn't think about that," Anika admitted. She smiled and gave a half shrug. "I guess Grady's going to have to teach you. We need to shop *and* give you dance lessons." She picked up the coin purse. "Now, take this. It's yours, and don't worry about spending Grady's money. Honestly, he's never had anyone to spend it on, so he's got plenty hoarded away."

As they walked to the market, Alissia learned some things about the design of the city. People and rickshaws traveled the main paths, while horses and carts traveled along separate ones that ran parallel, but hidden, behind a wall of trees.

Large canopies gave shelter to booths packed with all kinds of fascinating wonders. Fresh and organic fruits, vegetables, and herbs overflowed many barrels.

Alissia avoided going near the meat vendors, and Anika introduced her to a variety of dried leaves, roots, and herbs to be steeped into a hot drink called chet. They both enjoyed sampling new flavors at many of the tables.

The women dressed less formal than the night before, and with the sun shining down on her purple hair, many people stared at Alissia. She even overheard a small child ask her mother about "that strange lady."

Once back at the townhouse, the two women enjoyed a quick lunch before leaving again to walk around the city. They entered a variety of shops and looked around, and Alissia found another pair of hand-crafted sunglasses to add to her much needed collection. She also found some scarves she could wear over her head to conceal her hair.

At a small bookstore, she found a few books describing some of the natural resources. With nature being so important, she needed to learn the many varieties and uses for each animal, plant, rock, and even streams of water.

After they finished shopping, the two of them went home to prepare dinner. While Alissia chopped vegetables, Grady entered the kitchen. He walked directly over to her and gave her a peck on the cheek.

"Did you have a good day?"

Alissia smiled at his unexpected affection. "I did. How about you?"

"I think we'll be able to talk to Agro this week. It's not too difficult to track him down."

She stopped chopping the root in her hand and looked back at him in surprise. "How can you find him so fast?"

He gave a smug grin. "I work for the Eldership. All I had to do was go to the Eldership building and pull some information." Looking at the knife in her hand, he teased, "You haven't been getting any ideas with the knife have you?"

She laughed and shook her head.

As they ate dinner, Anika told everyone about Alissia needing dance lessons, and Grady seemed eager to begin. They cleaned the kitchen and cleared a space in the small sitting room. Then Alissia learned how they recorded music onto crystals that played on a music box.

Anika and Langley went to the kitchen to dance, while she and Grady went to the sitting area. They began with slow music, and Grady effortlessly moved her along the floor. Without knowing any of the steps, she found herself following his lead, dipping and spinning at his subtle promptings.

"You seem to have a lot of experience when it comes to dancing," she said.

He grinned and gave her a twirl. "I learned as a boy. We're not just taught book knowledge. We're also taught how to be ambassadors, and that means I've had a lot of social and etiquette training."

The four of them enjoyed their evening of dancing and laughing, and Alissia went to sleep smiling.

By now, waking up with the feeling of being watched during the night did not surprise her. After a lot of consideration, she decided she would not fear the ones responsible for the handprints on her body. They healed or even brought her back to life, and she believed they probably ran away because of Grady.

When she walked into the kitchen, the others were sitting at the table finishing their breakfast. The men decided to take the day off rather than spend their day getting wet in the pouring rain.

Alissia enjoyed spending the entire day with Grady. They sat together on the sofa and looked through a book about plants, and he explained each of their uses and where they could be found. She gave him a yoga lesson, and he taught her a new formal dance.

As the four of them ate dinner, they decided upon a fake history for Alissia. She would be from another big city south of Allure called Lanora. With the city so far away, there would be less of a chance of meeting someone from there.

They would say that she and Grady met while she visited Allure. They fell in love quickly, and they planned to marry at the end of spring. She wanted to buy a wedding dress from Pallen, and Anika wanted to spend the winter there with her husband.

After dinner, the four of them sat in the sitting room, and they ended their night with laughter and pleasant conversation.

The following morning Alissia joined Anika in the kitchen to find the men already gone, but they came home early in the afternoon with Agro's address. The four of them decided that Grady and Alissia needed to go alone to meet him, since Agro probably would not share as much with the others around.

She and Grady left after dinner in the early evening hours. He rented a rickshaw, and she sat next to him with a small blanket in her lap and his arm around her. They rode in silence for a long while, deep in their own thoughts regarding the meeting about to take place.

"What are your feelings toward Agro for bringing you here?" Grady asked, keeping his voice low.

Alissia looked down at her hands, a mix of emotions filling her as she carefully considered her words. "I'm mad about the fact that he brought me here without even caring if it would kill me." She let out a sigh before looking up to meet his gaze. "If I had died, it would have been because of what he did, and I consider that murder."

He pulled her closer and kissed the top of her head. "I don't know anything about him now, but I do know that he was in a very dark place when his mother died and his father was imprisoned. That's not an excuse for what he did, but I can't help but wonder why he sent me his notes. I'm with the Eldership, and it's my job to have him arrested. He could have just burned his notes and went on with his life. The Agro I knew years ago would have done that."

The rickshaw stopped at a small home on the outskirts of the city. Grady helped her out of it before paying the driver. Then he took her by the hand and gave it a light squeeze. "Ready?"

She nodded, and they walked the short distance to the house. Grady knocked on the door, and a woman about the same age as Alissia soon opened it. With long, curly and red hair, she wore a plain, yellow dress, and she carried an infant girl on her hip.

"May I help you?" she asked, with a friendly smile.

"My name is Grady, and this is Alissia. We're here to see Agro. Is he home?"

A look of alarm appeared on the woman's face, and her eyes went to Alissia. She quickly recovered and smiled. Moving aside, she politely said, "Yes, please come in."

The woman led them into the kitchen, where a man with light blonde hair and pale skin sat finishing his dinner.

"Agro, you have visitors."

He glanced at Grady before his eyes fell on Alissia, and a grave look appeared on his face. Turning back to Grady, he gave a curt nod. "Grady, I haven't seen you in a while." Motioning with his hand, he tried to smile as he said, "Both of you, please sit down. Have you eaten?"

Grady and Alissia nodded and took a seat at the small table, and the woman quickly cleared the dishes away. As she sat down next to Agro, their eyes met, and she gave an encouraging smile.

"This is my wife, Tia, and our little one, Faye." The somber look returned to his face, and he placed his elbows on the table. "I know why you're here."

"This is Alexandra," Grady said. "She now prefers to be called Alissia, and she was pulled through the window."

Tia took her husband by the hand and gave it a squeeze.

"I'm very sorry for what I did," Agro said, staring into Alissia's eyes, "and I wish I could undo it. I tried to find a way to reverse it, but I couldn't think of anything. When I realized there was nothing I could do, I sent everything to Grady. He's an honorable man and would help." He paused before asking, "Did you get hurt coming through the window?"

Alissia looked at Grady, not trusting herself to speak. Agro seemed remorseful, and she knew she would eventually forgive him—but not tonight. It took all her strength to fight against the fiery rage stirring within her, as she did not want Grady to see that dark side of her.

Beneath the table, Grady took her hand in his and rubbed his thumb along her palm. "We don't really know what happened when she came through," he answered, "and we still have a lot of questions. What do you know about the cave she landed in?"

"All I know is that nobody ever goes there," answered Agro, with a shrug, "and I could get there within an hour on horseback from the Eldership. It's not far from the trails, so the risk of an animal attack is low. I found it while researching some maps of the mountains. The cave only showed on one of the maps, so I went there for myself. When I moved here, I knew that I couldn't get there in enough time."

He paused, glancing at Alissia. "Grady," he said pleadingly, "I'm not the same person I was back then. I was too consumed with myself to care about anyone else, but I've now learned to have peace through my Creator. I'm very sorry for what I did and wish that I could undo it."

Alissia focused on her breathing, all too aware of her chest rising and falling at a rapid pace. "You know," she said, through clenched teeth, "I was in a very dark place years ago too, but I never tried to kill anyone—by accident or on purpose."

After a moment of uncomfortable silence, Grady said, "I looked at the window after she came through, and the hole didn't get bigger. It looks as though she was squeezed through." His eyes locked onto Agro's, and he said firmly, "And her body suffered greatly when she came through. Do you know of a way that she can get home? Any idea whatsoever?"

Agro shook his head. "I worked through everything I knew so that I could get through, and I didn't even get close to accomplishing anything. The only thing I managed to do was throw a little connection into her reality. I stopped experimenting shortly after I left Allure and gave up."

He paused before adding, "As far as I know, there's no way back. I found the jade in some of my father's belongings, and even if we did know of a way, I'm guessing it won't have enough power to send her back."

After a moment of silence, Grady stated, "Then I'll close the window."

The finality of his words stunned Alissia. Although she expected that she would never be able to return to her reality, no one had ever said the words out loud and with such decisiveness.

Grady stood and pulled Alissia up next to him. Then he smiled down at Tia. "It was nice meeting you, Tia." Turning to his former friend, he said, "Agro, I'm happy you've found peace and hope you continue with that. I wish the best for you and your lovely family. You've answered all our questions, and I think it's time we leave."

Tia and Agro followed them to the door, where Grady stopped and turned around. "Nobody knows about this," he said firmly. "You know what the Eldership would do to all of us, especially her, if they ever found out. You can never tell anyone about her. Is that understood?"

The two of them adamantly agreed they would never speak of it to anyone, and she and Grady left. Thankful for his silence as they walked toward the city, Alissia thought of her mother and sister, and she imagined them crying over her disappearance.

"Grady," she said, not looking at him, "whatever happened to my diary?"

"I picked it up when I found you and placed it under your mattress at Anika's house. I never read a page, and I've been waiting for you to ask for it."

"So, it's not in my reality for anyone to see?"

He lifted her hand and gave it a kiss. "It's not in the other reality, and your family will never see it."

Although Alissia always feared allowing someone to know her true self, she liked how Grady seemed to continuously know what she was thinking. He always seemed to say and do the right things at the perfect moment.

Once they got closer to the city, they found a rickshaw, and they rode in silence until it stopped in front of a small café. After paying the driver, Grady led her to a table and sat down close beside her.

"What are we doing here?"

He smiled and set a menu down in front of her. "We're having dessert. I know you're upset right now, and I honestly don't want you to go to bed tonight with a heavy heart."

Not knowing how to respond, she looked down at the menu and read through her choices. She soon decided upon a piece of pie made with an unknown ingredient and a new flavor of chet to drink.

"I'm sorry I don't know how to get you back to your reality," said Grady, after the waitress left their table. "All I can do is help you in this one. Langley would love for you to work on his ranch. You have amazing abilities, so you don't have to worry about not being able to take care of yourself." He smiled hopefully. "You might even learn to like it here."

"I love it here," replied Alissia, trying to return his smile. "I just hate that my mother and sister will suffer even more because of my disappearance."

"I understand," he said, nodding.

While eating, he successfully got Alissia to laugh a few times. She could tell he was really trying to make her feel better, and she took comfort in knowing he cared about her happiness.

They strolled through the gardens on their way home and enjoyed the living statues and music. As they turned into their alley, he said, "We can start research at the library to see what we can find on the Lamians. HHThere are a lot of historical books we can go through."

Alissia nodded, still not having much to say. At the door, he took her into his arms and gave her a long kiss.

"Do you feel better?" he asked, stroking her hair.

She smiled up at him. "Yes, and thank you for tonight."

He kissed her forehead before letting her go, and then he opened the door.

Alissia said nothing as she passed Langley and Anika sitting on the sofa, and she quickly readied for bed. Staring up at the stars through the clear ceiling, thoughts of her mother and sister kept her awake.

Late into the night, a sudden idea came to her, and she shot out of bed and crept downstairs. Silence filled the air, and an occasional heat stone put out a soft, red glow in the darkened townhouse. She tiptoed to the sofa, where she leaned down and whispered, "Grady. Grady, I need to talk to you."

"Alissia?" has asked, sleep and confusion filling his voice.

He rolled onto his side and slid over before lifting the blanket and pulling her onto the sofa. "What's wrong?" he asked, putting his arm around her and pulling her in close so that her back nestled against his chest.

"I have an idea. Can you leave the window open and keep recording the area around the tree?"

"I can. But why do you want this?"

"I want to see my mom and sister through the recordings. I know they'll go there often, since that's the last place I was. I just want to see them."

"Alissia," he began hesitantly, "you know how sad they'll be. Are you sure you want to watch it?"

"I'm sure," she asserted. "And maybe one day, we can find a way to send a message through to them."

His body tensed. "We can try."

She rolled over and studied his face. "Is there a problem with this request?"

"Not really. I already knew that I'm going to have to distance myself from the Eldership."

"What do you mean?" she questioned. Her brows drew together, and she frowned. "Why would you distance yourself from your career? I thought you were in line to be an elder one day."

"I don't think I'm going to be able to hide you, do illegal experiments, and be in the Eldership at the same time. I'm going to have to leave the Eldership."

Seeing the sadness in his eyes, she shook her head adamantly. "Grady, I never meant for you to leave your career, and I don't want you to do that for me. We could just leave the window open and never experiment. I could live outside Allure, somewhere away from the Eldership, and you could still have your job."

He gave a light, sarcastic laugh. "So, I would keep my job and live in Allure close to the Eldership? And you would live somewhere away from the Eldership . . . and me?"

"I don't want you to leave what you've worked your entire life for. It wouldn't be right," she insisted. "Technically, you don't even have to be doing any of this for me. I'm beyond grateful. You saved my life, but I'm not your respon—"

His unexpected kiss sent shivers throughout her entire body, and she relaxed in his arms, responding readily to his touch.

"So," he whispered, pulling away, "we just walk away from this? Is that what you really want?"

She stared into his questioning eyes and answered softly, "I don't want you to give up your career because of me."

"What if I want to?" he said firmly. "It's my decision, isn't it?"

Alissia sucked in a breath, her eyes suddenly wide with fear. She had never talked commitment with anyone. Wasn't it too soon for that? They only knew each other for a few weeks, although they practically lived together and saw each other throughout each day and into the night. Surely, that would count for more than a few weeks.

He pulled her into his arms and held her close. "I've scared you. We have a lot of time before any decisions have to be made. We're spending the entire winter in a beautiful city, and we don't have to think about any of this right now. Let's just focus on trying to find out what's going on with you. Does that sound better?"

She nodded her head against his chest, and it did not take long for her pulse to return to its normal pace. The steady rhythm of his heartbeat at her ear, along his woodsy scent, gradually soothed her fears away.

He rubbed his hand along her back, and then he lifted her head up by her chin. As his lips came down on hers, heat rushed throughout her entire body, and she eagerly returned his kiss.

What started out as soft and slow, soon turned to a passionate need, and her body yearned for his touch. Then he abruptly pulled away.

"You should get back to your bed before it's too late. I want to do this right," he said huskily. He kissed her forehead and let out a long, shaky breath. "This is going to be hard."

Without a word, she left him on the sofa and fled to her room, where she no longer thought of her mother and sister. Instead, thoughts of Grady consumed her mind.

She eventually found sleep, and when she awoke the next morning, it took longer than usual for her to get out of bed. Although she did not get much sleep, she still woke up with the usual feeling of being watched during the night.

When she stepped out of her bedroom, Grady walked out of the bathroom with wet hair, and a fresh scent filled the air.

"Good morning." With a knowing look, he asked, "How long did it take you to fall asleep last night?"

She grinned. "How long did it take you?"

He laughed and headed down the stairs as she walked into the bathroom.

During breakfast, she and Grady decided to spend their day at the library doing research, while Langley and Anika chose to walk around the city. Her friend was eager to spend time in Pallen with her husband, and she had a long list of places she wanted to visit.

Once at the library, Grady laughed at Alissia's overwhelmed expression. "We're only here for history, and we know what years we want to start with. We don't even have to read half these books."

She smiled. With the amount of books in this vast library, there had to be information about the Lamians.

Chapter 8

Two weeks later, they had still not discovered anything regarding the Lamians, but Alissia did find that she could now read and understand the old language. Frustration grew as each day passed, and it did not help that people constantly stared at her. Her monthly never started, and she wondered if she was even a human female anymore.

One afternoon, as she and Grady ate lunch at a small café, a man walked over to their table.

"Grady?"

"Langston, how have you been? I haven't seen you in years." Grady motioned to a chair. "Would you like to join us? This is my betrothed, Alissia. Alissia, this is Langston, an old friend of mine from the Eldership."

"Betrothed?" Langston sat down and grinned at Alissia. "I didn't think anyone could ever distract him from the Eldership." Turning to Grady, he asked, "What are you doing in Pallen?"

"You know how all the women adore Pallen's fashion," Grady answered, leaning back in his chair. "Alissia wanted a wedding dress, and since my cousin, Anika, wanted to spend the winter here, I decided to come along. How do you like living here?"

The man grinned. "I'm married now."

"You're married?" Grady's eyebrows lifted. "Now I'm the one surprised. I didn't think that was your style."

Langston shrugged. "Neither did I. I fell hard and fast." He turned to Alissia. "You should meet my wife. The Eldership is having a ball Friday night." Turning back to Grady, he asked, "Are the two of you going?"

"I hadn't planned on it. I'm on vacation and haven't been close to the Eldership since I've been here."

Langston's face took on a look of mock surprise. "You haven't been close to the Eldership since you've been here?" He turned to Alissia. "What have you done to this man? He's always close to the Eldership." To Grady, he said, "Seriously, you should join us. You know how women love to get all dressed up for these things, and you know how we like to see them all dressed up."

He pulled a card from his front pocket. "Here's the information, and don't forget to bring your Eldership I.D. Pallen's parties are even better than those of Allure."

As Grady took the card, Langston said, "I'll let everyone know you're in town, and they'll want to see you." He shook his head. "I can't believe you haven't let anyone know you're here."

"I did stop by the Eldership when I first arrived and saw a few people."

"Hah! The wrong ones, since they didn't let anyone else know you're in town. The men are going to be happy to see you, and none of them will believe you're finally engaged. We all had bets on how soon you'd be an elder." He turned to Alissia with a grin. "You've saved this man from a life of drudgery."

Grady laughed. "Who all is here that I know?"

As the men continued their conversation about various people within the Eldership and shared some of their old memories together, Alissia considered what Langston said about Grady becoming an elder one day.

Her thoughts stayed with her throughout the rest of the afternoon, and he asked her more than once what she was thinking. She knew he did not believe her excuse of being tired, and she also knew he would not stop asking about it until she gave a direct answer.

She dreaded their walk home and tried to think of an excuse to avoid their daily stroll through the gardens. Once home, she planned to stay close to Anika so that Grady would not have a chance to ask questions, as she did not know how to tell him how she felt.

While carrying a small stack of books to be put away, a man bumped into her, knocking them from her hands. He was blonde, well-dressed, and appeared to be in his late thirties. He bent down to retrieve the books, and as he straightened, he said, "I'm sorry. I wasn't paying attention. My name's Holt. What's yours?"

Remembering to talk with her practiced accent, she returned his smile. "I'm Alissia. Thank you for helping with the books."

"It's the least I could do, since it was entirely my fault." He glanced at the books in his hands. "You must like history. What are you searching for? I'm a historian, and I might be able to answer some questions for you."

Even if he could answer questions about the Lamians, she dared not mention their name, as she knew she resembled them too much. She quickly decided to change the subject. "Where do you work as a historian? You're local?"

He shook his head. "No, I'm actually just visiting Pallen and love their library. I think I saw you in here the other day, too. You must love it as much as I do."

As he carried her books to the bin, she did what her friends advised her to do when meeting someone from this reality. She acted shy and smiled a lot.

When they arrived at the bin, he read each of the titles before setting them down. Then he turned and said, "If you like these, I believe I know of another one you might like from this time period. It's a lot more interesting. Are you going to be here tomorrow? I can bring it to you."

"Um . . . I think so. My fiancé . . ." Remembering that word was not used in this reality, she stammered, "I mean . . . my betrothed and I are usually here almost every day." She took a few steps toward her table. "If I'm not here tomorrow, I should be here another day."

He grinned, walking beside her. "Good! I'll find it and bring it to you."

"That's nice of you," she said, wanting to be rid of him. "Thank you."

"Are you from around here?"

"No, we're just visiting the city." She stopped walking and turned to him. "It was nice meeting you. Maybe I'll see you tomorrow."

He gave a curt nod. "I'll be here."

She walked alone the rest of the way back to the table, and noticing her sudden mood change, Grady asked, "What are you smiling about?"

She grinned even bigger. "I just talked to my first stranger all by myself. And y'all were worried I couldn't do it!"

He gave a mock look of surprise. "And what did you talk about?"

"He's a historian and wants to bring me a book like the ones he carried for me."

"Oh, so he carried your books?" he teased, his brows raised.

"He carried my books, because he made me drop them when he bumped into me." She laughed. "You aren't jealous, are you?"

He chuckled lightly as he walked around the table. "No, I'm not jealous." He gave her a quick kiss on the forehead.

"Are we ready to leave?" she asked. He nodded and took her by the hand, and as they walked toward the door, she said, "Do you think it might be raining outside?"

His smile faded. "No, but I can guess that you want it to be."

"And why would I want to walk home in the rain?" she asked, trying to sound lighthearted.

"That's easy, Alissia. You've been thinking about something all afternoon." After a pause, he added, "And you're not tired, but since you want me to believe you are, I know of the perfect bench in a nearby garden where you can rest."

"But I think I just need to go to bed early tonight."

He stopped walking and asked gravely, "Is it that bad?"

She tried to smile. "Is what that bad?"

"Whatever it is you don't want to talk about, is it bad enough to make you want to avoid me?"

Glancing down at her shoe, Alissia chewed on her bottom lip. She hated to see him hurting. "I don't want to avoid you. I just . . . don't usually talk about everything."

He squeezed her hand, looking intently into her eyes. "If you don't talk to me about it, how am I supposed to help you?"

Grady led her to a private bench near the back of one of the gardens. After they sat down, he turned to face her.

"Does this have anything to do with our conversation with Langston today?"

"Yes," she answered softly, looking down at her hands. She began to fiddle with the engagement ring.

"Does this have to do with my job at the Eldership?"

She nodded. "Yes."

"Would you like to tell me, or shall I continue with the questions?"

Letting out a deep breath, Alissia stopped fidgeting with the ring and turned to face him. "You've worked your entire life to become an elder. That's been your dream since childhood, and it's one that you can make come true. Then I fall into your reality, and you immediately feel obligated to help me. You've spent a lot of money on me, you've traveled through the mountains with me, and now you're talking about leaving the Eldership because of me."

With pleading eyes, she stated, "Langley said I could get a job on his ranch. I can then take care of myself. You're not obligated to give up everything to protect me from the Eldership, and I could live a quiet life."

Grady crossed his arms and leaned back in the bench, staring at the statue in front of them. Alissia watched him, while chewing on her bottom lip.

"Are you upset?" she asked.

He turned to face her, his eyes full of sadness. "You think I'm doing all this out of obligation to you." He let out a breath before asking softly, "Will you ever allow anyone to just love you? Nothing complicated. No hidden motives. Can you understand that to me, you're more important than the Eldership? If I do what you propose and went back to the Eldership while you live your life elsewhere, I would be miserable. It's not what I want. I've known it from the day I met you but didn't want to scare you by moving too fast. Now, I'm scaring you away because I'm moving too slow. You really don't know how I feel about you, do you?"

He sighed and looked intently into her eyes. "Alissia, I want you more than anything I've ever wanted, and I want you for as long as I can have you."

He took her by the hand. While rubbing his thumb along her engagement ring, he said, "I don't want you to ever take this ring off your finger, and I want to place another ring beside it one day."

Alissia's heart fell from her chest.

He continued, "It may be too soon for you, and I don't want you to say anything in return to what I'm about to say." He paused, staring hard into her eyes. "I love you. I don't want the Eldership. I want you. I will follow you on this journey to find out what's happening to you, but I'm not doing it out of obligation. I'm doing it because I'll be miserable if I don't do it." He shook his head. "I'm not walking away from you."

A mix of emotions raged within Alissia as she turned to stare at the statue. She never imagined love to be a part of her life. And did he just propose?

Not knowing how to respond, she said, "I won't mention it again."

"Mention what?" he asked, confused.

She turned to him and tried to smile. "The Eldership. I won't mention them again, but I want you to make sure you don't feel obligated to do anything for me."

He nodded. "Have I scared you?"

She thought for a moment before answering, "I've just never heard anything like that before, and I wasn't expecting it."

"But have I scared you?" he asked again, his eyes searching.

She gave a reassuring smile. "No, you haven't scared me—surprised, but not scared."

He smiled and leaned down to give her a long, tender kiss.

As they walked the rest of the way home, Alissia mulled over their conversation. She never allowed herself to imagine a future with anyone. Could Grady be different?

Later that evening as she and Grady ate dinner with Anika and Langley, Grady said, "I saw someone from the Eldership today, and he invited us to a ball on Friday night."

"It's been a long time since I've been to a ball," Anika said. Then her expression changed to concern. "Do you think Alissia should go to a ball at the Eldership? Would that be safe?"

Grady leaned back in his chair and shook his head. "It won't be safe but not going won't be any safer. Langston will tell everyone I'm in town, and they'll begin to wonder why I haven't visited with anyone or been active at the Eldership. If we miss the dance, some of them will begin to look for me and will want to meet Alissia. I think we should go and end everyone's curiosity in one night."

"Why don't you go without me?" Alissia asked.

He shook his head. "He'll tell everyone I'm engaged. If I show up alone, that would draw more attention to us. Even if I told them you were sick, they would want to meet you later, and I would rather you meet them in a crowd than in an intimate setting. I think we're going to have to play this out." He looked at Langley. "I need for you and Anika to come with us. That way, Alissia will have Anika by her side in there. You know how some of these women can be."

"Do you think Anika can handle all those women?" Langley asked.

Anika swatted her husband on the shoulder and laughed. "I've been to plenty of these things before I married you. I can deal with them."

Getting a little worried, Alissia asked, "How bad can they be?"

"Some women like to tear other women apart when they feel threatened," replied Anika.

"And why would they feel threatened by me?"

Using her fingers to count, Anika said, "Because you're a female, you're new, and you're pretty. It only takes one of those reasons for an Eldership woman to feel threatened."

"What about her hair and eyes?" Langley asked.

After a moment of silence, Anika responded, "There's no way we can hide her hair. As for her eyes, she'll have to wear dark glasses, and we can say she has a medical condition that makes her eyes sensitive to light. I think she should even wear a dress that matches her hair, and she should act as though nothing is wrong. Although she's different, she was born this way, and it's natural."

"Natural?" asked Alissia, with a sarcastic frown. "Have you ever heard of anyone born with purple hair, nails, and eyes. And let's not forget about my shimmery skin?"

"No," countered Anika, "but I have heard of a baby born with three arms. Sometimes, unnatural things happen naturally, Alissia. There are those rare occasions."

"I think that's all we can do. We can't hide it," Grady said thoughtfully. He smiled at Alissia. "You're just a rare beauty."

Anika turned to Alissia with an excited grin. "This means we need to go shopping for a dress and have our hair and nails done." She looked down at Alissia's nails and frowned. "Well, I'll need to have my nails done."

Alissia rolled her eyes and shook her head. *Great! More shopping. And more spending of Grady's money.*

Chapter 9

Anika and Alissia spent the next day shopping for ball gowns. With Pallen having a reputation for fashion, the women had plenty of stores to browse. After making their selections, they paid extra for express alterations and arrived home in time for dinner.

Over their evening meal, Anika excitedly described their dresses to the men and informed them that she and Alissia would be going shoe shopping the next day.

Shoe shopping always challenged Alissia, as most stores never even carried her small size. The same was true for this reality, and it took them the entire day to find the perfect shoes to fit her.

That evening, she and Grady practiced dancing. She greatly enjoyed his lessons, as he always found a way to make it fun and romantic at the same time, and she went to bed smiling on each of those nights.

On the day of the ball, Alissia and Anika went to a spa, where they enjoyed full body massages before sitting in a pool of something warm, green, and floral-scented. A thick cream removed the unwanted hair from their bodies, leaving Alissia's legs smooth and shiny.

Her purple hair caught a lot of attention from the workers, and she acted shy, letting Anika do most of the talking. She only took off her glasses a few times—keeping her eyes closed each time. As an extra precaution, she also kept them closed the entire time a woman cut and styled her hair.

As she looked at herself in the mirror that evening, she could barely recognize her reflection. She wore a strapless dress with a sweetheart neckline and an empire waist. The lightweight fabric, with a sheer outer layer, hung loosely above her matching ballet slippers. A long slit ran along the left side of the dress, which matched the same deep shade of purple as her hair.

She loved the feel of running her hands along the outside of the dress. When she moved, it shimmered in the light.

Her hair, pulled onto her head and held in place by pins that shined like jewels, sparkled with glitter. A few of her long curls hung loosely around her lightly made-up face, and her purple nails and skin shimmered in the light.

Not wanting to spend too much of Grady's money, she chose not to buy jewelry and continued to wear her imitation diamond stud earrings.

Alissia frowned as she picked up a new pair of tinted glasses and put them on. Although they matched perfectly, she despised having to wear dark glasses at night. She also hated how much money her growing collection of handcrafted sunglasses costed Grady.

A light knock sounded on the door, and she hastily grabbed her intimate clothing scattered around the room. After hiding them beneath the pillow on her bed, she opened the door.

Grady smiled, causing her heart to flutter. He wore black dress pants with a matching frock coat. His dark burgundy double vest had a white, lace neck wrap hanging out from it, and he held a black box in one hand.

"May I come in?"

Alissia gave a nervous smile and stepped back. "Yeah, come in."

As he entered the room, she chided herself for not being in control of her emotions, and she forced a cool smile onto her face. He took her by the hand and kissed it lightly while gazing into her eyes. "You're beautiful. I don't think I'm going to be able to take my eyes off you all night."

She felt herself swallow. "Thank you."

"I got you a gift," he said, releasing her hand and holding out the box. "I hope you like what I selected."

Alissia focused on trying to keep her hands from shaking as she accepted the box and lifted the lid. She instantly took in a sharp breath, and with wide eyes, she stared down at a deep purple, jewel drop necklace and matching earrings.

"I tried to match them to your hair, because I've come to love that color," he said softly. He took the necklace from the box and fastened it around her neck, where it rested against her bare chest. Standing behind her, he turned her to face the mirror. "Do you like it?"

"I love it," she stammered, reaching up to trace her fingers along the necklace. "Thank you."

He took the box from her other hand and began to pull one of the earrings from it, and she quickly removed her fake studs. Once she finished putting in the new earrings, he stood behind her, and the two of them stared at their reflection in the mirror. Shivers went through her entire body when he kissed her shoulder.

"You make them look beautiful," he said. He then surprised her by reaching up and pulling the tinted glasses from her face. "You're beautiful—especially your eyes—and I love to look into them."

She frowned and shook her head. "They don't even look normal."

He turned her around and gazed into her eyes. "No, but that doesn't mean they don't look beautiful. I love the rare occasions when I get to see them, and I'm thankful that I'm one of the few people that get to see them."

He kissed her forehead before handing back her glasses. Taking a step away, he held out his arm. "Shall we go? I believe we have a ball to attend."

As they walked out of the bedroom, he added, "Anika's probably pacing the floor by now to see your necklace. She's not very happy with me for making her wait."

They found Anika and Langley waiting for them at the bottom of the stairs. Anika wore a long, gold, shimmery dress with a pearl necklace and earrings, and her long, auburn hair was pulled onto her head. Langley wore a suit similar to Grady's, with a deep olive colored vest.

Seeing Alissia, Anika darted over. She eyed the necklace and earrings before a broad grin spread across her face. "I'm impressed," she said, turning to Grady.

He laughed heartily, and the four of them put on their formal cloaks and gloves. They walked to the awaiting carriage in the alley, and as they traveled the back paths through the city, Alissia felt as though she lived in a fairytale.

They stopped at a stone path, and Grady helped her out of the carriage. The short trail led through a beautiful garden filled with statues, glow stones, fountains, and various colored bella flowers.

The music from the ball could be heard as they walked along the path, and they soon came to a large, two-story building. Grady explained that the building was actually a massive gazebo made with double supporting beams all around. Long, thick, burgundy curtains surrounded the building between each set of beams, and white, glowing bella flowers covered each beam.

Two guards dressed in matching uniforms and topcoats with gloves and hats stood at the entrance. Alissia stopped walking and watched as a couple walked up to the guards. The man showed his pass before the guards stepped to opposite sides of the entrance. As they pulled on separate golden cords, the curtains opened. Once the smiling guests walked through, the guards released the cords, closing the curtains.

"Wow! I've never seen anything like this," Alissia said, grinning excitedly.

Grady responded, "The curtains are only up during the cold season. There are heat rocks inside, and the thick curtains help to keep the heat from escaping."

Anika pulled her cloak tightly around her body. "Then I think we should go inside. I need some of that heat."

After the guards approved them, the curtains opened, and the four of them stepped into a foyer surrounded by more thick curtains. A group of men dressed in matching uniforms took their cloaks and gloves to be put away. Then more curtains were pulled back, revealing a large, open area filled with talking and laughing guests. At the back of the room another set of curtains held open by thick, golden cords revealed people dancing beyond the opening.

Large heat and glow stones set in elegant fixtures hung down from the rafters of the clear ceiling. White bella flowers covered each supporting beam with their roots hidden inside the base. Glow stones and something resembling marble formed the floor, each floral-shaped glow stone set in place with the marble, similar to interlocking tile.

All the women wore long, elegant dresses of various colors, and some had glitter in their hair and shimmery body lotion on their skin. The jewels Grady gave her would not stand out in this room, as it appeared as if all the women wore jewels of their own. The men wore suits similar to Grady's with various colored vests beneath their jackets.

Anika smiled at Alissia. "Is this what you were expecting?"

Alissia, still mesmerized by her surroundings, shook her head and continued to look around the room.

Grady linked his arm into hers and led them into the crowd, and it did not take long before someone recognized him and called him over.

"Grady, it's been a long time. What are you doing in Pallen this winter?"

"I'm on vacation. My betrothed here wants a dress from Pallen, and I couldn't say no." Motioning to Alissia, Grady added, "Jarek, this is my lovely bride-to-be, Alissia. Alissia, this is Jarek. He worked with me in Allure." Gesturing to Anika, he said, "I'm not sure if you already know my cousin, Anika, and her husband, Langley. They're serving as our chaperones."

Jarek grinned at Langley. "Yes, I know both Langley and his father. Bought my best horse from them." He shook his head, adding, "Although, I don't do much riding since moving here to Pallen."

After Jarek introduced his wife, Keara, and all the others in the group, the men began to discuss the Eldership, while the women talked about the décor in the room. That topic did not last long, and the women soon began to ask personal questions about her and Grady. She politely answered some of them using her fake accent, but Anika answered most of them for her.

They began to inquire about Alissia's childhood, and although Anika subtly tried to change the subject more than once, the women seemed intent on quizzing Alissia.

During the attack on her privacy, Alissia continued to smile, but her patience ran out when a woman named Dhara asked snidely, "Why are you wearing dark glasses at night, at a ball? You do realize it is night, don't you?"

As she opened her mouth to speak, Anika interjected, "She has a medical condition she was born with, leaving her eyes sensitive to light." She linked her arm into Alissia's. "Now, if you'll excuse us, ladies, we just got here and haven't had a chance to walk around." She then got the men's attention before leading Alissia away.

"What was that all about, and why didn't they ask questions about you?" demanded Alissia.

"Because I'm not betrothed to one of Allure's most eligible bachelors known for choosing his career over women." Anika stopped walking and turned to look into Alissia's eyes. "I'm not a future wife of a future elder. I don't come from a distant land. I don't have purple hair, and I'm not the one wearing dark glasses at a ball at night. I'm a married woman, and my husband and I don't have anything to do with the Eldership. They have no interest in me. They are, however, interested in you, and they were testing you to see how you would respond."

Alissia glanced over her shoulder to find Grady watching her. Although he smiled, she thought she noticed worry in his eyes. She gave a reassuring smile before turning her attention back to Anika. In a calmer tone, she asked, "Why would they test me?"

"Alissia, look around the room at the women." Anika paused before stressing, "I mean, *really* look at them." Alissia began to scan the room, and Anika continued, "Most of the women here put a lot of effort into being the wife, or date, of an Eldership man, and they worked hard to get close to the man they're here with.

"Being a member of the Eldership is the highest respected position within our land and comes with a lot of wealth and power. The people at the top even get to live in castles." Placing both of her hands on her chest, she added wistfully, "Young girls *dream* of living at an Eldership castle and going to balls like this."

She dropped her hands and frowned. "As for the young boys selected to receive Eldership training, their early years are filled with hard work. Their childhood is much different than others, and they only get to see girls on the occasional holidays they spend with their families. Once they graduate and begin to work within the Eldership, everything suddenly changes for them. They no longer live at the school, and they can have somewhat of a normal life. At the same time, they begin to attend balls like this all throughout the year."

She shook her head in disgust. "You'd be surprised at how many young women see unmarried Eldership men as prey, and they'll do just about anything to become married to one. They'll lie, manipulate, and hurt anyone that gets in their way. In doing so, friendship isn't important to them."

Alissia's eyebrows rose in disbelief, and Anika nodded adamantly. She touched Alissia's arm, adding, "And it's worse if their father's in the Eldership. The young boys strive hard to make their parents happy by getting selected for training. If one son is selected and another one isn't, it usually devastates the one not chosen. Imagine being a boy with an Eldership father that expects the same from you, yet you're not chosen while your brother is."

Alissia cringed.

"Exactly!" said Anika. "And for the daughters, they usually go to private schools surrounded by other Eldership children. Most of their social skills come from their mothers, so they learn at an early age to put themselves first. By the time they're grown, they're experts at making other women look bad so they can look good. They spend all their youths pursuing Eldership men, and they spend the rest of their lives trying to keep them." She leaned in closer, raising her eyebrows. "And a lot of these men have mistresses."

"But I thought this reality didn't do that," said Alissia, her face twisted in confusion. "Grady and I needed a chaperone just to travel together, and he said people waited until after marriage before doing anything like that."

Anika smiled. "That's because Grady and most of our society hold onto the laws of our Creator. They stay strong in their faith. Having a mistress is highly shameful and disliked, and it can ruin a career."

She shook her head, her smile fading. "However, there are plenty of women in this world that don't care about that. If they can't marry an Eldership man, they don't mind being his mistress. It's all about the money. These men are constantly pursued by women, and sometimes they succumb to the temptation—not all of them, but some."

Scanning the room, she added, "And not all the women in this room are horrible. You just have to discern between the good and bad."

Looking back at Alissia, she asked, "So do you see why I came with you, and you had to come? Grady has a reputation for being married to the Eldership, and people will be very curious to know who has won his attention. He usually doesn't pursue a woman or pay attention to the women that pursue him."

"Why doesn't he?"

Anika cocked her head thoughtfully for a moment. Then she smiled at Alissia. "Most people think it's because he's obsessed with his career and doesn't take the time, which is true, but I also believe it's because he's like me somewhat.

"Our family's from Allure, and we have a lot of relatives within the Eldership. Although my father is not of the Eldership, my mother's brother is. I went to a private school filled with Eldership children, and I witnessed their insecurities." She shook her head, admitting, "I actually felt sorry for them—even as they tried to hurt me. I was lucky because I had parents that loved me and truly loved each other."

Her eyes drifted to Langley, and she smiled. "Although I've gone to a few balls within the Eldership with someone from my past, in the end, I chose to walk away from that lifestyle. I chose Langley, and I chose to live outside the city on a ranch."

Alissia smiled, agreeing with her friend's choice.

"As for Grady," said Anika, catching the eye of her cousin, "he spends his spare time at our ranch. To me, that means he enjoys our lifestyle and personalities over those at the Eldership." She grinned. "And believe me, our lifestyle is *very* different from most of the people in this room."

Watching Grady and Langley walk toward them, Alissia could not understand why a man like Grady would be willing to give up everything for her, and she wondered how many women have tried to gain his attention.

"The two of you look as though you're plotting something," Langley teased.

Anika laughed. "No, I was just explaining Eldership society to Alissia. She didn't have much fun with the women we just met."

Grady looked at Alissia with concern. "The best thing for you to do is act nervous and shy. Try to let Anika talk for you as much as possible."

"I can handle the Eldership women," Alissia asserted, "and I don't need Anika to speak for me."

He chuckled, shaking his head. "I know you don't need Anika, but I think it would draw less attention to you if you acted shy. The women will be less interested if you don't have much to say." He took her by the hand. "I'm hoping you never see any of them again, so don't worry about trying to impress any of them. The less you say, the less they'll turn the conversation to you."

"He's right," said Anika. "Your silence will make them uncomfortable. You don't even have to act interested in the conversation and can act as if you're not paying attention. You can even watch the people across the room."

"You've got to try not to get noticed," Grady stressed, giving her hand a light squeeze.

Alissia frowned. "I have purple hair, and I'm wearing sunglasses at a ball. Although that's not as noticeable where I come from, it doesn't blend in the land of nature people."

"Maybe no one will notice," said Langley. He smiled. "It's not as if we're in a room full of unaccepting people."

At that moment, one of Grady's colleagues interrupted the conversation, and Alissia spent the next hour meeting various people. She allowed Grady and Anika to speak for her as much as possible, and she spent a lot of time looking around the room, not paying much attention to those around her.

At one point, she noticed the man she met at the library standing across the room. He grinned at her, and she politely acknowledged him with a smile of her own before turning away.

She also noticed a man that seemed to be watching her. At first she thought it was her imagination, but each time she glanced his way, his dark, penetrating eyes bore into hers.

Except for a white ascot at his neck, he dressed completely in black. His olive skin tone and dark hair made him look like a foreigner compared to most of the others in the room, and unlike Grady's short, perfectly styled hair, his was longer, with a naturally disheveled look to it. His strong facial features gave him a fierce and dominating presence, overshadowing the men around him.

Beginning to feel self-conscious, Alissia decided to meet his gaze, thinking he would guiltily look away. Instead, he acknowledged her with a private nod, and she quickly turned her head.

HA few minutes later, Grady asked, "Shall we dance?"

"I thought you'd never ask," she answered, with a grin.

He took her hand and led her through the curtained entrance leading to the dance floor, where a small orchestra in the corner of the room played a slow song. Guests sat at tables and chairs arranged along the curtained walls of the room.

As she and Grady waited for a new song to begin, Alissia watched the couples dancing gracefully in the middle of the room. Recognizing the waltz they performed, she grinned up at Grady.

With the first two of their dances being fast paced, she giggled at Grady's playfulness as she moved along with the music. When a slow song began, he pulled her into his arms.

"I've been dying to hold you all night."

She smiled up at him but said nothing in return, too busy enjoying the moment. The music, ambiance, his embrace and smell—everything soothed her and filled her with happiness. She told herself she would never forget this moment.

After two slow dances, he kissed the top of her hand and led her away from the dance floor. They soon found Anika and Langley sitting at a table with a man she did not recognize. As she and Grady sat down at the table, Anika said, "Edric here was just telling us some interesting things about the Eldership in Pallen."

Edric looked to be in his late thirties, with dark blonde hair. After being introduced to Alissia, he turned to Grady and said eagerly, "I was just telling them about a hidden room recently discovered within the castle. It contained some old scrolls written in the ancient language, and from the small portion that's been translated, we know they were penned by a man from our kingdom that was spying on King Octavious."

He lifted his drink and took a few gulps before setting it back down. After wiping his hand across his mouth, he continued, "Nobody really knows what happened during that war, and we hope these scrolls will tell the story of how our kingdoms became united."

He leaned in closer to Grady, his expression animated. "But that's not all. The scrolls mentioned an unknown magical race of people. The Eldership has brought in some of the best translators, and we hope to soon know more about them."

Alissia stiffened, and Grady found her hand under the table and gave it a gentle squeeze. He began to rub her palm with his thumb.

"How many scrolls are there?" he asked calmly.

Edric leaned back and relaxed in his seat. "A lot, and they all have different dates on them."

"And what do they know about this group of people?" asked Grady.

"We've only had a few of the first scrolls translated so far, but we think King Octavious used them to win the war. We don't know how yet. We only know they were extremely important to him, and he sought their help."

Grady nodded. "I'd like copies of your notes as you get them. I'm sure the elders in Allure will find this information fascinating. I'll get back to you, and we can discuss this in more detail over lunch next week."

Edric seemed happy to find another person interested in the scrolls, and after guzzling down his drink, he began to retell the story. Losing interest in the conversation, Alissia went back to scanning the room, and her heart immediately fell from her chest as her gaze locked onto the same dark, piercing eyes from earlier.

The mysterious man watched her from a crowded table, and once he stopped talking, those around him laughed. He then had the audacity to wink at her, and she instinctively turned to Grady.

It took all her willpower to keep her eyes from returning to the nerve-racking man. She and Anika soon made their way across the room to the bathroom, and as they walked back to their seats, Alissia accidently knocked into someone.

"We just can't seem to stop bumping into each other, can we?"

Alissia smiled back at the man from the library. "I'm so sorry. I wasn't paying attention."

He dismissed her apology with a wave of his hand. "I found that book for you, but I didn't see you again."

"I had to go dress shopping." She turned to Anika. "Anika, this is someone I met at the library the other day." She looked back at him apologetically. "I'm sorry. I'm horrible with names. What's your name again?"

"Holt."

Alissia said to Anika, "He's a historian on vacation and said he knew of another book similar to the ones I was reading."

An attractive, tall woman with long, light blonde hair walked up to Holt, and he introduced her as his wife, Nevara. She gave a friendly smile to Alissia and asked, "Do you work with the Eldership?"

"No, my betrothed works for the Eldership in Allure. We're actually here looking for a wedding dress." Motioning to Anika, she said, "Anika and her husband are our chaperones."

She noticed Grady and Langley walking up to them and added, "Oh, here he is now. Grady, this is Holt and his wife, Nevara. Holt's the man I met from the library the other day." She then gestured to Langley. "And this is Anika's husband, Langley."

Langley politely addressed them before asking Anika to dance. As the two of them walked away, Grady turned to Holt. "Alissia told me you're a historian. Do you work here at the Eldership?"

Holt grinned, shaking his head. "No, I'm completely on vacation right now. Nevara's doing some consulting for them, so I came along to enjoy the city."

"What kind of consulting do you do?" Grady asked Nevara.

"I'm helping them translate some old documents they recently found."

"Ah," said Grady, lifting his brows, "I just heard about the recent discovery. Sounds exciting."

"There are so many mysteries hiding in those scrolls," she replied longingly. "I'm thankful the Eldership sent for me."

"As a historian, I'm eager to know what's in them," said Holt. "We've never been able to find much information about that time period, so these scrolls are a fascinating find."

The four of them enjoyed a polite conversation before Grady asked Alissia for another dance. As they shared their last slow dance of the night, she noticed the mysterious man standing at the edge of the dance floor. He seemed to be in a deep conversation with another man, and since he was not looking her way, she pointed him out to Grady. "Who's that man standing over there? The one in black."

He glanced over his shoulder. "That's Luke Harrison. He's a member of the Eldership in one of our northern territories." His eyes narrowed, and he teased, "Why? Do I have competition?"

She shook her head, smiling. "No competition. I've caught him staring at me a few times tonight and don't know why."

"You don't know why?" He lowered his head to her ear and whispered, "Alissia, you're the most beautiful woman in this room. I'd be staring at you, too, if I were him." He straightened and gave her a flattering smile. "But, luckily, I'm the one that gets to hold you."

The song ended, and he pulled away and kissed the top of her hand. He led her away from the dance floor, and searching for Anika and Langley, the two of them strolled into the other area of the gazebo. As they made their way across the room, people continuously stopped Grady, and each time, he kept the conversation short and said his goodbyes.

With dark hair fading to grey, an overweight man with the same tanned complexion as Luke Harrison walked up to them. In a cheerful, unfamiliar accent, he said, "Grady Bolair, I didn't know you were expected in Pallen. The elders sent you to check on things here?"

Grady smiled and answered politely, "No, I'm on vacation and in Pallen for a personal visit."

"And would this beautiful young lady have anything to do with your unusual distraction from the Eldership?" he asked, eyeing Alissia.

"She does," answered Grady, with a nod. He placed his hand on Alissia's back. "This is Alissia, my recently betrothed. Alissia, this is Alrik Durst."

The man held out his hand, and when she accepted it, he lowered his head and swept his lips lightly across the top of her hand. "You have soft skin and delicate hands," he said, turning her hand over and lightly inspecting it. "Where are you from, dear girl?"

Before she could answer, Grady responded, "She's from Lanora. What brings you to the city?"

Alrik released Alissia's hand and straightened. "I've some trade business to work out with the Eldership." He placed his hand on Grady's shoulder. "In fact, I was hoping I could discuss some things with you. I have some questions about the new tax bill that was just passed. I also need your opinion on a proposal I'm considering bringing to Allure. Maybe you can take some written proposals back with you."

In a polite, but straightforward manner, Grady responded, "I'm not doing any official business at this time. However, I understand Morton is here for the winter review, and he'd be happy to help you in any way he can."

Alrik smiled and nodded, releasing his grip on Grady. "I apologize. You're on vacation."

A large man slammed into Alissia from behind, and as he tried to regain his balance, he knocked her glasses from her face. She immediately closed her eyes and looked down.

Grady hastily retrieved her glasses and gave them to her before pulling the drunken man away. With her glasses back on, Alissia watched Alrik seize the top of the man's vest.

"Young man," warned Alrik, in a low, firm voice, "you seem to have had an immense amount of alcohol tonight, and I think you need to leave. You should know this is not appropriate behavior here."

Grady turned his attention to Alissia. "Are you all right?"

She nodded. "I'm fine."

Alrik motioned to a nearby server and discreetly told him to make sure the intoxicated man made it safely to a carriage. He then turned to Alissia. "You aren't hurt, are you?"

It was a subtle incident, only noticed by those nearby, and Alissia was almost certain no one saw her eyes. She smiled politely. "I'm fine. Thank you."

"You'll have to excuse us," said Grady, taking her by the hand. "We were in the process of looking for our chaperones. It's getting late."

Alrik gave a curt nod. "I wish you both a pleasant ride home. It was very nice meeting you, Alissia."

She smiled and nodded, and as Grady began to lead her toward the entrance, she noticed Luke standing near a curtained wall not too far away. He watched Alrik, but then his gaze turned to her. Instead of acknowledging her with a wink or a nod as before, his dark, piercing eyes turned cold and calculating, sending fear down her spine.

Chapter 10

A light snow fell outside as they walked along the path leading to the row of awaiting carriages. Once inside the privacy of one of them, Anika snuggled close to Langley and gave a contented sigh. "That was fun. It's been a while since I've been to an Eldership ball." She smirked at Grady. "Reminds me how blessed I am that I didn't marry into that."

Grady's body shook with laughter. "It wasn't that bad, was it?"

Before she could answer, Langley asked somberly, "What do you think about these scrolls?"

Grady thought for a moment. Then he shrugged. "We've searched for weeks and haven't found anything. Part of me is happy the scrolls could tell us more, but at the same time, I'm worried. I've already considered that Alissia's new appearance could resemble whoever changed her. My biggest concern is that the scrolls will describe them, and they'll look like her. If that happens, we'll have a problem—especially after tonight."

"I shouldn't have come," Alissia fretted.

"There was no other way," Grady responded. He pulled her closer and gave her a quick peck on the cheek. "I still think it was better for everyone to meet you in public rather than in a private setting. Besides, if it weren't for the scrolls, there wouldn't even be a threat. Although your appearance is very unique compared to others, I'm sure nobody thought of you as a Lamian. The Eldership doesn't even know about them, and we still haven't found anything about them in the historical records."

"Well, they all know what she looks like now," Anika declared. "All they need to do is find a description in the scrolls, and they'll easily think of her at the ball."

"If they come for her," Langley began, "we can't go back to the mountains right now. We'd have to go in another direction."

His statement unsettled Alissia. "What will happen to you and Anika if anyone finds out about me?"

"Nothing," Grady answered. "If someone finds out about you, the two of us will travel in the opposite direction and leave them behind."

"That's not going to happen," Anika asserted.

Grady responded firmly, "When you agreed to travel with us, there wasn't a chance of you being in trouble with the Eldership. Nobody knew anything about her or this new race of people, but now we're at a higher risk. From the moment I took her to your home, I already decided that you wouldn't take any blame for this. You'll say that I was the only one to know the truth about her. I introduced you to my new betrothed and asked you to spend the winter with us in Pallen. You never suspected a thing."

"But—"

"Anika!" Grady leaned forward, staring hard at his cousin. "If you leave with us, there'll be consequences, and I won't be able to get your life back."

"I don't want y'all to go with us," blurted Alissia, "because I don't want to be responsible for ruining anybody else's life."

Grady leaned back and let out a sigh. "Alissia, you're not responsible for ruining anyone's life, and you've actually made mine a lot better."

"How?" she demanded. "By making you lose everything? And now you might have to go on the run, too."

The carriage came to a stop, and they silently entered the townhouse. After removing their cloaks and gloves, they sat down in the small sitting room.

"We'll stay and claim our innocence," Langley said to Anika, breaking the silence, "and they won't have any proof that we know anything." He turned to Grady. "Where would you go? They know you wouldn't travel toward the mountains, and they'd search all the nearby villages."

"We'd keep moving, and when spring comes, we'd turn back toward the mountains. All her answers are in those tunnels, and we'll stay there as long as it takes to find them."

"Grady, not only do you need to get close to Edric," Anika said firmly, "but you need to try to get close to some of those translators. They're the first to know what's in the scrolls, and you'll need to know immediately if they describe someone like Alissia."

Grady nodded. "I'll start spending my evenings where some of them like to go after work. Alissia and I will pack our bags and be ready in case we have to leave quickly, and we'll go the moment I think they're getting too close. Translating is a slow process, so hopefully we'll have some time. As soon as the mountains are safe to travel, we'll leave."

He smiled at Anika. "Alissia will need the warmest traveling clothes and gear available in case we have to leave early. Do you think you can buy what she needs?"

"Another day of shopping with your money?" Anika gave a smug smile. "That doesn't sound too hard."

Everyone laughed and agreed to the plan, and Anika and Langley said their goodnights before going upstairs. Once alone, Grady turned to Alissia. "Will you please get ready for bed and come back down? I think we need to talk."

Alissia did as he asked, taking the time to pull out all the pins from her hair and putting it into a ponytail for the night. By the time she went back downstairs, all the glow stones were covered, and the roots of the bella flowers were pulled from their water. The heat rocks on the stone pedestals in front of the large windows produced a soft, red glow in the room. The thick curtains were drawn for privacy.

Grady lifted his blanket, and she climbed onto the sofa next to him, with her back against his chest and her head under his chin. He wrapped his arms around her, and they remained silent for a while, each in their own thoughts.

"Anika and Langley won't get into any trouble with the Eldership," said Grady softly. "There's no evidence they know the truth about you."

"What would happen if the Eldership finds out about me? What would they do?"

"Agro and I would go to prison for—"

"Why would you go to prison," she interjected, "when you're not the one who pulled me in? All you did was find me."

He let out a sigh before explaining, "What I did was highly illegal. Nobody is to try to get anything through a window. I also didn't report Agro's package when I received it, and it contained a rare jade that only the Eldership is supposed to have. I kept it secret, and I'm in the Eldership." He shook his head slightly. "There wouldn't be any excuse for that."

After a pause, he continued, "I would go to prison, and you'd become their new secret project. They wouldn't want anyone to know it's possible to pull someone through a window. If people knew, they might try experimenting. The Eldership would always have to keep the truth hidden, which means they'd always have to keep *you* hidden. Only a select few would even know about you, and they'd be the ones that would want to learn from you. You'd never be allowed true freedom.

"You'd also prove there's a hidden race of people that can save someone from death. The Eldership would search the tunnels until they found them. We still don't know whether the Lamians are good or bad, but we do know they saved your life. Wouldn't you rather find them for yourself?"

Alissia remained silent, her brows pinched in worry. Then she remembered the man at the ball, and she told Grady about him, ending with, "Why did he look at me as if I'd done something wrong?"

"I don't know," Grady answered thoughtfully. "Luke isn't from Pallen, and I don't think he's involved with the scrolls. He's from the North, and history isn't something he'd be concerned with."

"What would he be concerned with?"

"He's more interested in politics and military," replied Grady. After a pause, he added, "Tomorrow I'll get everything we need packed and ready in case we have to leave quickly, and I need for you to do the same as soon as Anika provides you with some winter clothing."

As she nodded, she remembered something that tugged at her thoughts all evening. "Are there any women in the Eldership?"

"No."

"Why not?" she asked defensively.

"You would ask that," he answered, his chest trembling with laughter. "Alissia, the Eldership was founded long ago, and nothing has changed since then. Things are a bit different than where you come from."

She frowned. "Do y'all think women can't do the job?"

"I don't think any such thing," he asserted. "It's just the way the Eldership was designed. In fact, you met a woman tonight that's translating the scrolls for the Eldership."

"She just can't have an Eldership title or pay because that's reserved for the men," Alissia said bitterly. "Do they even pay the women as much as the men doing the same job?"

"They get paid the same. The woman you met tonight is being paid *very* well for her time in Pallen."

Alissia stared out in front of her, frowning, and Grady took her by the hand. He rubbed his thumb along her palm, and she closed her eyes, letting his touch soothe her.

"I need for you to stop thinking you're responsible for any of this," he said softly. "Agro pulled you into this reality. Langley and Anika made a choice to help you. And I've already told you how I feel. I'd rather be hiding from the Eldership with you than living the life I had before I met you. I wish you'd believe me when I say that."

Nothing he said could take away the guilt she felt. Although she was not the one responsible for the trouble, her presence put each of her new friends in danger.

She remained silent and soon fell asleep, only to jerk awake a few hours later.

"What's wrong?" Grady asked. He rolled her over and pulled her in close.

Alissia trembled in his arms. "I think the presence I've been feeling every night is scared."

He stroked her hair, and with the sound of his steady heartbeat at her ear, she soon fell back to sleep.

*****

"I think we failed as chaperones, Langley."

"What are you talking about?" Langley asked, sauntering down the stairs. "Oh," he added, joining his wife.

Grady lifted his hand and gave a feeble attempt to wave them away. "Nothing happened. You didn't fail."

"Not even close," mumbled Alissia, still half asleep.

Langley laughed as he turned and entered the kitchen, and Anika's eyes narrowed. She eyed her wards for a moment before following her husband out of the room.

Grady and Alissia chuckled, and she rolled over so that her back rested against his chest. Comfortable in his arms, she did not want to get up, and they both began to fall back to sleep.

A short while later, they awoke to the sound of Anika yelling from the kitchen that breakfast was ready.

"I could stay here all day," murmured Grady, squeezing Alissia.

She grinned. "This is a comfortable couch, isn't it?"

His body shook with laughter, and they both got up to join the others in the kitchen.

A thin layer of fresh, white snow covered the ground outside. While Alissia and Grady spent the day sorting through their traveling gear, Langley accompanied Anika on a shopping spree for Alissia.

That evening, Alissia tried on all her new clothing. Her gloves and boots were waterproof, both lined with fur. Her long, black cloak was thick and hooded, and as she rubbed her hand along the soft, foreign material, fear began to settle in.

She ended her day falling asleep with visions of her and Grady escaping in the night.

Chapter *11*

Over the next few weeks, Grady spent his weekdays at the library. On his way home, he would stop by one of the pubs near the Eldership, surrounding himself with people working on the scrolls.

Everyone agreed that Alissia should not go out in public, so she spent her weekday mornings teaching Anika and Langley yoga and Pilates. In return, the two of them gave her vocabulary lessons. She could now fake an accent easily, and she continuously learned new words.

Each night, she and Grady stayed up late talking about the differences between their realities. He explained what his people knew about the Creator of the two realities, and she told him what she knew. He would often surprise her with mouthwatering treats or new books, and she anticipated his arrival all throughout each day.

Translating the scrolls was a slow process. So far, they mainly described King Octavious's kingdom and how he desired finding the mysterious people. He believed they would give him the power to win the war, and he sent many of his men to search for them.

Alissia loved the weekends, as Grady would not go to the library or pub during that time. On those days, she would teach him yoga and Pilates, and they would spend their afternoons playing various card and dice games. They sat for hours talking, and they ended their nights dancing in the small sitting room.

After three weeks of this schedule, Grady walked through the door one night with a broad grin. He plopped down next to her on the sofa and gave her a quick peck on the cheek. Handing her a small box of sweets, he said, "I finally found a book with some information on the Lamians, and tomorrow I may be able to find more."

She set his gift aside, giving him her full attention.

"I'm quite sure the Lamians are responsible for your healing," he stated. "It described them as having purple hair, glowing purple eyes, and they're around four feet tall. The reason we haven't been able to find anything about them in the historical section is because they aren't considered real. I started looking in books that have to do with fantasy and mythical creatures, and I found a story with them in it. It said people tortured and killed them, and a lot of them suffered painful deaths. It seems people believed the Lamians could give immortality and riches, but they denied having these powers. A lot of people tried to force them into giving them what they wanted."

"How were they tortured and killed?"

He hesitated before responding, "They were burned alive."

She hoped her face did not give away the fear and pain she tried to hide as she envisioned various burning and screaming Lamians.

Grady took her by the hand. "I'm hoping to find more information tomorrow, now that I know where to look."

Alissia did not respond, and he removed her tinted glasses and tilted her face up to him. "Let's go out for dinner tomorrow night, just you and me."

Her brows furrowed in confusion. "But I thought I didn't need to be seen right now."

"You don't, but you've been locked away for over three weeks." He smiled, dropping his hands from her face. "I'll take you somewhere far from the Eldership, on the other side of the city, and you can wear one of your head scarves and a pair of glasses. Everyone's wearing hats and covering up in this cold weather, and it'll be dark outside. I truly don't believe it'll be a problem."

He tucked a few strands of hair behind her ear and added, in a troubled voice, "Alissia, I don't know how much longer we'll be in Pallen. It's only a matter of time before the scrolls reveal the identity of these people, and if I find more information about them in more than one book, there's a possibility that the Eldership isn't our only threat."

Seeing her confused expression, he said, "You're safe if nobody knows about the Lamians. The good news is that we've only been able to find two books that have mentioned them, and we've done a lot of searching. The bad news is that we weren't looking in the right place, and I don't know how much information we'll find now that I know where to look. The less information I find about them means the less other people know about them. I don't remember learning about them in any of my classes, but legends are not something I've ever paid much attention to. I'm more of a realist. If there are a lot of books out there describing the appearance of a Lamian, there's a chance you may have already been recognized by someone."

A worried frown creased Alissia's forehead as she silently stared across the room in thought. Although she hoped that once she found the Lamians she would want to stay with them, she may not have a choice in the matter. Just the thought of being burned alive was enough to make her want to remain hidden with the Lamians.

Grady removed his boots and pulled his legs up and onto the sofa. With his back against the corner and her back against his chest, he held her in his arms.

"I've upset you," he said, slowly tracing his fingers along her right arm.

She closed her eyes, enjoying his touch. After a while, his fingers left her arm, and he pulled her hair to one side and brushed his lips across her neck, sending shivers throughout her entire body.

"I miss spending my days with you, and I think you miss me, too," he said softly at her ear.

She smiled to herself as his hand made its way to the engagement ring on her finger. He rubbed his thumb across the ring a few times before positioning her body so that her shoulder rested against his chest. With their faces only inches apart, he gazed intently into her eyes.

Her pulse quickened as he leaned in closer, and when their lips met, his hand went to her back, pulling her in to him. Her hand made its way to the back of his neck and stayed there until the kiss ended. He then placed a kiss on her forehead before settling back into the sofa and closing his eyes.

Alissia rubbed her fingertips along the side of his face, and he smiled. He opened his eyes and stared up at her. "I'll come home early tomorrow night, and we'll leave. I've got something special planned for you."

She pulled her hand from his face. "What?"

"It's a surprise," he said, grinning.

She batted her eyes and gave an innocent smile. "What is it?"

"A surprise. I do believe that's a word used in your reality."

She leaned closer, putting more effort into wooing him. "Give me a hint?"

Laughing out loud, he sat up and pulled her into his arms for another long kiss. Just when she thought she would melt into his chest, he pulled away and let out a shaky breath.

"Soon, but not tonight. In fact," he added, tapping the tip of her nose with his finger, "you should escape up to your room. It's getting harder to pull away from you. You have my heart, and my body wants you as well."

He kissed her forehead and nudged her from his lap. Halfway up the stairs, she heard him let out a shaky breath.

While preparing for bed, she pondered what Grady said about the Lamians. Each time she envisioned herself being burned alive, she turned her thoughts to his embrace.

In bed, she smiled as she recalled how pleased he looked while she trailed her fingers along his face. Then her eyes widened in realization, and her smile fell.

Grady was now in a position to hurt her. The last person with that honor had been her father, and her love for him had almost destroyed her.

Staring at the stars above, she whispered, "I'm in love with him."

Chapter 12

The next morning, Alissia walked into the kitchen to find Anika and Langley sitting at the table. Grady left earlier than usual, but not before telling Langley what he learned about the Lamians. Langley also knew of their plans for that evening, and he decided to take Anika on a date of their own.

Everyone agreed it would be good for Alissia to get out of the house, as long as she stayed far away from the Eldership with Grady by her side. After being stuck inside for so long, she anticipated a night out, and her excitement grew throughout the day.

She began to get ready that afternoon and spent a lot of time and effort on her appearance, choosing to wear a long, black dress with a matching, shimmery headscarf.

Once satisfied with her appearance, she smiled nervously at herself in the mirror. "I love you," she whispered, practicing her surprise for Grady. She let the foreign words roll off her tongue a few more times before grabbing her cloak and gloves to go downstairs.

She found Langley sitting on the sofa reading a book, and she sat down in a chair across from him. A few moments later, Anika came down the stairs dressed in a long, blue gown and her pearls. She sat down beside her husband and joined the conversation, but Alissia could tell they both wanted to be on their way.

She urged them to leave, but they refused, not wanting her to be alone. An hour passed before she insisted they leave while there was still enough time for dinner before their show. Reluctantly, they agreed, and Anika hugged her before walking out.

Alissia checked her appearance again in the mirror. Then she sat down on the sofa. Without a distraction, she soon began to worry about Grady, and she stood.

Pacing the floor, she imagined the Eldership questioning Grady about her, and she tried to think of something she could do to help. The thought of not having any control quickly led to panic, and she jumped when a knock came at the door. She stood frozen, staring at the door, when someone knocked again. She considered peeking out from the closed curtains as she walked over to the door, but she knew she would be seen.

"Who is it?" she called out.

"It's Holt from the library and ball. Remember Holt and Nevara? I have some news about Grady."

With shaky hands, she quickly pulled the headscarf up to conceal her hair. Although he had seen it before, she did not want him or anyone else to see it again.

She closed her eyes and took a deep breath. "Get it together," she told herself. Forcing a smile onto her face, she opened the door.

"Did something happen?" she asked, focusing on her voice.

"Grady isn't hurt," Holt announced, holding up his hands. "In fact, he's at my house. May I please come in?"

The troubled look on his face worried her, and she stepped aside, motioning for him to enter. He sat down on the sofa, and she sat down in a chair across from him.

Leaning forward with his hands clasped together, he seemed uncomfortable. "I'm sorry to intrude like this," he stammered. "It looks as though you were about to leave. This will only take a moment of your time."

Trying not to sound impatient, she responded, "Why is Grady at your house?"

He hesitated before answering, "I don't know how to tell you this, and you probably won't believe me." Tears shimmered in his eyes, and he looked down at his hands for a moment. Looking back up, he cleared his throat.

"Nevara and I have been having problems with our marriage for a while, and I thought this time in Pallen would help our relationship." He gave a half shrug. "I think it did in the beginning, but about two weeks ago, she came home later than usual one night. Since then, she's been going out every night during the week."

He let out a deep breath before looking her in the eyes. "Alissia, Nevara and Grady have been spending a lot of time together. They've been going to dinner almost every night, and I've seen them kissing. He even gave her a necklace. She left work early one day, and they spent most of the day together."

Alissia's chest felt heavy, the room suddenly hot. "No," she said, shaking her head, "Grady wouldn't do that."

"Then where has he been every night instead of here with you, and how did I know where he lived? I've followed him home before." In a loathing voice, he added, "After I watched him kiss my wife goodnight."

"I know he's been going out with his friends from the Eldership," she replied, her fake accent faltering. "He wants to see them while in town."

He frowned. "Maybe that's where it started. I knew she was unhappy, but I never thought she'd do this." He shook his head, adding, "We were going to fix things."

Alissia clasped her hands together in her lap, in an attempt to appear calm and unmoved.

"They're together right now," Holt continued. "I told Nevara last night that I unexpectedly found an old friend visiting the city, and we planned to have dinner and drinks tonight. I led her to believe I wouldn't be home until very late, just to see how far she would go."

He paused. "I watched her leave work early, and I followed her to the library. She found Grady, and they went out for drinks. Then she took him home."

He closed his eyes tightly. When he looked back at Alissia, a tear escaped, leaving a wet streak down his face.

"The first night I tell her that I won't be home," he said softly, shaking his head, "and she brings him to our house."

Alissia silently stared back at the man sitting across from her. He seemed sincere, and she did not know how to respond. Her mind struggled to find an alternative explanation, but Grady had mentioned Nevara's name more than once. He often met with her, along with others, at the pub.

Holt stood abruptly. "I plan to confront them together tonight." He attempted a polite smile and added, "I just wanted you to know before your wedding, and I'm sorry I'm the one to tell you." He started walking toward the door. Once there, he turned around and said softly, "At least now you know the truth."

"What are you planning to do?" she asked, standing.

"I plan to go home and find them together. After that . . ." He paused and shook his head, giving a shrug. "I don't know." He then opened the door and walked out, closing it behind him.

Alissia stared at the door in confusion. Looking up at the ceiling, she let out a frustrated groan. Then she turned back to the door with a scowl. "I just can't sit here." Without hesitation, she rushed into the alley and called out, "Wait!"

Holt stopped, his foot on the bottom step of a carriage. He turned and stared back at Alissia expectantly.

"I . . . uh . . . want to see for myself."

He nodded.

She pointed over her shoulder. "Will you wait while I write a note telling the others where I am?"

"I'll wait," he answered, stepping away from the carriage.

After Alissia locked the house, Holt helped her into the carriage, where they rode in silence.

They stopped in an alley lined with small townhouses, similar to where Alissia stayed, and Holt politely helped her out of the carriage. As he paid the driver, he said, "Wait here, please. Miss Alissia will probably not want to stay long, and you can take her back home."

Her body trembled as she followed Holt the short distance to the door. He pulled out a key and carefully inserted it into the lock. Turning to her, he placed his finger to his mouth, requesting silence, and she nodded.

He unlocked and opened the door, and she followed him inside.

Chapter 13

Alissia stared in disbelief at the sight of Grady sleeping peacefully on a sofa. He was shirtless, with a blanket over the lower portion of his body and a large beer stein located on the floor beside him.

Nevara entered the room, wearing nothing but Grady's white poet's shirt. A look of panic appeared across her face, and she rushed to Grady's side and shook him roughly.

He slowly opened his eyes and glanced around the room before looking down at his shirtless body. He then looked up at Nevara and turned to meet Alissia's gaze, where a look of pure terror replaced his confused expression.

"Alissia, this isn't what it seems."

He threw the blanket from his body and stood, as all eyes in the room went to his unbuttoned pants. He glanced down and then back to Alissia before crossing the short distance between them.

"Alissia," he pleaded, grabbing her by the arm, "please listen to me."

Everything within Alissia died in that moment. Without even trying to hide her natural accent, she said coldly, "We both knew it wasn't going to work, and the only reason I was with you is because I needed you." Sneering up at him, she added, "Why do you think I never even told you I loved you?"

Even though she felt a stab to her heart with each word she spoke, she continued, "I've never been a good liar, so I chose not to say anything at all."

"Alissia, please let me talk. It's not what you think," he begged, tugging her arm.

She jerked out of his grasp. "You'll never touch me again," she vowed, her eyes boring into his.

As she turned to open the door, he grabbed her arm again, and she spun around and slapped him hard across the face. Before he could respond, she walked out of the house, slamming the door behind her.

She rushed to the carriage and looked over her shoulder to find the door still closed, and a sob caught in her throat. She cried the entire ride home, and she could not meet the driver's eyes as he helped her out of the carriage.

"How much do I owe you?" she asked weakly.

"Nothing, ma'am. It's been paid for." In a concerned voice, he added, "Are you all right?"

Without answering, she turned and darted to the townhouse. In the privacy of her room, she threw herself on the bed and wept even more.

She eventually stopped crying, but the pain stayed with her. Staring up at the stars, she decided she did not want to feel anything anymore. The last time she cried this hard was when her father first started hitting her.

Feeling nothing at all would be better than the intense pain she now felt. She could not control it, and it hurt too much. She wanted to go back to the old Alissia. Not the one from her childhood, but the one that left Georgia and put herself through school while working. During those years, she only felt cold and numb, giving her the strength she needed to survive on her own.

Alissia closed her eyes and began to think of her childhood. Instead of fighting the memories, she welcomed them like an old friend. Something within her told her to stop, but she ignored the warning. She knew the consequences of shutting off her emotions. She would feel nothing but emptiness. But to her, that was better than the pain.

Her struggle continued as a thought came to mind of how happy she had been over the past few months. She then reminded herself of all the pain she now felt. No amount of happiness was worth this amount of pain, and she did not want it anymore. She did not want to feel anything.

Her resolution momentarily shook, knowing the worst part of shutting off her emotions would be how it would affect her faith. If she stopped feeling anything and only depended on herself, her prayer life would become empty. Her heart would harden like stone, and she would feel nothing.

As memories of her father filled her mind, a familiar sadness began to seep in. The words he often shouted in her face caused more damage than his fist, each painful memory a cold reminder of what trusting someone meant for her.

No longer feeling the uncontrollable pain caused by seeing Grady with Nevara, Alissia went to the bathroom and washed her face.

"This is your fault," she hissed, glaring at her reflection in the mirror. "You knew better than to trust someone."

A distant memory surfaced, making itself real again.

A teenage girl's green eyes glared into a bedroom mirror, her face swollen with tears and a bag of bloody clothing clenched in her fist.

Staring at herself in disgust, she vowed, "Never again. You will never be a victim again."

A tear threatened, and she lifted her chin determinedly. "And there'll be no more tears from you, either. You knew love wasn't meant for you, and you should never have expected it."

Alissia closed her eyes as the memory faded. "You put yourself in a position to get hurt," she whispered. "Grady only did what was to be expected."

With a fresh new purpose in mind, she rushed to the bedroom and quickly changed into her new traveling clothes. She took off the engagement ring and placed it on the bed next to the jewelry Grady gave her.

Although her pride told her to leave the money, she knew she could not survive without it, and she loathed herself as she poured the money from the frilly purse into a leather pouch strapped to a belt at her waist.

She ran downstairs to sort through their travel bags and emptied one of the backpacks before filling it with some of the food and other supplies already packed in various saddlebags.

She did not have a plan. She just wanted to get away, and she never wanted to see Grady again. She thought of Anika and Langley and how much she liked them, but she quickly pushed those thoughts aside and reminded herself that she needed no one.

Full of determination, she put on her gloves and lifted the hood of her cloak before stepping into the cold, winter air. When she noticed a carriage parked at one end of the alley, she turned in the opposite direction. Knowing it would be more expensive to stay in the city, she found a rickshaw and told the young man to take her to an inexpensive inn near the gates.

During the long ride, she was left alone with nothing but her thoughts. She struggled mostly with the memory of Nevara walking into the room wearing Grady's shirt. Although the haunting memory no longer caused the uncontrollable pain, it brought a dull sadness with it.

Why did he act as if he loved her if he was seeing Nevara? And why did he act so honorable with her when he obviously did not have a problem taking things further with Nevara?

Alissia would never have believed or accepted it, if not for seeing them together with her own eyes. She wanted to believe he had gotten drunk and never meant to do anything. However, that was still no excuse, and she definitely did not need another drinking man in her life.

Once the rickshaw came to a stop, she unloaded her belongings and paid the man. Staring at the door of the inn, she took a shaky breath. Then she lifted her chin, squared her shoulders, and made her way to the door.

Inside, a pleasant smell of food reminded her that she only ate a light lunch that day. Although she never craved food while stressed, she knew she needed to eat something.

She easily found a table in a back corner of the room, and shortly after sitting down, an older woman walked over and explained what was left in the kitchen.

Alissia ordered a plate of cooked vegetables and some bread before asking about a room for the night. The waitress told her one would be waiting for her when she finished eating. She then headed to another table, leaving Alissia alone to study her new surroundings.

Unlike the ambiance within the city, modest furnishings adorned the inn, and the people dressed less elegantly. Glowing, white bella flowers covered the walls and ceiling, and each table held a small, clear container with a glow rock inside. Although heat stones were positioned at every window of the room, one of the walls held a stone fireplace with a warm, blazing fire.

As she watched the strangers in the room, Alissia thought about how alone she truly was. Feeling drained from her intense crying, she looked down and rested her forehead in the palms of her hands, where she considered some of the overwhelming challenges she would have to deal with for the rest of her life if she did not find the Lamians soon.

"Alissia?"

She looked up to find Holt standing before her with an uncertain smile on his face. He wore a backpack and held a traveling bag in his left hand.

"I didn't expect to see you here," he said. "May I join you? I haven't eaten, and I'm starving."

Although not in the mood for company, she remembered his tears and did not want to add to his pain. She forced a smile and nodded. "Yes, that's fine."

He set his bags on the floor and sat down across from her, just as her food and water were placed on the table. The waitress explained what was left in the kitchen, and Holt ordered his meal, along with two drinks. Alissia was staring down at her plate when he turned his attention back to her.

"Don't wait on me," he said, motioning. "Please eat."

The food looked delicious, but the idea of eating made her feel sick to her stomach. She picked up her fork and took a small bite of the vegetables.

Holt leaned back in his chair and watched her for a moment. "Do you have anywhere to go?"

"I'll think of something," she answered, faking a smile.

After a bit of silence, he said, "I'm sorry I was the one who ruined your night. I believe this is worse for you than it is for me. I've spent the last year struggling to save my marriage, but you seemed to be very happy—and in love." He paused before adding, "Maybe I shouldn't have told you, but I know I would have wanted to know the truth before I married."

She could feel the numbness inside of her pushing back the pain. "I'm glad I know the truth now."

The waitress set two drinks on the table, and then she made her way back to the kitchen.

"I usually don't drink," he said, lifting one of the mugs to his mouth, "but I'll need some help getting to sleep tonight."

When she did not pick up her drink and join him, he leaned in closer. "The only reason I ordered this drink is because it's known to help people fall asleep. You should try it. You won't get drunk from a few sips, but it will help to settle your mind so that you can fall asleep." He paused before emphasizing, "And I think we're both going to have a hard time with sleep tonight."

Alissia took a small sip of the strong drink before making a face and setting it back down.

Holt laughed as the waitress placed his soup in front of him. He waited for her to leave before asking, "You don't drink, do you?"

She shook her head. "Just an occasional wine."

"It's up to you," he said, shrugging, "but just a few more sips is all it will take."

Knowing her restless mind would have a lot to think about that night, Alissia forced herself to drink some more.

He took a few bites of his soup and wiped his mouth with a cloth napkin. "Seriously, do you have any family on this side of the mountains you can go to?"

She shook her head, and he set his spoon down, looking intently at her. "You mentioned tonight you needed Grady. Do you need help with something?"

At the mention of Grady's name, she immediately reminded herself that she needed no one.

A sudden, sharp pain shot through her stomach, and she began to feel nauseous. She put her hand to her mouth and quickly got up from the table before running out of the inn, barely making it outside before losing her dinner.

Her stomach churned in pain, and she slowly straightened and closed her eyes, leaning against the soft bella flowers growing along the inn.

The sound of fighting caught her attention, and she turned to find a man striking Holt in the face. A few punches later, Holt fell to the ground, where he remained motionless, and his attacker ran into the inn. He soon came back out carrying Alissia's traveling bags, and he rushed over to her.

"You're in danger," he warned, breathing heavily, "and I need to get you out of here."

She barely understood his foreign accent, much different from Grady's. After a moment of confusion, she recognized him as the mysterious man from the ball. Still fighting the pain in her stomach, fear slammed into her as she remembered he worked for the Eldership—the military department of the Eldership.

"I'm not here to hurt you," he assured, raising his hands in surrender.

Alissia glared at him as she pulled her body from the wall. "I'm not going anywhere with you," she declared venomously, using her fake accent.

A look of surprise flashed across his face before he let out a sigh and scowled. "You're not going to make this easy for me, are you?"

"I told you. I'm not going anywhere with you." Her expression dared him to touch her.

He laughed, glancing over his shoulder. "We really don't have time for this. Just think of me as your knight in shining armor. Come now, let's go."

As he went to grab her arm, she kicked him in the groin and bolted. She rounded the corner of the building before he tackled her to the ground and rolled her over. With his body on top of hers and both her hands pinned above her head, he rested his forehead on her shoulder.

After a few heavy breaths, he said in a restrained voice, "I'm *really* trying to help you out here, and you're trying to kill me."

Alissia thrashed beneath him, but he effortlessly held her in place. After a while she stopped moving, and he lifted his head. She glared up at him, her breathing heavy.

"I didn't ask for your help, so walk away," she spat.

He cocked his head to the side, and his body tensed at the sound of horses stopping in front of the inn. His left hand let go of hers, and he firmly placed it over her mouth. With his lips touching her ear, he whispered sternly, "If you don't want to get caught, be quiet."

Alissia closed her eyes and listened carefully to the voices of two men.

"What if she's not in there?"

"He said she was here."

"What's that?"

The man on top of Alissia whispered, "If I have to fight them, you need to stay hidden and wait for me."

From the front of the inn, she heard, "Looks like he lost a fight, but we don't have time to mess with him. Let's get her and go. He's waiting."

After the two men entered the inn, Alissia's aggressor said sternly, "We need to leave *now*. They're probably not the only ones looking for you tonight, and you need to trust me. I'm trying to get you out of here safely."

Reluctantly, she nodded, and he lifted his hand from her mouth. He stood and helped her to her feet before grabbing her two packs from the ground. She followed him to two horses hidden beneath a group of trees, where she mounted the one wearing a saddle. He tied her bags onto the other horse that seemed to be carrying his traveling gear as well.

He pulled something out of one of his bags before swiftly hopping into the saddle behind Alissia. With his arms around her, he grabbed the reigns, and neither of them spoke as he led the horses toward the city gates.

No longer distracted by the fight, her attention went back to her pain, and she winced.

"This might help ease the pain in your stomach," he said, holding a vial of liquid in front of her face.

Alissia could not see colors with her night vision, and she wondered what the liquid truly looked like. Her eyes narrowed with suspicion. "How do you know my stomach hurts?"

He lowered his hand. "Probably because the drink you decided to try tonight is also known as cock ale. It's made with chicken, and I've read Lamians have problems with eating meat."

His answer confirmed what she already knew. He recognized her as a Lamian, and the other men at the inn knew about her as well.

"I don't trust you," she replied.

His chest shook with laughter. "Look, if I wanted to hurt you—and there was a moment I was tempted—I would have done it already." He added with emphasis, "Do you even have any idea how much that hurt?"

"That was the idea. It was supposed to hurt."

He held the vial in front of her face again. "Do you want it or not? It's up to you, but it should help to ease the pain in your stomach."

Alissia let out a frustrated sigh and took the vial from his hand. Although she did not trust him, the pain was intense. As she opened it, he said, "Only take two small sips and no more."

She lifted the vial to her nose and instantly thought of the lavender-scented lotion and bath oil she often used before coming to this reality. She then took two sips before closing the vial and passing it back to him.

"You recognized me as a Lamian the night of the ball. Is that why you were staring at me?"

"That's one reason."

Alissia thought for a moment before continuing, "Then you waited for the first opportunity to go after me, and tonight was the first night I've been out since the ball. You've been waiting for this moment ever since that night, haven't you? You've been watching me."

"You've got it wrong. I didn't plan any of this. In fact, I'm not the one who tried to sneak out of the city late at night, all by myself, and with a crowd following me." He lifted his finger for emphasis. "I'd also like to remind you that I had nothing to do with you trying a new drink tonight. This was all your doing, not mine, and as far as watching you, I have not." He lowered his hand and said, "I paid someone else to do it for me."

Alissia's face twisted in confusion. "Why did you hire someone to watch me?"

"Because I had other things to do."

A strange sensation rose within Alissia, and she suddenly could barely keep her eyes open.

"What did you give me?" she asked, in a slurred voice. She shook her head, attempting to stay awake, but she could not fight against the darkness, as it immediately overtook her.

Chapter 14

Alissia slowly opened her eyes and stared up at the bright, sunny sky through a clear, tinted ceiling. The events of the night before began to play through her mind, and she closed her eyes and rolled onto her side. At the memory of being drugged, her eyes shot open, and she sat up.

White bella flowers covered the walls in the small room, which held a simple nightstand and dresser, along with the small bed she rested in. Her traveling bags were in a corner, along with her cloak and boots.

Trying not to make a sound, Alissia left the bed and slightly opened the door. When she did not see or hear anything, she gradually opened the door and stuck out her head.

She cautiously tiptoed through a sitting room and entered a small kitchen. On the table, she found a note that read:

Dear Alissia,

I am guessing you are a bit angry as you read this, and I hate that I'm not there to see you. I've gone to get you a horse and will be back shortly.

There's food in the kitchen when you get hungry. For your safety, this cabin is extremely isolated, so going for a long walk in the forest is not recommended.

Luke

Alissia clenched her teeth as she read the note again. *He drugged me and left me in an isolated cabin for my safety? What if something happens to him, and he never comes back? Did he plan for that?*
As she washed her hands, she envisioned all that she would say to him when he returned. Her temper grew even stronger when she walked outside to find it already early in the afternoon. She stormed back into the house and searched the small, one-bedroom cabin. It appeared as if no one lived there, and she found nothing personal.
Alissia forced down some food before taking a bath. The bathroom was not as fascinating as Anika's with water flowing down the wall, and it did not have a blue, glowing light at the bottom of the pool. Glowing bella flowers covered the walls, and other flowers and greenery abundantly filled the room.
While sitting in the warm, soothing water, her thoughts turned to Grady, and she immediately replaced her pain with a mix of anger and strong determination.
By the time she finished dressing, she felt stronger than she had in years, and she felt unbreakable. She knew it would only take a few

more days to completely harden her heart, and then she would feel nothing. She would be untouchable.

She opened the bathroom door to find Luke reading a book while lounging on the sofa.

"Feel better?" he asked cheerily.

Alissia ignored him and went to the bedroom to put away her things. Her explosive temper raged within her, but she told herself her vengeance would have to wait. Too many questions needed answering.

Once partially calm, she opened the door and walked into the sitting room. Luke set his book aside and looked up at her. The innocent look on his face fueled her temper, and she took a deep breath as she sat down across from him.

"So, I was right about you being angry?" he asked.

Her cold glare turned into a look of disbelief. "You drugged me! You told me that it would help my stomach, and you put me to sleep!"

"It's all I had, and I was right," he calmly responded. "Your stomach didn't hurt anymore after you took it, did it?"

"I didn't feel anything," she said, between clenched teeth. Her eyes narrowed. "And what happened when you put me to bed? You took off my cloak and boots. What else did you do?"

"Do you really think I'm that desperate?" he asked, chuckling. "Would it help if I said I was sorry?"

"No," she declared, crossing her arms, "because you obviously don't mean it."

He laughed, shaking his head. Lifting his hands in surrender, he said, "I promise I'm sorry. Our journey's going to be miserable if you don't forgive me soon."

"What journey?"

He sat up and put his feet on the floor. "Well, where were you going before I rescued you?"

"That's none of your business, and I wasn't in trouble," replied Alissia, uncrossing her arms. "Why did you attack Holt? Did you kill him?"

"So that was his name." Luke shrugged. "He was in the way, and he looked suspicious. He's sore but still alive."

Alissia rolled her eyes. "And how did he look suspicious?"

"Why else would he order that drink for you?" he asked, leaning back. "I'm thinking you didn't order it."

"He said it would help us sleep, because that's what the drink is known for."

"It is known for that," he said, nodding.

Alissia scowled. "Do you realize that if he's innocent, you attacked someone that just caught his wife with another man? And in his own home. Do you know how bad he already felt? His life was already ruined, and then you used his face for a punching bag."

"But," he said, pointing into the air, "what if he wasn't innocent?"

"And why would he try to get me sick?"

Luke lowered his hand with an annoying smirk on his face. "Maybe it was his way of proving you're a Lamian. It could have been a test."

"And why would he do that?" Alissia challenged.

"Why wouldn't he? I wasn't certain you were a Lamian until I saw you get sick. I mean, I thought you were, but the drink confirmed it." He paused before adding, "In fact, that was a clever idea."

Alissia shook her head. "He could have easily kidnapped me the moment I stepped into his carriage or when I went inside his home, but he didn't. Instead, he paid the driver to take me home."

Luke's smile faded, and his expression turned serious. "I'm curious to know what happened last night. I'm assuming the man he caught his wife with was Grady, and he wanted you to see it for yourself." He raised his eyebrows. "Are you certain Holt's innocent?"

Not wanting to talk about Grady, she answered his question with a defiant glare.

"Did you actually see Grady with this man's wife," he asked, "not just together in his home? Did you see Grady *doing* anything with her?"

Alissia looked away and stared at the wall, her jaw firmly set.

"All right, I see you don't want to talk about it." He stood and walked to the bathroom. "But," he said, turning around, "you do realize the best way for Holt to get close to you would have been to destroy your trust in Grady to make you feel alone? Maybe the plan was to get you to trust him, so he wouldn't have to force anything from you. I can easily see how that would have worked more in his favor than kidnapping you."

He gave a half shrug. "You should have told me. I would have asked Grady when I saw him today."

He closed the bathroom door, leaving Alissia completely dumbfounded. Ignoring her strong desire to beat on the door and ask questions about Grady, she looked down and began to massage her temples.

Moments later, Luke stepped out of the bathroom. He did not even look her way as he walked to the kitchen.

Determined not to give him the satisfaction of knowing he was irritating her, she tried to force herself to wait on him to come out of the kitchen. However, her resolve only lasted a minute, and she scowled in frustration as she stood from the chair.

Luke sat at the table eating a dried strip of meat when Alissia sat down across from him. She smiled slightly. "So where did you see Grady today?" she asked, trying to sound casual.

He took a bite of his meat strip and began to chew. "He was at the Eldership."

"And what was he doing when you saw him?"

Luke swallowed and bit off another chunk. "Walking down a hall."

Alissia's smile tightened. "Did he look upset?"

"No, he looked normal."

Losing her patience, she dropped the pretense and blurted, "Why was he there, and what were you doing there? And what does the Eldership want with me?"

She silently screamed as she watched him slowly finish off the strip of meat. Then he leaned back in his chair.

"I don't know why he was there, because I didn't talk to him. I was there to let them know I was returning home. And as for the Eldership, it depends on which one."

Alissia's face twisted in confusion. "I thought there was only one Eldership."

"There is only one Eldership, but there are different places within the Eldership. Right now, we're in a southern city that's near the Eldership's central location. I'm from a northern city—far from here. And as for what the Eldership wants with you, it depends on which one finds you first."

"What do you mean, finds me?" she asked suspiciously. "They don't know I'm with you?"

Luke grinned and shook his head. "Nobody knows you're with me."

"Then why am I with you?" she questioned, wringing her hands beneath the table. "I thought you were with the Eldership, and that's why you kidnapped me."

"First of all, I never kidnapped you. I saved you," he emphasized, pointing into the air. He dropped his hand into his lap. "As for why you're with me, I'm sure you're not going to like my answer."

Concealing her fear, she asked coolly, "Why am I here with you?"

"I plan for the North to find you first," he said, meeting her gaze, "so we're going on a little journey."

She gave a sarcastic laugh. "I'm not going anywhere with you."

"I knew you'd say that," he replied smugly.

Alissia glared. "I mean it. I'm not going anywhere with you, and you can't make me."

He chuckled, causing her to loathe him even more. Then he took a sip of his drink. Setting his glass down, he studied her face for a moment.

"What do you plan to do if I leave you?" he asked calmly. "It's obvious I'm not the only one to recognize you for what you are."

"What do you mean? Nobody knew about the Lamians until they found the scrolls, and they didn't know anything the night of the ball. Grady can't even find anything about them at the library, so how did you know?"

"The king couldn't erase everything about your people's existence," he answered, "no matter how hard he tried. He destroyed as much evidence as he could, but he couldn't destroy word of mouth. And eventually, things were written down again."

Realizing he knew things about the Lamians and could possibly give her some answers, Alissia's heart began to pound excitedly within her chest. She leaned back in her chair, trying to appear relaxed.

"What do you mean, the king tried to erase our existence?" she asked, her voice steady. "How much do you know about the Lamians?"

"You know about your people's past."

"Pretend that I don't know anything about my people," she said, with a forced smile, "and you explain it to me."

He studied her face for a moment, and then he nodded. "All right, I'll pretend you don't know anything, but we both know you do."

"Start from the beginning. I want everything you know about my people." She cocked her head and gave a slight grin, taunting, "And maybe I'll tell you if it's true."

Luke nodded, and his brows furrowed. His gaze drifted in thought, and he said, "Your people were first on this land and resented the immigrants that came here. You tried to live peacefully away from my ancestors, but soon there were more of us than you. The land filled with kingdoms, and war became common. Rumors eventually spread that your people had special powers, so the humans began to hunt your people and try to force things from them."

His eyes met hers. "It's said that many Lamians died keeping their secrets, but some weren't as strong."

Alissia stared back at him for a moment, and then his gaze went to the glass on the table. He picked it up and took a sip. Setting it back down, he said, "Back then, the northern kingdom held the most wealth and power and usually won the majority of the wars. It's said that King Octavious—whose kingdom is now the city of Allure—decided upon a plan that would help him and the Lamians. He made a deal with them. He would help them settle in a hidden location and would erase their existence from our history if they would help him win the war."

Giving a bitter smile, Luke added, "Your people not only helped him win the war, but you helped him conquer the entire land."

He paused, as if waiting for a response, and she stared blankly at him.

"Once he conquered a kingdom," Luke continued, "he would destroy most of their historical records. He was able to erase most of our history, and of course, no one ever saw or heard from the Lamians again. To this day, most of what happened during that time is unknown."

Propping his elbows on the table, he leaned closer. A smile crept to his face, and he whispered animatedly, "But a few scrolls were hidden across the land."

He sat back in his chair and studied her response. She continued with her poker face, hoping he could not tell she was listening intently to every word he spoke. She tried to appear unimpressed.

"In the North," he continued, "there are many tales and stories about your people that have been passed down through the years, and everyone's heard of the small, magical Lamians with purple hair and eyes. It's told they give riches and power to those they favor."

Alissia looked down at her hands resting in her lap, hoping he did not notice the jolt of surprise his last statement caused within her, and she wondered why the Lamians decided to favor her.

Luke continued, "King Octavious erased your existence the best he could, but he could never control the bedtime stories told to the next generation. He had more control in the South where he lived, and that's why not too many people know of the Lamians here.

"And nobody really believes in the legends." He shrugged, "Well, they didn't until you came along. So why are you in Pallen?"

Alissia contemplated her existence. She proved the Lamians' were real, and she knew from history what men were capable of doing. Genocide still happened in her reality, and if people already tortured the Lamians to get what they wanted, they would do it again.

She looked up to find Luke watching her. "What powers do you think the Lamians have?"

"You look surprised," he noted, his brows drawn together. "Why don't you tell me your version of what happened?"

With his dark eyes boring into her, it took an immense amount of effort to appear indifferent. She shrugged. "I don't have a version. I was just wondering what powers people think I have. What did my people do that won the war, and if we're so powerful, why are we hiding?"

Alissia felt the blood rush to her face from the intensity of his stare, and she smiled and lifted her brows expectantly, grateful for a skin tone that did not reveal her true emotions.

His gaze relaxed somewhat, and he responded, "It's said that your people are peaceful and never fought in the war, but they helped the king by making him extremely wealthy and powerful. Some stories even say they gifted him with their powers. His wealth helped to build a formidable army that continued to grow with each kingdom he conquered. People began to want to be conquered by him. He brought wealth to each kingdom, and he promised peace within the land. He designed the Eldership to keep that peace after his death, and there hasn't been a civil war since."

"So if everything's so good, why would the Eldership want me?"

"If your people have the power to conquer an entire land, I'm sure a lot of people will want to meet you, and not all of them will be good."

"Then why don't you just take me to the Eldership in Pallen?" she asked, frowning.

Luke shook his head. "The Eldership's controlled in the South, and over the last few hundred years, things are getting better for the South and worse for the North. Tension has been building for a long time, and it's still rising. The last thing we need is for history to repeat itself."

Alissia's face hardened. "I'm not going with you to the North."

"You're going to the North with me, and it's for your own safety," he replied calmly.

"You plan to kidnap me, but it's for my own safety?" she asked incredulously.

He leaned across the table and looked hard into her eyes. "Did you forget the part about your people being tortured to death? In fact, I have no doubt that the man with you last night deceived you into leaving Grady, just so he could get you alone to gain your trust."

Luke leaned back in his chair looking annoyed. "I'm still trying to figure out why a female Lamian openly went to an Eldership ball and is now wandering around alone for everyone to see." His palm slammed onto the table. "And you seem completely oblivious to your danger."

He stood and declared, "We leave early tomorrow morning, and I need for you to show me what you've packed so I can make sure you have everything you need. Unfortunately, it's going to be cold."

"What do you mean, you have no doubt Holt tricked me?" she demanded, staring up at him. "How would you know whether or not Grady was with his wife?"

Luke gave a sarcastic laugh. "Because Grady's on his way to becoming an elder, and he has a spotless reputation. I've met him, and it doesn't fit his character—at all. He wouldn't give up the respect he's worked for all these years in the Eldership for a married woman. He could have just about any woman in Allure."

With a smug grin, he added, "I'm willing to bet you didn't see him actually in the act of doing anything with the woman, but I'm sure they made him look guilty."

"No," she said, trying to sound sure of herself, "but I saw enough. She was wearing his shirt, and his pants were undone."

"Was Grady even conscious when you found them together?" Luke questioned. "He could have easily been drugged, just as you were last night. Then Holt followed you to the inn to comfort you." He scoffed, "And I'm sure he offered to help you since you were all alone."

Not trusting herself to speak, Alissia stood and walked toward the kitchen door. Luke grabbed her by the arm, and within inches of her face, he said coldly, "You need to understand that you can't trust anyone now. You were deceived last night. You put yourself in danger the moment you stepped into that man's carriage, and I can't protect you if you do something like that again."

Alissia yanked her arm away. "You only want to protect me, because you want something from me, too," she spat. "I'm your prized Lamian that you found, and you want to take me home to show me off to your Eldership." She paused before adding, "But I promise you. I *will* make your life a nightmare, and I'll leave you the first chance I get."

As she walked out of the room, Luke said under his breath, "And I believe that."

Staring at the glowing bella flowers along the wall in her room, Alissia squeezed her pillow. She recalled the look of surprise and terror on Grady's face when he woke up on the sofa. He pleaded with her to listen, yet she did not even give him a chance to speak. Her memory of looking him in the eyes and telling him she never loved him hurt the most.

A lone tear escaped and fell onto the pillow. Last night's pain turned her bitter and numb—the complete opposite of how she now felt. She no longer felt angry, hurt, and betrayed. Instead, she felt sorrow and guilt, knowing she ruined something perfect.

Deep down, she knew Grady was innocent. He had been willing to give up everything for her.

Now, she did not think she would ever see him again. She imagined how upset and worried he must be because of her disappearance.

Thoughts of Anika and Langley brought even more guilt, and as tears filled her eyes, she vowed to find a way back to Pallen.

She stayed in the fetal position, staring at the wall, for over an hour before she heard a light knock on the door. Although her tears stopped long ago, she still did not want to face Luke any time soon. She ignored his knock, but he opened the door and let himself in.

Alissia regretted not pulling the bella flowers from the water and covering the glow stones. She closed her eyes, hoping Luke would believe she was asleep.

She heard him set something on the nightstand, and then she felt him sit down beside her on the bed. She could feel his body against her back, but he waited a while to speak.

"I'm sorry, and I mean it this time," he said solemnly. "I just want you to understand how bad this is. I don't know who else knows about your people, but I know I'm not the only one. I also don't know what they know about you, but if people believe you can make them rich and powerful, some of them will come after you. Some will try to win your trust, and others will try to force things from you.

"I don't know what powers you have, and I don't care. What I do know is that you're in danger. I offer you the protection of the Eldership, but it has to be the northern Eldership. I don't expect you to trust me, but I will say that I'm not here to hurt you."

He stood. "I put some food on the nightstand, and I promise I didn't put anything in it. You need to eat, because this will be the best meal you'll get for a while. We'll be leaving early in the morning."

Alissia heard him walk out of the room and close the door. She continued to stare at the wall a bit longer but eventually sat up and looked at the food. Seeing the warm vegetables and bread made her stomach growl, yet her stressed body did not want anything. She forced herself to eat and got a lot of it down before getting ready for bed.

Sleep did not come easy, and she woke often through the night.

Chapter 15

Alissia awoke to Luke pulling back her covers and telling her to get dressed. Seeing the stars in the dark sky above her, she scowled and pulled the blanket back over her body before rolling over. He then yanked the blanket from the bed, picked her up, and set her onto her feet.

She glared at him, hoping her strange eyes scared him. Then she grabbed one of her bags and stomped to the bathroom. A spiteful grin spread across her face as she locked the door, deciding to take a long, hot bath.

Stepping into the pool, she remembered a voice in the night pleading for her not to use any of her new abilities. She needed to keep them hidden and trust no one. Too real to be a dream, she knew the voice came from the presence she felt each night. She wondered why the Lamians had never spoken to her before, and it bothered her that it took so long for them to reach out to her.

Luke soon knocked on the door and told her to hurry. Alissia grinned as she continued to take her time washing her hair.

Shortly thereafter, the door slightly opened. "You have until the horses are loaded before I come in to get you." The door closed, leaving Alissia staring in disbelief. She let out a groan and dunked her head.

After dressing in extra layers of clothing and putting away her things, she walked to the kitchen. A bowl of warm oats was on the table, and she sat down to eat. She took a few bites before Luke walked in and sat down across from her. Alissia acknowledged him with a cold stare.

"I see you like to use the silent treatment when you're angry," he taunted. He shrugged. "I guess that's better than screaming. At least we'll have a peaceful journey."

She scowled. "Do you try to annoy me, or does this come naturally for you?"

"So much for the peaceful journey," he said, looking heavenward while stretching.

She decided to ignore him and continued with her breakfast. As she took her last bite, he pulled a wedding ring out of his front pocket and set it down in front of her. She looked at the ring and back at him.

"I measured your finger when I put you to bed the other night, so it should fit." He lifted his left hand, revealing his ring finger. "I've got a matching one, and we're married now—unless you want to travel as my mistress." He shrugged. "I'm fine with that, too, but if you're going to keep eyeing me like that, we definitely look more like a married couple."

Alissia picked up the ring tiand stared at it. Grady's mock proposal came to mind, and she recalled their first kiss.

"Look, it's the best thing to do," Luke urged, his voice suddenly gentle. "It's more for you than me."

She quickly put on the ring and went to clean her teeth, leaving him to wash the few dirty dishes. When she walked out of the bathroom, he stood waiting for her at the door. He watched as she put on her gloves and cloak before wrapping her damp hair in a thick headscarf. As he bent to pick up her bags, she asked, "What if I refuse to get on the horse? What would you do?"

He left her bags on the floor and straightened. As he stared down at her with a stern look, she noticed his height. Although Grady was only a few inches away from six feet tall, she guessed Luke to be at least a whole foot taller than her. With a dominating presence, she knew Luke easily put fear into many men.

"I'm not your enemy," he said firmly, "and I'm giving you my protection, along with the protection of the Eldership. To do that, you have to be in the northern territory."

Refusing to look away, she countered, "Grady was already doing that, and I don't want your protection. I want to go back to Pallen to find Grady."

Luke shook his head. "This isn't Allure, and Grady isn't even aware of what's happening here. From what I've witnessed lately, I believe Pallen's Eldership is corrupt."

He picked up her bags. "And as for refusing to get on the horse, I may be here for your protection, but that doesn't mean you're going to like the way I do things. You *will* get on the horse, and I'd prefer you do it without my help."

Clenching her teeth, Alissia walked past him, and once outside, she asked which of the four horses was hers. As Luke secured her bags to one of the packhorses, she turned her back to him and bonded with her horse. She made sure to tell the horse to pay attention to the trail, because they would be returning.

The two of them rode in silence as Luke and his packhorse led the way. Although tempted to have him thrown from his horse, Alissia remembered the words told to her during the night. She also feared what he would do to the horse.

He did not like to stop, and she worried about how fast they traveled. Paying close attention to the trails, she tried to think of a way to escape. She also tried to come up with ideas of how she could slow down their progress.

If she was to be his prisoner, she would act like one. With that mindset, she sat down and watched him do all the work of setting up camp and cooking dinner that night. He did not seem to notice or even care, and she soon learned how efficient he was at getting things done. Obviously, he traveled often.

It did not take long before Luke sat down by the fire with a bowl of hot food. Alissia got up to get her own and then sat down across from him.

Cold weather always made her hungrier than usual, and with a light lunch, she was too famished to care that the soup was thick and slimy with hard lumps in it. Then she took her first bite and gagged.

"What is this?" she asked, frowning in disgust.

"It's food, and it's very filling and healthy. It's made with murdock root and will help to keep up our energy as we travel."

Alissia looked down at the soup. Shaking her head, she turned back to him. "I'm not eating this."

Luke frowned. "We've got a long way to go, and it's winter. I'm trying to get you to the Eldership quickly. Once we get there, you can eat anything you want, and you can have your own comfortable bed. Life will be great, but you're going to have to give up some things while we travel."

"What? Heat, food, and sleep?" she asked, with a scowl.

He stared at her for a moment before standing. She watched as he went through some bags, and then he returned with some cheese and bread. When he held out the food, she exchanged her bowl for it.

After washing the dishes íand securing their food for the night, he readied for bed and came over to stand in front of her. His expectant stare annoyed Alissia, and she glared up at him in defiance.

Luke sighed heavily. Then he swiftly picked her up and threw her over his shoulder. He ignored her fists beating against his back and her kicking feet, and he carried her into the tent.

"I tried it your way, and it didn't work," he said calmly, after setting her down.

Alissia's hands balled into fists at her sides. "I need to get ready for bed, and that includes some privacy outside."

As she took a glow stone from his hand, she thought about how lucky she was to still have on her gloves. He did not seem to know about her night vision or ability to charge things, and she wanted to keep it that way.

"Don't take too long, or I'll come after you," he warned, stepping aside.

Alissia snatched up her pack and hurried out of the tent. As she walked to a group of trees, she got an idea, and her mouth twisted into an evil grin.

She set the glow stone down behind the trees, and while cleaning her teeth, she mentally reached out to the animals in the area. Once she found the one she wanted, she willed it to her. She then left the glow stone and crept over to the horses.

She untied Luke's horse before bonding with him, and during the bonding process, she poured energy from her body into him. She told the horse to wait until she began to scream, at which point he was to start walking back to the cabin.

As she crept back to the glow rock, she picked up the furry, little animal resembling a large mouse without a tail. She retrieved the glow rock and made a few noises so that Luke would think she was still getting ready for bed. Then she quickly bonded with the animal and put it in her bag.

Alissia did not look at Luke as she set her bag down at the foot of her blanket. Keeping her back to him, she took off her outer clothing, glasses, and boots. Then she crawled under her thick blanket and rolled over.

He covered the glow stones, leaving a dim, red glow coming from a small heat rock between the feet of their blankets.

"I'm a light sleeper," he warned.

She smiled to herself and willed the small critter to her. While petting her, Alissia gave the animal her instructions.

It took Alissia a moment to build up her courage before she let out a deathly, loud scream. Luke immediately snatched the cover off the pile of glow stones and stood over her with a knife in his right hand. Although the fierce look on his face scared her, she continued to scream, and his expression soon twisted into confusion.

"What's wrong?" he yelled.

Alissia continued to scream hysterically as she sat up and tried to push him away. She began to yell at him for scaring her with his knife, and he stared down at her as if seeing someone with three heads.

She tried to sound as if she were crying while screaming, and lacking confidence in her performance, she soon decided to act crazy and frantic.

Just as she was about to fake hyperventilating, he sheathed his knife under his shirt. He then sat down in front of her and took hold of both of her hands. In a soothing voice, he said, "It's all right. Tell me what's wrong. I can't help you if you don't tell me what's wrong."

She pretended to cry loudly when she got out of her blanket and stood. He stood again, and she looked away when a smile threatened her face. Seeing him confused and helpless was not something she had predicted, and she took great satisfaction in making him feel powerless.

Although she expected his horse to be gone by now, Alissia wanted to be certain Luke would not hear any branches snapping. She threw herself into his body and put her arms around him, screaming about something touching her.

He pried her away and lifted her bedding to reveal the small animal. As he reached for his knife, Alissia smacked him on the shoulder.

"No! Don't hurt it!" she screamed. "You can't kill it! Why would you kill it?"

He studied her face for a moment and shook his head before reaching down to pick up the animal. The critter ran to Alissia's feet, and she screamed even louder. It took a few minutes for Luke to catch the mouse-like animal, and then he set it outside and turned back to face her.

Alissia stared back at him awkwardly and attempted to smile, suddenly feeling like an idiot.

He said nothing as he fixed their bedding, and then he watched her crawl under her blanket. She attempted another smile before rolling over, and he covered the glow stones.

Staring at the wall of the tent, a malicious grin filled Alissia's face, and it did not take long for her to fall asleep.

Chapter 16

Alissia's eyes shot open as her blanket was yanked away. Luke grabbed her hand and pulled her to her feet before dragging her out of the tent.

She forced herself not to cower beneath his fierce glare as he tossed her riding boots, gloves, and cloak—each landing with a thud at her feet. Once she finished putting them on, he swiftly picked her up and placed her in the saddle of her horse. He then handed her a small bag before pulling her sunglasses from his pocket. She accepted them, and he jumped into the saddle. As they began to ride toward Pallen, she frowned up at the few stars left in the sky.

After a while, a smug grin crept to her face. "Is something wrong?" she trilled innocently. "What are we doing?"

Luke said nothing, his body tense. She opened the bag in her hand and pulled out some dried fruit, and although the food was not something she would normally eat, she enjoyed her breakfast.

Alissia spent most of the day sleeping against Luke's chest, and they rode in complete silence with few stops. They returned back to camp with his horse late that afternoon, and while he tended to the horses, she washed up and found something to eat. She then changed into something to wear for yoga and tried to find a grassy area as far away from Luke as possible. While going through her poses, she noticed him watching her as he built a fire, and she turned her back to him.

Once finished, she told Luke she needed some privacy in the tent. With the heat stone still absorbing sunlight outside the tent, she wished she could charge it and bring it in with her. Instead, she endured the cold while undressing and washing with the cleansing gel. She then put on a thick layer of clothing and crawled beneath her blanket.

A strange noise from outside soon caught Alissia's attention, and she stepped out of the tent to find Luke going through a fast-paced sword routine. Completely focused, he did not notice her, and she watched him for a moment before sitting down by the fire.

It was dusk by now, and she took advantage of his not knowing she could see in the dark. As she held her hands up to the fire, her eyes never left him. Although cold outside, sweat glistened on his shirtless, lean body, and with every skillful lunge and slice he delivered through the air, his toned muscles flexed beneath his skin.

His movements eventually slowed, and she noticed a tattoo on the left side of his chest. A chain hung from his neck, holding a large ring that moved with each heavy breath he took.

When he looked her way, she quickly turned her attention to the fire, and he walked over and wiped the sweat from his body with a small towel. While rubbing cleansing gel over his torso and through his hair, she awkwardly pretended to focus on warming herself. Relief filled her when he finally picked up a glow stone and entered the tent.

After a while, Alissia's thoughts turned to Grady. She recalled the nights they danced together and how happy she had felt in his arms, each memory reaffirming his innocence.

When she heard Luke coming out of the tent, she forced her thoughts aside, and her expression hardened. She did not even look his way until he sat down across from her with a bowl of food. He wore fresh clothing, and his usual disheveled hair looked combed, with the stubble on his face gone.

He smiled and put a bite of food in his mouth, and she recognized it as the same horrible meal from the night before. He did not even take the time to warm it over the fire. She mentally screamed, deciding he was the most Spartan person alive. Enjoying food and sleep seemed foreign to him.

She got up and found some crackers and a container of unpleasant nut spread that Luke served for lunch the day before, while telling her how filling it was. She rolled her eyes, thinking how he only packed food that served a purpose other than taste.

By the time she sat back down by the fire with her food, Luke was finished eating. He watched her eat with a strange smile on his face, making her uncomfortable.

"That was pretty clever what you did with the horse last night," he eventually said.

She gave an innocent smile.

"You do realize now that I know what you're capable of, I'm going to have to watch you even closer. In fact, I'm glad this happened on our first day, because now I know I underestimated you."

His smile grew, and he pulled out a set of leather restraints from behind him. Holding them up in the light of the fire, he said, "I hoped that I wouldn't have to use these while on this journey, but luckily, I've been taught to always be prepared."

Alissia stared back at him in disbelief. Catching herself, she lifted her chin and met his gaze defiantly. "You may get those on me, but I promise it won't be easy. And I promise you'll get hurt in the process."

Luke burst into laughter, strengthening her desire to hit him. When he finally stopped, he wiped a tear from his eye and grinned.

"And I believe you," he said, standing to his feet.

After cleaning the dishes and putting away the food, he got ready for bed. Then he walked over to her.

"Are we going to repeat last night?"

"I don't know," she retorted. "Are you going to boss me around and try to control me every day?"

His mouth twitched. "That depends on you. Are you going to do what needs to be done on your own, or do I need to help you?"

Alissia glared up at him for a moment. Then she stood and readied for bed. Hours later, she was restless and fully awake, staring at the wall of the tent. No matter how hard she tried, she could not stop thinking about what she left behind in Pallen.

Frustrated, Alissia sat up and watched Luke for a moment. He had to be exhausted from all the traveling and getting up so early, and he was most likely in a deep sleep by now. Chewing on her bottom lip, she wondered if this could be her opportunity to escape.

The best outcome would be that she never see him again. The next best thing would be to have him catch up with her tomorrow, as it would still be another wasted day. She did not want to get any farther from Pallen. Although she knew she would probably get caught, she had to try something.

Alissia looked over at the heat stone and frowned. Although the rock only let out a dim, red glow, she wished she could cover it.

She kept her boots, gloves, and cloak under her blanket to keep warm during the night. Her clothing pack sat at the foot of her bedding, while the other pack remained outside.

Adrenaline kicked in as she slowly picked up her gloves and pushed them into her boots. Without making a sound, she set the boots at the entrance of the tent. She then did the same with her bag.

She inched her way to the opening and held her breath as she carefully undid a button of the tent flap. Because of her small size, she only needed to undo two of the large buttons for a hole big enough to slip through.

Once finished with the buttons, Alissia looked down at Luke. She now sat less than a foot away from his face. He still slept and had not even twitched since she began to move around.

She listened and looked around the tent for any movement from the wind. Once satisfied she would not have to deal with a breeze when she opened the flap, she slowly slipped her boots through, one at a time. She could hear her pulse in her ears, and her hands shook as she carefully placed her bag outside, setting it on top of her boots.

Looking down at Luke, Alissia grinned excitedly. She watched him for a long moment before she found the courage to creep through the small hole.

She could barely breathe as she cautiously inched her way through the opening, and once outside, she almost burst into tears of joy.

A strong grip suddenly seized Alissia's right ankle and yanked her body back through the opening, where she landed in a tight grip within Luke's arms.

He covered her with his blanket before propping himself on one of his elbows, reaching over to fasten the buttons of the flap. He flopped back down and locked her in his embrace, with her back against his chest and her head beneath his chin.

Once the shock wore off, Alissia began to struggle within his arms. He let her squirm for a moment before sternly whispering in her ear, "It's either this or the restraints tonight, and don't say you weren't warned."

She stopped writhing. "You were awake the whole time, and you waited until I was outside. Am I right?" she panted.

His chest trembled with laughter. "I told you I sleep lightly. You're the one who chose to ignore my warning."

Alissia closed her eyes, focusing on her heavy breathing. Tears of rage threatened to break free. She loathed Luke for making her feel powerless—just like her father.

Chapter 17

An awareness of someone tugging on her ear pulled Alissia from her sleep. Not ready to wake, she gave a soft moan and nestled into the warmth at her side. The tugging persisted, and she frowned, covering her ear with her hand.

The sound of laughter, along with a shaking body, pulled her back to reality, and she opened her eyes to find Luke staring down at her. Propped on his elbow, he watched her from the light of the glow stones.

She turned her face to the side, covering it with her arm. "This is not how I want my day to start," she muttered. "It's still nighttime."

"Good morning, Pixet," he said cheerily. "You really are hard to wake. I'm thinking if I slept like that you would have succeeded in getting away from me last night."

She turned her back to him and closed her eyes, only to have the blanket yanked away.

"I *really* don't like you," she scowled. "You do know that, don't you?"

He laughed heartily as he stood and began to get ready.

Alissia sat up and pulled her boots into the tent. Then she stared down at them in dread. They were cold—very cold. The smirk on Luke's face confirmed what she thought.

"You did this on purpose, didn't you?"

"I'm not the one who put them outside last night. You made that choice, not me." He lifted his brows. "In my opinion, I think you should have left them in the tent where they belonged."

She threw both of her gloves at him, and he left the tent laughing. After dressing, she stepped outside with her pack, and Luke brought her a steamy mug. Although she craved a hot, morning drink, she did not trust his sense of taste.

"How bad is this?" she asked, sniffing the drink.

He lightly blew into his matching cup and took a sip. "I drink it all the time, and it'll help to warm you." He smiled and added, "I know you're angry with me for interrupting your escape last night, and I'm sorry you're angry. I offer you peace."

Alissia frowned, noticing his apology was not for anything he did.

The drink smelled all right, so she decided to taste it. However, she regretted that decision the moment the liquid entered her mouth, and she immediately spit it out. She continued to spit, but the foul taste stayed on her tongue.

Luke took the mug from her. "Does this mean there won't be peace today?"

She glared at him for a moment before stomping away.

His cheery attitude did not lighten her mood all day, and she believed he thrived off her unhappiness.

He set up camp that night near a stream, and he surprised her after dinner by preparing a bath. He used the same kind of foldable material she used in the mountains, and he filled it with water from the clear stream before placing a small box with a botch stone in the corner of the bath. He also took the time to tie a thin rope between two trees, so he could hang his blanket to work as a wall.

The simple pleasure of a hot bath softened Alissia's mood, and as she sat by the fire drying her hair, her eyes became heavy .

Luke sat down across from her and shook his head roughly before running his fingers through his wet hair. He watched her for a moment. "Are you still angry?"

"Why can't I go back to Pallen?" she asked softly, not in the mood to fight. "I could find Grady, and then we could leave and go far away where no one can find me."

"You love him?"

She stared at the fire and thought about his question. Telling Luke how she felt about Grady seemed wrong. She never even told Grady her feelings. He needed to be the first person to hear those words from her mouth, not Luke.

"He was willing to give up everything for me, even being an elder," she said, her eyes never leaving the fire. "He loved me."

Not wanting Luke to see her sadness, she got up and readied for bed. By the time he joined her in the tent, she was already asleep.

*****

Alissia did not argue with Luke as they continued to travel for the next two days, but she did not talk to him much either. As each day passed, her heart grew heavier at leaving Pallen and Grady behind. She grew tired of getting up each morning before dawn and spending her days on a horse. She was always cold, and although Luke now attempted to find something she would eat, she was tired of eating the same unpleasant food.

They now rode beside each other when the trails allowed, and she gave Luke a questioning look when she noticed a village in the distance. He stopped his horse, and she did the same, surprised by the sudden hard look on his face.

"Fix your headwrap so your hair's hidden," he said firmly.

She stared back at him defiantly, and he let out a sigh. Although the look on his face did not change, his voice softened somewhat as he said, "For your safety, you need to conceal your hair."

"Are you asking me, or are you telling me?" she questioned, her eyebrows raised.

A muscle in his jaw twitched. "I'm asking you."

Alissia pulled her hood back and rearranged her headscarf so the wrap covered her thick hair. Once finished, she lifted her hood back over her head. With a patronizing smile, she said, "You know, people can still see my eyebrows if they get close enough. Besides, I thought I was just a legend, and nobody from Pallen knows I'm with you."

"We're still not far enough away from Pallen. The farther we get, the harder it'll be for someone to follow you. We're not traveling on any of the main roads, and that means the paths we're taking are out of the way."

He added with emphasis, "And since we lost a day of travel, if anyone is searching for you and they're going in this direction, they would have gotten here first."

He nudged his horse forward, and she did the same. They rode to the stables at the back of an inn, and a boy looking to be around eleven years old met them. Luke gave him a coin and told him he would be rewarded if he took special care of their supplies and horses. When the boy noticed the sword on Luke's horse, his face lit up. Luke told him to keep the sword hidden and not to mention it to anyone, and the boy nodded excitedly, suddenly looking at Luke like he was a celebrity.

It was just beginning to get dark as they walked into the inn, and Luke found a table in a back corner of the crowded room. He sat where he could watch most of the people, and it took a moment before a young lady came to take their order. Alissia's stomach growled as she went over the food choices.

Luke watched the room while devouring his meal, and half of Alissia's food was still on her plate when he finished eating. Although he did not rush her as she savored every bite, he seemed distracted. When she finished, she looked expectantly at him.

"What's for dessert?"

He smiled for the first time since arriving at the village. "You can eat more?"

She grinned and nodded.

He motioned for the waitress, and as she began to clear their table, Luke asked her about the desserts. Alissia did not recognize any of them, and she told the waitress she needed a moment to think before making a decision. The woman nodded and walked away.

Alissia chewed on her bottom lip, staring at Luke. He seemed interested in something behind her.

"Um . . . can you explain what the desserts are?"

His eyes focused on her. "You really are far from home, aren't you? I already knew that from the way you talk. I've never heard your accent or a lot of your words, and I know quite a few languages."

"I've been hidden away all my life, remember? Grady would explain things to me, and he didn't ask questions about it."

Luke nodded and began to describe the desserts, and she chose something similar to a fruit cobbler. He did not order anything for himself, and shortly after her dessert arrived, he abruptly stood and said he felt sick.

She could barely understand him as he put his hand to his stomach and began to speak quickly in his strong accent. He told her she needed to hurry and finish eating, and then she was to ask the waitress to have someone show her to their room. She would be safe if she went straight to the room immediately after she finished, and he should be there by then.

She watched in shock as he grabbed his pack and rushed away from the table. She turned around and watched him walk to their waitress, who called for a young girl. The girl began to lead Luke up the stairs, and Alissia stared with wide eyes as they disappeared from her sight.

Her hands shook when she turned back around and took two quick bites of her dessert. She grabbed her two bags and rushed to the door, nearly laughing out loud as she stepped out into the cold, night air.

Although dark outside, the glowing bella flowers growing up the sides of the inn put out enough light for people to see. Alissia turned the corner and began her way along the path to the stables. Her body trembled with adrenaline, and when she heard a man's voice behind her, she jumped and let out a small shriek before turning around.

"I'm sorry," said a young man, smiling politely. "I didn't mean to scare you."

Someone cried out behind her, and Alissia spun around to discover Luke pulling a man's arm high up into his shoulder blades. He glared fiercely at the man standing behind her.

Just as Alissia felt a hand on her arm, Luke knocked the feet out from under the man he held. He ran over to her and kicked a knife out of the hand of the man attempting to grab her. After punching him in the face, Luke grabbed the man's hand and pulled it behind his back, high up into his shoulder blades.

Seeing the other man about to run, Luke pulled a knife from his side and held it up, ready to throw it.

"I'm with the league," he warned. "Don't make that mistake."

Fear immediately spread across the man's face, and he put both of his hands in front of his body with his palms up, as if holding an invisible tray.

Luke smiled. "Smart choice. You may get to live another day after all."

He shoved the man he held, and they walked over to his accomplice. When Luke told them to sit down, they both obeyed while begging for their lives. He shushed them before turning his attention to Alissia.

"Well done, Pixet," he said, smiling. He gave a curt nod. "You were perfect."

Recognition dawned on Alissia's face. "You mean . . . you planned this? You used me?"

He laughed and looked down at his captives, and she wondered why they did not make an attempt to knock him down or tackle him. She would still be fighting, and there were two of them against one.

Luke turned his attention back to her, still grinning. "I told you that you'd be safe if you went to the room immediately after you finished eating. You're the one who chose to put yourself in danger." He gave a half shrug. "I'm beginning to believe I'm here to save you from yourself."

Alissia's grips tightened on her bags, turning her knuckles white. "You do realize I didn't even get to finish my dessert."

He chuckled. "I guess you didn't want it that bad."

Before she could respond, he looked down at the two men. "I'm guessing you have a room here. Am I right?"

They both nodded.

"Here's what we're going to do. We're going to quickly and quietly walk to your room, and then I'm going to ask you a few questions."

Luke's face hardened, and he pointed into the air for emphasis. "I'm a fair man, but any mistake you make could easily become your last, and I think we all know how this night could end."

Once in the men's room, Luke ordered his prisoners to sit on one of the two beds.

"What are your names?" he asked firmly.

The man that attempted to grab Alissia answered, "I'm Nolan, and he's Slade. I think this is a misunderstanding. I only wanted to ask her if she knew of a place I could buy another horse. We've never been here, and I only wanted directions. I only pulled my knife out when

I saw you holding Slade, and I panicked. We mean no harm, and I'm sorry if we upset you."

Alissia flinched when Luke's fist slammed into the right side of Nolan's face—his left eye still red from the last punch. While searching through their belongings, Luke found two vials filled with black liquid, some rope, and restraints. He opened one of the vials and smelled it before replacing the top.

The men looked at each other knowingly as Luke took off his shirt and set it on the other bed. When he turned back around, they began to show signs of panic, both staring at his chest.

At first, Alissia thought they feared the knife he wore under his shirt, but they seemed to be looking at his tattoo. She could not see it from where she stood behind Luke, and she wished she had paid more attention to him the night he washed by the fire.

"I guess this night isn't going to end as I hoped," said Luke, in a low and threatening voice, while holding up the vials. "I'd like to know why you have two vials of leo and where you got it from. You know you don't have the authority to use this." He paused, setting the vials on the nightstand. "I've been patient. If you lie to me again, I'll escort the lady to her room, and I'll return alone. I suggest you tell me everything."

"I'll tell you anything you want to know, and you can arrest us, too," Slade whimpered, tears filling his eyes. "We messed up. I'm sorry."

"I'm guessing you planned to give it to her," said Luke, motioning to Alissia, "but it would only take one vial to kill her. Why do you have so much?"

Slade anxiously glanced at Alissia. "We were told to bring her back alive. We never planned to hurt her, but . . ."

"But what?" demanded Luke.

Slade cleared his throat before continuing, "But some people said she's not human. She has the power to kill us with her mind, and she would have to be kept asleep if we want to be safe."

He faltered as tears lined his face. "Please," he begged. "No one said she was with the league, and we wouldn't have even started looking for her if we'd known. If you let us leave, we can let them know she's under your protection."

"Who hired you?" demanded Luke.

"Alrik Durst," answered Nolan.

The name sounded familiar to Alissia, and she wondered if she met Alrik at the ball.

"How many others are looking for her?"

"He put a bounty on her. I don't know how many others know about it," said Nolan. "We found out through one of our friends, and we thought we'd try to find her first."

"How much is the bounty, and what exactly is the bounty for?"

Although Nolan looked terrified, he was more composed than Slade, and he seemed eager to answer Luke's questions. "Twenty thousand shecks. We were to find the Lamian and bring her back alive. She went missing in Pallen a few days ago, and he wants her brought back."

"How did you recognize her?"

"He's telling people she's short, has purple hair and eyes, beautiful, shimmery skin, and long purple nails," answered Nolan. "She wears dark glasses everywhere she goes, and she would probably try to keep her hair covered. We noticed her when she walked in tonight."

"When did you hear about the bounty, and how long have you been here?"

"Less than two days ago, and we left within a couple of hours. We just got here tonight."

Luke stared at the men thoughtfully for a long moment. "You do understand I have a problem now that you know where she is and who she's with."

Alissia stood frozen and watched as both men begged for their lives. They promised they would tell no one about her, and when their voices began to rise in panic, Luke struck each of them and warned them to calm down. He put restraints on them, and they looked at Alissia, whimpering, as if begging her for their lives.

She could stand no more. Hurting them was one thing, but killing them was another.

"Stop this, L —"

Luke's head shot up, and he snarled, "If you say my name, I'll kill them right now."

She tensed beneath his cold stare, never having seen him like this. By the time she thought of a response, he was tying a long sock around Nolan's mouth. Instead of demanding that he stop, she decided to try to talk to him as if talking someone down from a ledge.

"You really don't want to kill them," she said soothingly. "We can find a way out of this. I promise. We can figure something out. Just talk to me."

He grabbed his shirt and put it on, buttoning a few buttons. Then he turned to her. His hand went through his hair and he gave a tight smile. "All right, we'll talk about it."

He crossed the short distance between them and swiftly picked her up. "But not here."

He was fast, and he was strong. Alissia immediately found herself being carried down a narrow hall with Luke's arm under her bottom. His other arm held her firmly in place, locking her chest against his.

She struggled in his arms, wildly kicking both of her legs. She tried to lift her head, but his hand held it securely in place. She heard him excuse himself to someone, and he explained that she was a passionate lover.

"You know how Gazzerian women are," he said, laughing. Alissia wondered why her feet did not make contact with anyone.

She felt herself being carried up a flight of stairs, and that is when she was able to turn her head just enough for her teeth to find flesh. She took great satisfaction in hearing him groan as she bit down.

When she heard him unlocking a door, she let go of her bite. She focused her attention on holding both of her legs out so that they caught each side of the doorframe as he tried to walk through. After a short struggle, he made it into the room and closed the door. Then they fell onto a bed with him on top of her.

He caught both of her hands before they made contact with his face, and he dodged the headbutt she tried to deliver as he pinned them down. Struggling beneath his body, she recognized they were in the same position as the first night they met when he tackled her, with her body pinned beneath his and his forehead on her shoulder. As they both struggled with their breathing, everything within Alissia hoped her bite hurt him more than the kick to his groin.

Being held down made her feel powerless, and since she spent most of her childhood feeling powerless, Alissia loathed that feeling. She began to feel suffocated and out of control, and she started to writhe beneath him like a wild, trapped animal. When she finally stopped struggling, she could feel warm tears making their way to the front of her eyes. She refused to give Luke the satisfaction of seeing her weak, and she turned her head and closed her eyes in an attempt to regain control of her emotions.

Shortly after her body went limp, Luke lifted his head. He put his lips to her ear and said, "I'm not going to kill them. That has never been my plan, and if you stop fighting me, I'll explain."

She did not trust herself to respond.

"I'm not going to kill them," he vowed. "However, I do plan to scare them, so they won't talk when they get home. We don't need anyone to know which way you're traveling, and they don't need to know you're with me. I'm hoping I'll scare them enough that they'll go back home and never get involved in something like this again. They're young and inexperienced, and they made a mistake. That mistake could have cost your life, because they seem to have found a way to get leo. I plan to find out where they got it, so the league in Pallen can arrest whomever is responsible."

Alissia turned her head to look into his face. A lock of hair hung down into his eyes as he stared down at her.

"I knew while I watched them as we ate that they were inexperienced and were never a threat," he explained. "If I ever thought they were a true threat, I would never have left you alone for you to get yourself killed. What you witnessed from me tonight was nothing but fear and intimidation."

He gave a reassuring smile. "Why do you think I took off my shirt? The moment they saw my mark, they knew what I'm capable of doing. I don't have to prove anything, and I don't have to kill them. But they need to believe they came close to death tonight. They're very lucky I don't enjoy some parts of my job as much as some of the others in my profession."

He stopped talking and waited for a response. When she said nothing, he frowned. "It's either this, or I break all of their legs so they can't return to Pallen until they're healed. I'm showing them mercy. Do you trust me?"

She studied his face, her brows furrowed.

"I promise I'll take you back to the room once I'm done with them," he vowed, "and you can see for yourself that they still live. Now will you trust me?"

Alissia frowned. "I don't trust you, but I believe you."

His grip lessened on her hands. "If I let go of you, do you promise you won't try to kill me again?"

Her eyes narrowed. "I promise I won't try to kill you again today."

The corners of his mouth twitched, and he released her. As soon as he rolled onto the bed, she sat up.

"I need to go back to them now," he said. "They believe they're about to die, and they're both terrified."

Luke got up and walked over to his belongings, and Alissia wondered if he or the young girl brought them to the room. When he turned around with the restraints, she shook her head adamantly and said, "You're not putting those on me."

"We both know what'll happen if I don't do this," he said, suddenly looking tired, "and unlike earlier, now is not the time for you to go off getting into trouble—especially now that I know you have a bounty on you. Unfortunately, the two boys in the other room aren't anything compared to some of the others coming after you."

He took a step toward her. "Now, shall we do this the easy way or the hard way?"

Alissia lifted her chin, challenging him with her eyes.

Letting out a harsh breath, Luke shook his head. "You're not going to make this easy for me, are you?"

She stood from the bed, ready for another fight, and he frowned before walking over to her. He swiftly caught both of her wrists when she tried to hit him, and as she frantically kicked and struggled against him, they fell onto the bed with him on top of her.

She continued to move wildly beneath him, and as he attempted to put the restraints on her wrists, she delivered a headbutt to his nose. When he noticed his blood trickling onto the side of her face, he let go of her and stood back to his feet.

Alissia propped herself onto both elbows. With a smug smile, she watched Luke tend to his injury.

He turned to her with a frustrated look. "Why do you always have to be so difficult?"

"Why do you always have to be so mean?"

"*I'm* being mean?" he asked, throwing his hands into the air. "I've saved you twice after you've tried running off on your own, and I'm only trying to protect you."

Shaking his head, he let out a bitter laugh before meeting her eyes again. "I would think you'd be somewhat grateful for my protection, yet all you've done is complain and fought me since I've met you."

Alissia's eyes blazed with fury as she lurched into a sitting position. "You're only protecting me so that you can take me home to your Eldership, and that's the only reason you're protecting me. Don't even act like you're doing it because you care about what happens to me."

Pointing at the door, she said, "You're almost as bad as them. You want something from me, too. If you really wanted to help me, you'd take me back to Grady and let him take care of things."

"Grady?" he asked harshly, running his hand through his hair. "I'm still wondering why Grady took you to the Eldership ball and showed you off to everyone—especially to people rich enough to put a bounty on you."

He glared expectantly at her, and she turned her gaze to the nightstand.

"You don't know everything," she said softly. "Grady's done more for me than you know, so don't act as if he's done something wrong. We both didn't know people knew about the Lamians." She turned back to meet his gaze. "And it seems a lot of people know more about them than I even do."

His confusion gave her some satisfaction. She wanted him to know he did not know everything.

Luke's face softened, and he walked over and wiped his blood from her face. Setting the cloth aside, he picked up the restraints.

"You know I'm not leaving this room until this is done," he said solemnly. "Do we have to fight about it? Now that I know there's a bounty for you, things are going to be more difficult. Let me take care of those two boys in the other room. You know they're completely terrified right now."

He smiled. "When I get back, you can take a hot bath before bed, and if I hurry, I can even give our dirty laundry to the innkeeper's wife and pay double for her to find someone to get everything clean by morning. I'll even ask her about some food to take with us, and I won't try to feed you any more murdock root."

Without looking at him, she held up both of her hands and allowed him to restrain her to the bed. As soon as he stepped away, she glared up at him. "You will pay for this."

"I'm sure I will." He stared thoughtfully at her for a moment. "I won't do anything to your feet if you promise not to tear down the bed or try to break your wrists trying to get out of here."

She looked down and answered, in a resigned voice, "I promise."

As he tied a cloth around her head to cover her mouth, he said, "I wish I didn't have to do this, but I'm beginning to believe you'd bite off your own hands to break free of me."

He took off her boots, and she made an attempt to get comfortable on the bed. Then he left the room, locking the door behind him.

Alissia took in her surroundings. Unlike the men's room with two small beds, one large bed and a small sofa filled the cramped room. A glow-rock statue positioned on the nightstand by the bed gave out light, along with the glowing, white bella flowers. Various scented flowers adorned the simple room, and a window hid behind closed curtains. A heat stone hung down from the ceiling, and she could see the stars through the tinted, clear ceiling, which meant they were on the top floor of the inn.

She recalled Luke's conversation with the two men. If there truly was a bounty on her, she knew she had no other choice but to stay with Luke. Even though she hated how he tried to control her, she knew she would be much safer with him than on her own. He could protect her better than anyone else, even if his protection ended with her being given over to the northern Eldership.

She wondered what would have happened if she had not left Pallen. Although she and Grady had been ready to leave if they suspected danger, he could easily have been attacked or even killed if they left together.

Images of Grady being attacked by Nolan and Slade, along with even more experienced kidnappers, filled her mind. In the end, she decided leaving him was the best thing she could have done. She already hurt him enough, and it was best if he forgot about her and went back to Allure to be an elder. He could find a normal woman to marry, and he could have a long, happy life.

A tear slowly trickled down her face as she recalled what was said about her. She was no longer a human. She knew nothing of her future, and she had no control over anything in her life.

That thought scared her the most. Even as a teenager surrounded by chaos, she at least had a job and knew she would leave one day. She worked hard and went to school. She made a new life, yet she could do nothing here. She had depended on Grady for everything, and now she depended on Luke. She was completely useless.

When she heard Luke at the door, she hastily wiped her tears on her sleeves. It was not easy with her wrists restrained, and she turned her back to the door to gain more time. She stopped the moment she heard the door open, and she repeatedly blinked her eyes in hopes of making them look normal again.

He sat down next to her, and she forced a hard look onto her face before turning around.

He appeared tired as he silently took off the restraints and untied the cloth around her mouth. She noticed the marks on his knuckles but said nothing. After he stood, he asked, "Do you still want to see them?"

She nodded.

Once inside the men's room, she found them asleep on their beds, with their faces badly bruised and bloody. Staring down at them, she remembered the fear she felt while watching Luke question them, and she imagined what he did to cause such damage.

"I told you I needed to scare them enough so they wouldn't go back to Pallen and let Alrik know about you. If they tell him you're with me, he'll know what direction we're traveling."

He let out a tired breath. "I'm almost certain these two will go home and try to find a better way to make money, and they'll reconsider a life of crime. I told them the league in Pallen would be watching them from now on, and I'm sure they know I'm capable of finding them if they lead anyone to us."

He placed his hand on the doorknob. "Now we need to go back to the room, and I need for you to give me your clothes so you can get a bath before bed. We'll be leaving early in the morning."

They walked back to their room in silence, where she gathered her dirty clothing. Then he followed her to the bathroom and waited outside the door for her to give him the clothes she wore. He told her she would need to hurry, because everyone shared the bathroom on their floor. Just as she finished bathing, he knocked on the door, and she wrapped herself in a towel.

He gave her a clean gown he borrowed from the innkeeper's daughter, and Alissia wondered if the innkeeper let everyone use his family's personal clothing. After they got back to their room, she asked Luke about it.

"They're being paid well," he replied tersely.

He seemed tired and distracted as he pulled most of the bella flowers from their water. When he told her to go to bed, she was too tired to argue with him for telling her what to do. She crawled into the bed and rolled over.

Shortly thereafter, Alissia heard a noise and rolled back over to find Luke wearing nothing but his pants and doing one-armed push-ups. She watched him for a moment before rolling back over, and it did not take long for her to fall into a deep, dreamless sleep.

Chapter *18*

The sweet smell of honey, along with something warm rubbing against her lips, caused Alissia's eyes to flutter open.

Luke grinned, sitting on the bed beside her with wet hair. His face was free of stubble, and his fresh, woodsy scent blended with the sweet aroma in the room. He took a bite of the pastry in his hand.

"What? No evil face this morning?" he teased. "All it takes is the right kind of food to pull you out of bed willingly?"

She gave a big, showy stretch before smiling up at him. "Who says you're going to pull me out of this bed?"

He laughed as he stood. "We have to leave before someone else recognizes you."

"It's still dark outside, isn't it?" Alissia asked, frowning.

"Of course."

Ignoring her scowl, he set a basket of various pastries down in front of her and motioned to the glass of juice on the nightstand.

Alissia relished every bite of her breakfast, not caring that Luke found her smacking and moaning humorous. She finished the meal by licking the honey from each of her fingers. Then she greedily packed away the extra pastries to finish off later.

It was still dark outside when they left the village, and they spent the day traveling in silence. He rode in front of her with his pack-horse, and they did not stop long for lunch. Alissia spent most of her time thinking about the night before.

"Who's Alrik Durst?" she asked over dinner. "The name sounds somewhat familiar, and I think I met him at the ball."

Luke set his empty bowl aside. "Yes, you met him, and Grady introduced him to you. You were talking to him when your glasses were knocked off." His face twisted in disapproval. "That drunk wasn't an accident."

"Is that why you looked mad at me that night?"

He nodded. "I suspected Alrik. He's from the North, and he knows of the Lamians." He added bitterly, "He's a powerful and greedy man, and I'm sure he'd love to have you."

Alissia took a few bites of her food while she recalled meeting Alrik. She remembered him as a gentleman, with the same Latin appearance as Luke.

"What would he do if he found me?" she asked.

"He'd want everything you could give him, and that's why I need to get you under the protection of the northern league."

Alissia set her bowl down, giving Luke her full attention. "What exactly is the league?"

"It's a special division within the Eldership you have to be chosen for. To be in the league, you have to complete a specific type of training, and many of the chosen don't finish." His eyes clouded over, and he added, "They walk away."

"What kind of training?"

"The league's the Eldership's highest form of enforcement, and we're trained to protect and enforce." He picked up a stick and stoked the fire.

"And what makes it so different?"

"Not many complete the necessary training, so the league is a select group of people known for being able to withstand and complete certain things."

Alissia's brows furrowed. "If there hasn't been a war since the Eldership began, what do you actually do?"

He set the stick aside and looked at Alissia. "I said we haven't had a civil war since the Eldership began. That doesn't mean we haven't had wars against our bordering lands, and we've also had our ports attacked." His eyes went to the fire, and he gave a half shrug. "But I'm not considered a soldier and wouldn't serve among the troops if a war did come."

"What were you trained for then?"

He let out a sigh, keeping his gaze on the fire. "I was chosen as a child, and I'm skilled in many areas." Waving offhandedly, he said, "Spy, guard, and some other things."

"What other things?"

His face hardened, and he met her gaze. "Things most people don't enjoy doing."

After an uncomfortable moment of silence, Alissia asked, "What does the tattoo mean, and why did they seem so scared of it?"

"It confirms that I'm a member of the league, and they knew they had no other choice but to cooperate." His eyes locked onto hers as he added firmly, "But don't expect that reaction from everyone. I could tell from the beginning they could easily be intimidated, and they weren't experienced. Don't expect me to always be that nice. If those two boys had been more experienced at what they were trying to do, things could have easily ended differently."

Alissia turned away from Luke's hard stare. Chewing on her bottom lip, she watched the fire for a moment. Then she turned back to him and said, "Grady told me he was chosen at an early age to go into the Eldership. Is it that way for everyone?"

Luke took a sip of his drink before answering, "Everyone within the Eldership was chosen at an early age and are trained in the area they're best in. Grady and I were trained very differently, though. He's spent his entire life training in the government capital of Allure, and his training has a lot to do with interpreting the laws and codes of the Eldership. Although we both have the same basic training everyone within the Eldership has, my training is a lot more about enforcing the laws. I spent a few years training in Allure, and that's how I met Grady. Most of my training was in the North, though."

"But what about family?" Alissia asked, relieved the tension was gone. "Did you leave your family as a child and live in the school?"

Luke shook his head. "Grady's family lives in Allure, so he got to see them often. I never had a family, so I spent my childhood living at the Eldership school."

Although his last statement surprised her, she had more important questions to ask. "What will the Eldership do with me? You know . . . once you give me to them?"

He grimaced. "I'm not giving you to the Eldership. I'm taking you there for your protection. The northern Eldership is different from the southern Eldership in many ways. I also have more power there." He assured, "I can make sure you won't be taken advantage of, but I can't do that if you're in the South."

He frowned with disgust. "If you go to Allure, where everyone is power hungry, they'll all want to use you, and you'll be miserable."

Shaking his head, he added, "Not only that, but last night proved the southern Eldership isn't your biggest concern. It's people that think you can give them wealth and power.

"Alrik Durst is from the North but has spent the last twenty years getting wealthy in the South. I'm sure when he saw you at the ball, all those stories he remembered from his childhood came back to him.

His men were most likely the ones we heard at the inn. He had someone watching you, and nobody expected you to leave that night."

Luke gave a hard stare as he said, "You're lucky my man contacted me in time, and I was able to meet him in the alley." He let his words sink in before continuing, "I wasn't expecting anything that night, either. I think the only reason I got to you first was because I wasn't alone. I was able to follow you while Garrett went to the stables and got everything ready for us to leave. Once I got to the inn, I sent a message to the stables for him to bring the horses there."

Still giving Alissia a stern look, he said, "Alrik won't be the only person to recognize you, and I'm still confused how you've been traveling around out in the open without being noticed. How long have you been out of hiding?"

Alissia turned her eyes to the fire. Ignoring his glare, she asked firmly, "What will happen to me when I get to the North? What will the Eldership want from me?"

"The main thing is that I know exactly who to trust in the North, and you'll have protection. You'll live at the Eldership and be guarded at all times."

She gave a bitter laugh and turned back to him. "So I'll be a prisoner?"

"You won't be a prisoner," he assured. "They'll consider you an ambassador of the Lamians, and they'll treat you as such. You'll be given almost anything you ask for." Smiling, he spread his hands and added, "Isn't that every girl's dream?"

"Not mine," retorted Alissia, her face twisted in disgust. "I don't consider being told what to do and where to live a dream come true."

"They'll want to learn more about your people, and since you'll be an ambassador, you'll be treated as such."

"And what if I can't tell them anything about my people?" she snapped. "What if I can't even tell them anything about myself?" With pleading eyes, she asked softly, "What if I can't even answer a single question?"

She paused, her eyes never leaving his. Then she said, "They'll resent me, and I'll be of no use to them. Didn't you say they'd want to use me against the South?"

"No," he replied, lifting his finger for emphasis, "I said I didn't want the South to use you against us, as that's already happened in the past."

In frustration, Alissia looked heavenward. An idea came to mind, and she turned back to Luke. "What if I'm trying to find my people? What if I don't even know where they are, and that's all I want to do? If you take me to the northern Eldership to live, I'll never be able to look for them."

"Do you know where your people are?" Luke asked, watching her closely.

"No," she answered matter-of-factly, "I don't know where my people are."

His thoughtful gaze turned to the fire, and hope sprang up within Alissia. After a while, he looked back at her and said, "If you're alone, you'll need the protection of the Eldership more than you know. You can't walk around this land looking for your people and expect to be safe."

Alissia gave a loud groan, wishing she could hit him. She took a few deep breaths before trying again.

"But what if I'm not alone? What if Grady was willing to help me?"

Luke shook his head. "Then he doesn't fully understand the situation."

Alissia stared at him in disbelief. "He knows more about the situation than you do." When he did not respond, she added, "So I'm just supposed to give up and do nothing? Just quit? What would you do?"

"That's different."

"How's it different?"

"I can take care of myself."

The moment the words left his mouth, Alissia's frustration turned to fury. Glaring at him, her body trembled as she said indignantly,

"You don't even know me, and you know nothing about me. I've taken care of myself my entire life without any help, and now you're telling me I can't do it. You seem to have forgotten that I never asked for your help. In fact, I never wanted it."

"Have you even considered where you'd be if I hadn't shown up that first night? How about the second time?" He gave a smirk. "And I'm sure there'll be another time, because you can't seem to stay out of trouble."

That was it for Alissia. She knew if she continued the conversation, she would lose her temper. Without saying a word, she stood and left him by the fire. She quickly prepared for bed and crawled beneath her blanket.

When she heard Luke enter the tent, she pretended to be asleep. The next morning, he woke her before dawn, and she immediately gave him a cold look, refusing to speak.

At one point during their morning ride, he turned around and smiled. Within minutes, he wore bird droppings. He looked back at her suspiciously, and she glared at him.

Her silence continued into the night, and when she awoke the next morning, she had memories of the Lamians pleading with her not to use her powers. Her anger toward Luke carried over to them, as they seemed to have the ability to communicate with her, yet they only warned her not to use any of her abilities.

The next day, as she rode behind him in silence, she worried about how far she was getting from the mountains. She knew if Luke succeeded in taking her to the northern Eldership, she would never have a chance to go back to the Lamians. She would spend the rest of her life – however long that would be– not knowing anything about her body.

She spent her entire day trying to think of a way to escape, and she even considered using her power over animals. However, she knew that if she ever found the Lamians, they would know she used her abilities around Luke, and he would be a witness. That's when the idea of having an animal kill him came to mind, but the thought of murder was not an option for her. Although she hated him, she did not want to see him dead, and she was not a murderer.

As she tried to sleep that night, she finally thought of a plan. It was weak, but it was the best thing she could think of. It also went against her pride, but she was desperate by now. She would have to befriend Luke, and then she would tell him she thought the Lamians lived near the distant town she told everyone she was from. If he decided to help her get home, he would escort her back, and then she would find a way to lose him.

He only needed to be persuaded to turn around.

Chapter 19

Waking up before dawn again, Alissia scowled up at Luke. She immediately remembered her new strategy to befriend him, but it was too early for that. She could not force a smile onto her face, and she continued to glare at him.

After breakfast, she found she had more control of herself, and she smiled at him when she caught him looking her way. She even helped him pack, taking satisfaction in seeing the confusion on his face.

During their morning ride, she considered ways to befriend Luke, and it did not take long for frustration to set in. She never pursued relationships, but she did have plenty of experience walking away from people.

His silence suddenly bothered her, knowing she would have to be the one to start a conversation, and she did not have a clue what to talk about. Their last exchange proved they should not discuss their situation. She always hated it when someone asked about her past, so she did not want to do that. There was always the weather, but that did not appeal to her, either.

By late afternoon, Alissia still did not have an idea of how to start a pleasant conversation with Luke. She smiled at him often, but she could tell he was beginning to get suspicious.

When they stopped for the night, she helped him unload the horses, and she offered to assist with the tent. He let her help, and he even talked to her occasionally by pointing at something, telling her what else she could do.

She asked if he needed help with the cooking, but he declined her offer. She then sat down and began to watch him prepare the food. Smiling to herself, she wondered if she made him nervous.

"All right, what do you want?" Luke questioned, eyeing her suspiciously, as he stirred a small pot of soup over the fire.

Alissia grinned. "Nothing. I'm just watching you."

"And why are you watching me?"

"Why wouldn't I watch you?"

His eyes narrowed. "Whatever your devious brain is plotting, it's not going to work."

"Am I making you nervous?" she smirked.

"No, but you're confirming you're up to something."

She shrugged. "You were staring at me at the ball. I'm just doing the same in return."

"Yes, but something tells me you aren't thinking the same thing," he said, grinning.

"How do you know? I could be."

He gave a wink. "We could easily find out."

"All right, let's find out," challenged Alissia, letting her pride speak for her.

She knew she was in trouble the moment the words left her mouth. Luke pulled their dinner from the fire and set it down. Then he walked toward Alissia with a sly smile on his face.

Although she knew she should run, she lifted her chin and stared defiantly at him. He swiftly scooped her into his arms before heading toward the tent.

"All right! Stop!" she shrieked, kicking her legs. "I was thinking something else!"

Laughter erupted from Luke as he set her back down, and with a smug grin, he filled their bowls. Alissia stared at him in annoyance, deciding he only smiled when she was miserable.

"So, if that wasn't why you were staring at me, then why?" he asked, as they ate by the fire.

Ignoring her decision to befriend him, Alissia glared at Luke and took another bite of her food.

Although she was not able to force a smile onto her face when he woke her early the next morning, she resisted the urge to scowl at him. The thought of trying to have a conversation with Luke did not appeal to her, and she immediately dreaded the day.

Alissia spent her morning ride trying to think of how to start a conversation that would not end with him wearing a smug grin, and it was shortly after lunch when she got an idea.

"I want you to teach me self-defense," she stated, breaking the long silence between them.

His horse immediately stopped, and he turned around to look at her.

She stopped next to him and said, "I'm going to need it if I have so many people after me, and you're the perfect person to teach me."

"And when do you want to start these lessons?" he asked suspiciously.

She gave an innocent smile. "Tonight."

He eyed her thoughtfully before giving a nod. "All right. Tonight."

After dinner, he placed glow stones on the ground in a circle not far from the fire. He decided to focus on what to do if someone tried to attack her from behind, and she spent most of the lesson being roughly pulled into his chest.

By the end of the lesson, she knew a few things about defending herself, but the memory of his firm chest and strong arms stayed with her the most. Although she truly loathed him, her body did not seem to share her feelings of disgust.

Even though it did not come natural, Alissia smiled when Luke woke her the next morning. He saddled the horses while she ate breakfast, and hearing the faint sound of laughter, she jumped in surprise and turned around.

Using her night vision, she scanned the thick forest, and just as she was about to turn back around, she heard the laughter again. Noticing a dim, green light behind one of the outer trees, she reached out with her mind, and although many animals were around, she did not detect one in that area.

Out of curiosity, she set her bowl down and walked slowly toward the light. She soon found herself staring into the eyes of a tiny, translucent being.

It appeared to be a wingless fairy about the size of Alissia's hand. A dim, green glow surrounded her body, making it hard to see her features clearly.

The tiny being did not seem scared and even smiled as she hovered in front of Alissia's face. She giggled softly, and Alissia smiled back in wonder before glancing over her shoulder.

The fairy shook her head frantically.

"He can't see you," Alissia whispered.

The fairy responded by floating down to Alissia's hands and tugging on one of her gloves. Alissia removed the glove and held out her right hand, and the creature touched her tiny palm to Alissia's.

A feeling of great euphoria immediately filled Alissia, and the green light surrounded her. It only lasted for a short moment before the fairy pulled her hand away, and Alissia found herself back in reality. She instinctively glanced over her shoulder to find Luke still tending to the horses.

The fairy laughed, and Alissia smiled. When the fairy expectantly held her hand back out with her palm down, Alissia did the same. The fairy grinned up at Alissia before hovering over the top of her hand.

Alissia yanked her hand away, almost crying out in pain from what felt like a bee sting. Looking down, she noticed a small puncture wound on her hand, and she scowled at the tiny creature.

The fairy grinned, and Alissia stared back in confusion while massaging her hand. Hearing a sound behind her, she quickly turned around to find Luke strolling toward them. When she turned back around, the fairy was gone.

She hastily put on her glove and grabbed her bowl.

"I thought I heard something, but it was nothing," Alissia replied, scurrying past Luke.

Chapter 20

uckily, the trail was too narrow for them to ride beside each other that morning, and Luke did not notice how distracted she was. The skin around the puncture wound turned a pale blue color, and although she considered asking him about it, he did not even know the true color of her blood.

During their quick stop for lunch, she casually asked, "Do you know what a fairy is?"

"Never heard of it. Why?"

Alissia shrugged. "I just heard the word once and didn't know what it meant."

Once the trail widened that afternoon, they rode beside each other, and she smiled to herself when Luke immediately began to discuss self-defense techniques. Obviously, she found his passion, and he enjoyed talking about it. They were finally having conversations that did not end with her hating him and his warped sense of humor.

At one point, she got him to share some of the legends he knew about. However, nothing he described sounded similar to the creature from that morning, and she feared asking too many questions.

When they stopped for the night, he seemed eager to give her another lesson, and they rushed through their evening chores. She spent another night continuously slamming into his chest and falling onto the ground.

Alissia slept with her gloves on so that Luke would not notice her hand, and after a week of this routine, frustration rose within her. Although they no longer fought with each other, he did not seem to even consider turning back when she mentioned wanting to find the Lamians.

Her anxiety grew each day they traveled in the opposite direction of the mountains. She hated getting up before dawn to ride a horse all day in the cold, and her baths only came when they camped near water. Their meals consisted of the same things, and she desperately wanted a break from traveling.

Although her hand no longer bothered her, eight pale blue lines streaked away from the wound, making it resemble a tattoo of an eight-pointed star. At first, Alissia was terrified the lines would take over her entire body, but they stopped growing after a few days. Not wanting to deal with more uncertainties, she told herself it was only a scar.

About half an inch in size, the star was located on the meaty part of her right hand, between her thumb and pointer finger. It looked as though it was under her skin, and it did not hurt when she pushed down or rubbed on it.

Late one morning, Luke said, "Rain's coming, but there's a place we can go until it clears. We'll be there this afternoon."

Alissia looked up at the sky and saw no sign of rain, but she did not say anything. The idea of sleeping in a warm bed and having a hot bath filled her with excitement.

Once they neared the small village, they stopped and Luke dismounted.

"You need to fix your headscarf, and you're going to need to stay very close to me tonight." He added sternly, "I'm warning you now. This isn't the place for you to leave my side, and things will end a lot darker this time."

As she covered her hair, he unpacked his sword and attached it to his belt. She waited until he sat back in his saddle before asking, "Why are you wearing your sword?"

"Because we've been taking the fastest route, not the safest one." Luke nudged his horse forward. "Not many people travel this way, and there's a reason why."

"What do you mean we're not taking a safe route?" questioned Alissia, catching up to him.

"I've been this way many times." His eyes roamed her body, and he frowned. "Although, I don't stand out as much as you."

Before she could respond, his face hardened, and he turned his attention to the town.

Traveling through the village, Luke appeared dominating and fierce. With a set jaw, he intently took in everything around them.

As they walked away from the stables, he grabbed her by the hand, and once inside the inn, she instinctively stepped closer to him—immediately deciding not to attempt an escape that night.

Scanning the room, she tried not to meet the eyes of the sinister-looking men leering at her, and she noticed the women lived a very different lifestyle than her.

A bulky man strolled over to them, and Luke told him they needed a room for the night and food for their journey. The man nodded and led them upstairs to a small room with scarce furnishings. Although only one bed, the room appeared clean.

Once alone, Alissia dropped her bags and turned to Luke with accusing eyes. "Where have you taken me?"

He shrugged. "It was either this or the rain, and yesterday you were in a bad enough mood without the rain." He motioned to her bags. "You need to get your things so you can bathe before dinner, and I'll need your dirty laundry."

"When are we leaving?"

"Once it stops raining."

Alissia rolled her eyes. "It doesn't even look like it's going to rain."

"But it will."

Shaking her head, she began to pull the dirty clothes from her pack.

Luke stood outside the bathroom while Alissia bathed, and then he walked her back to their room. After putting her things away, she turned around to find him holding up the restraints.

Her eyes narrowed. "What are you doing?"

"I'm going to bathe, and I barely feel comfortable leaving you here by yourself." He added sternly, "I'm not walking out of this room until you're safely restrained."

Alissia crossed her arms and scowled, "You're doing this for my safety?"

"I am."

"Do you really think I'd leave this room after what I saw downstairs?"

Luke frowned. "At this point, I believe you're capable of anything."

Although Alissia knew it was useless to fight, his tone bothered her, and she struggled against him. Shortly thereafter, she found herself sprawled across the bed with him on top of her.

"Ew!" she groaned. "You smell like a horse, and I just bathed. Get off me!"

"You knew how this would end the moment you started to fight. Are you going to be still now?"

Glaring up at him, she remembered the mark on her hand, and she promised to cooperate. As soon as he released her, she scooted to the headboard and held out her hands, palms up, and he fastened the restraints. Once alone, she struggled to get comfortable on the bed and soon fell into a deep sleep.

*****

Alissia awoke to the sound of laughter coming from downstairs. Dark outside, the only light came from a small glow stone on a nightstand and a sparse amount of bella flowers growing along the walls. A heat stone rested on a small table by the window, putting out a red glow.

Uncomfortable and with sore wrists, Alissia noticed Luke asleep beside her, and she slowly lifted herself up to look at him.

She assumed he was exhausted from all the traveling. While thankful for her body's healing ability, she wondered if Luke's muscles were sore from riding in a saddle every day.

Never having observed him this close, his peaceful expression surprised her. Although he smiled and laughed often while teasing her, he usually kept a hard expression on his face.

After over two weeks of traveling together, she did not know anything about him, and he did not know her. Neither of them seemed eager to talk about themselves, and neither of them asked personal questions of the other, although they continuously found something to argue about.

Luke smelled fresh and woodsy, with his face free of stubble. A lock of hair hung down into his eyes, and she noticed a small scar under his chin. With his hands resting on his chest, she saw a scar across two of his fingers.

A corner of Alissia's mouth lifted as she stared down at his face. He was highly attractive, and for just a small moment, she wondered what it would be like if he actually cared for her.

Then she thought of Grady, and she reminded herself of Luke's annoying, controlling, and egotistical personality. Although he was the perfect eye candy, physical appearance was not everything.

Luke's eyes fluttered open, and Alissia thought she noticed a tender look on his face before his expression hardened. He sat up and went to undo her restraints, and she quickly positioned her hands to hide her scar.

She immediately felt relief once free of the restraints, but as she pulled her hands back, he grabbed her right hand and turned it over.

"What's this?" he demanded.

She tried to pull her hand from his grip, but it would not budge.

"It's a tattoo," she answered, sitting up.

"It's not a tattoo, and you've only had it for a week," he countered, still gripping her wrist. "What is it?"

Alissia smiled innocently. "Luke, it's been there for years. You just didn't notice it."

"I notice everything," he said firmly, staring hard into her eyes. "I notice now that you're lying, and I want to know the truth."

His authoritarian tone bothered her, and she looked back at him defiantly.

"And I want to turn around," she griped, "but you're forcing me to do something against my will." Her eyes bore into his as she venomously added, "You may be able to physically push me around, but you'll never be able to force me to talk."

Scowling back at her, Luke let go of her hand and stood. "We slept too long, and things are getting disorderly downstairs. We need to eat."

Alissia gave a smug grin, enjoying her small victory.

Neither spoke as he led her to the bathroom, and then he took her by the hand on their way downstairs. His eyes seemed to challenge everyone around them, and his mannerisms, along with his sword, made him a formidable presence, reminding Alissia of his controlled brutality.

The inn was much more crowded than earlier, and the people seemed less sober. Alissia tried not to look at anyone as she ate in silence, but everyone seemed to be watching them. The men's ogling left her feeling dirty and somewhat anxious, while the women openly stared at Luke.

As she took a sip of her drink, she compared herself to the other women in the room. With her high-priced clothing and long, glittery nails, along with her dark glasses and headscarf, she imagined she looked like a refined woman trying to hide from everyone in the room.

"They think I have money, don't they?"

Luke stabbed at his food. "That thought did cross my mind."

"Then why didn't you tell me?"

He laughed bitterly. "What good would it have done? All of your clothes are like that." Meeting her gaze, he sneered, "It seems someone has expensive taste."

"I didn't pick out any of them. Anika did, and she told me I had to wear the best since I'd be traveling with Grady."

"And she was right," he muttered.

She set her fork on her plate, giving him her full attention. "What do you mean by that?"

He took a bite of his food and swallowed before answering, "If you're with Grady, you have to dress the part."

"It was so we'd be less noticeable. If I was going to travel as his betrothed, it had to look real."

"Oh, it looked real to me," he retorted, "and I only saw you together once."

Alisisa glared back at him. "Why do you do that?"

"Do what?"

"Every time we try to have a conversation about something other than fighting techniques, you try to make me angry? Why can't you just be nice?"

He shrugged. "This is who I am, and you don't have to like me. I'm just here to protect you until you get to the northern Eldership."

A large, drunk man walked up to the table. Scowling down at Luke, he sneered, "The lady doesn't look like she's having much fun with you. How about I fix that?"

Luke's chair instantly crashed to the floor as he pulled a knife and grabbed the man's arm, lifting it into a painful position behind his back. With his knife to the man's throat, Luke glanced around the suddenly quiet room.

"I'm really not in the mood for this right now," he warned loudly, "but if anyone wants to try, I'll play."

"I'm sorry," the man stammered. "It's all just a misunderstanding. I was wrong."

Luke shoved the drunkard away and picked up his chair before sitting back down. Ignoring everyone's stares, he turned his attention back to his food.

Alissia remained silent for the rest of the meal. No one leered at her anymore, and most of the men immediately looked away if she glanced in their direction. The women, however, kept their eyes on Luke.

After dinner, he stood outside the bathroom while she prepared for bed. Then she allowed him to restrain her before he went to the bathroom. They did not speak for the rest of the night, and just as he started a workout while she tried to go to sleep, a heavy rain began to fall.

Chapter 21

Alissia smiled and squeezed her pillow, enjoying the rare moment of waking on her own timing. The sound of rain, along with the warm room and soft bed, soothed her. She rolled over to find Luke reading beside her, and she frowned. She threw her face into the pillow and let out a miserable groan.

"I thought you were going to sleep all day," he said cheerily.

"And why would I want to get up today?" asked Alissia, turning to face him.

"You don't have to, but I'm about to go downstairs to eat. You know what that means." Luke cocked his head and grinned. "Although I didn't restrain you when I left the room earlier. Somehow, I knew you'd continue to sleep soundly, and I was right."

"Are you trying to annoy me the moment I wake up? I'm really not in the mood for you."

It continued to rain throughout the day. Other than doing a long and intense yoga workout, Alissia spent most of her time napping, while Luke read a book.

He wrote a letter to the northern Eldership and sealed it with hot wax before stamping it with the ring hanging from his neck. When she asked how the letter would get to the Eldership, he explained how they used birds to carry messages. Each village housed a large supply of birds, and each bird followed a trained route.

Although not fond of the village, Alissia hated to see it stop raining that evening, and she prayed for a storm. It saddened her to know that one day at a cheap inn now felt like a vacation to her.

Her thoughts turned melancholy as she tried to fall asleep that night. She eventually rolled onto her back and let out a long sigh. Not knowing if Luke was still awake in his make-shift bed on the floor, she asked, "So your plan is to get me to the Eldership and dump me? I'm just a package you need to deliver."

It took a while before he replied, "I never said that."

"You said you're just here to protect me until you deliver me to the Eldership."

"I've already told you. You'll love living at the Eldership, and it should be a dream come true for you." He muttered, "You're being difficult over nothing."

"Nothing? You're forcing me to leave my people," she griped.

"I thought you didn't know where your people were."

"I know they're on the other side of the mountains, and when spring comes, I need to cross those mountains."

After a moment of silence, he said, "I thought you just crossed the mountains before winter. What made you decide you were going in the wrong direction?"

Alissia chewed on her bottom lip for a moment. "I had something to do in Pallen, and now I'm done. I can go back."

"What was so important in Pallen for you to cross the mountains?"

"That's something you'll never know," she answered firmly.

He did not respond, and after a while, an idea came to mind. Alissia's face twisted into a cunning smile.

"Luke, if I get too far from my people, I'll die. We need each other to survive, and I can't live without them. In fact, that's what this mark is. It's just the beginning." She paused before pleading softly, "You're going to kill me if you take me to the North. I'll die."

A long silence passed between them, giving Alissia hope.

"Luke?"

"I can't believe you thought of that, Pixet, and you sounded sincere, too. That was good, and most people would've believed you."

Alissia frowned. "You don't?"

"I do not."

"But, it's true."

"We both know it's not."

"I'm going to die, Luke," she implored softly.

"Not any time soon."

Giving up on the façade, she asked crossly, "And how do you know that?"

"You still have plenty of life in you. In fact, sometimes I think too much."

She gave an angry sigh and rolled over. Remembering what Nolan and Slade said about her, she grinned deviously. "You do know I can kill you with my mind, don't you? I've been nice, but you're leaving me no other choice."

Luke laughed. "If that were true, you would have killed me the moment you met me. In fact, you've already tried more than once."

Alissia chose not respond, and she soon fell asleep. The next day, they rode in silence, and she spent her time trying to think of another plan. Befriending Luke did not seem to be working. No matter what she said, he never even considered turning around.

She fell asleep that night thinking about how far they had traveled from Pallen, and her anxiety grew strong. Her worry continued throughout the next day, and her thoughts turned desperate. The Lamians warned her not to let anyone know of her talents or see them, but what if she did something subtle?

Although a lot of animals were in hibernation, Alissia had heard many wolves as she traveled. More than once, she even considered having them attack Luke, but no matter how much she despised him and dreamed of beating him herself, the thought of having him badly hurt and ripped apart by an animal did not appeal to her.

She needed to find a way to escape. Then she could get a wolf to travel with her. They were extremely vicious in the movies and had fur to help keep her warm when she slept.

Alissia wondered if she could reach out with her mind far enough for a wolf. Although she often heard them, they never seemed nearby. Hoping to expand her range with practice, she closed her eyes while riding in her saddle and focused on the animals around her. She chose a bird at a great distance away, and with all her might, she willed him to swoop down at Luke.

Shortly thereafter, Alissia laughed to herself at the sight of Luke dodging the bird. When he turned around and eyed her, she gave an innocent smile.

She spent the rest of the afternoon practicing, and as she sat by the fire that evening, she silently stared at a pebble, hoping to move it. However, no matter how much willpower she put into it, the rock would not budge.

She then stared hard at the fire in hopes of controlling a small movement, but that experiment did not work either. Neither did the one where she tried to start a small flame on her own.

"What are you doing?"

Alissia looked up to find Luke eyeing her with suspicion. She gave an innocent smile. "Nothing. Why?"

"You look as if you're doing something. What are you doing?"

She lifted her right hand and began to rub her fingers together as a smug grin crept to her face. "I was just wondering whether it was time to kill you with my mental powers. You know, you still have a chance to turn around before I actually do it."

He frowned and shook his head before standing. "Ready for some more training on how to really defend yourself?"

Later that night, Alissia mentally searched for wolves, and without success, she fell asleep.

The next day, she stayed deep in thought while riding behind Luke, and she finally came up with an idea. It consisted of going through his bags in hopes of finding something to use against him, and the only chance to search his bags would be on a bath night. She hoped for one that evening.

She knew he carried a map, and during their afternoon ride, she asked, "What was the name of the last village we were in?"

"Why?"

"Because I'm planning an escape and want to go back there since it was such a lovely place," she responded sarcastically. "Can't you just answer one question without suspicion? I'm a female. I'm curious."

Luke frowned. "Lorain."

"Why's it called Lorain?"

"I don't know. It's always been called Lorain."

"Do you go there often?"

"Only when I need to."

She smiled. "All right, that's all I wanted to know."

He responded with his usual frown and headshake.

Although they did not camp near water that night, Alissia remained happy. She finally had a solid plan. She would soon be traveling back to the mountains, and she would be in charge of her own life again. She did not need Luke for protection. She would find a wolf for that.

Alissia talked Luke into letting her help prepare dinner. She smiled as they discussed self-defense techniques, and she pretended to be eager for the evening lesson.

The next day excitement and anxiety filled her. When not reaching out with her mind in search of a wolf, she discussed fighting techniques with Luke. He seemed to be in a good mood.

Alissia focused hard to appear composed as she helped to set up camp that night near a stream, and Luke let her help with dinner as he prepared their bath.

While bathing, she tried not to think about what would happen if he caught her going through his pack. She knew she would never have another chance if she failed. Her entire plan depended on what she was about to do, and by the time she stepped out of the bath, her hands shook. She focused on appearing calm as she passed Luke and sat down by the fire.

She watched him gather his clothing bag before walking behind the blanket. As soon as she heard him enter the bath, she took a shaky, deep breath and crept to the blanket, careful not to let her shadow fall across it.

Alissia peeked around the edge of the blanket and smiled when she found the pack within reach and behind Luke's back. With trembling hands, she slowly lifted the heavy pack an inch from the ground and carefully pulled it to her body.

Grinning excitedly, she crept away from the blanket and began to search the bag. A leather trifold case with a tie around it immediately caught her attention, and she opened it to find an assortment of vials held in place by straps.

She began to open each vial to sniff the liquid within and soon found one containing the familiar scent of lavender. She quickly hid the vial in the pocket of her cape before putting everything back the way she found it. She then crept to the corner of the blanket, and while holding her breath, she cautiously set the pack on the ground.

Her body trembled with excitement as she made her way back to the fire. Sitting down, her face twisted into a malicious grin. Not only would she escape, but she would also use the same drug Luke had used on her—giving her revenge at the same time.

Chapter 22

Alissia rode beside Luke the following day, and they discussed pressure points and various defense techniques. She did not get annoyed with him, and she stayed engaged in the conversation. By the time they stopped to set up camp, they had enjoyed a pleasant day together.

While cooking dinner, Alissia added too much seasoning to the pot and apologized. As she began to ladle the soup into bowls, she mentally commanded the horses to make a commotion. Luke went to check on them, and she hastily drizzled a small amount of the sleeping drug into his bowl before stirring it in.

She gathered her food and drink and sat down by the fire. It did not take long before Luke Joined her, and she tried not to watch him as he devoured his food. She hoped the strong seasoning would disguise the taste of the drug, but at the speed in which he ate, she also wondered if he could even taste his food.

She had only eaten half of her dinner by the time he set his empty bowl aside, and when he noticed her watching him, he raised his eyebrows questioningly.

"Am I making you nervous?" she teased.

Luke grinned. "I believe we've had this conversation before."

"Yeah, but this time you're not going to win."

"Why's that?"

She took another bite of her food and chewed. After swallowing, she gave a smug grin. "Because it's my turn."

He opened his mouth to respond, only to close it abruptly as a look of dread filled his face. His eyes met hers knowingly.

Alissia stared at him, licking her spoon dry. Then she placed it in her bowl and set it aside. With her eyes boring into his, she said firmly, "I told you. It's my turn."

She never saw fear in Luke until that moment, as he implored, "Don't do this."

She leaned toward him. "I don't need anyone, and I can take care of myself."

Luke's gaze never left hers as his body slowly made its way to the ground. "You need me," he whispered. Then his eyes closed.

Filled with adrenaline, Alissia jumped to her feet and rolled Luke onto his back. After checking his pulse, she let out a sigh of relief, and then she dragged him a short distance from the fire. With trembling hands, she searched his body, amazed by the amount of knives hidden beneath his clothing. She chose a small one and moved her moneybag to the left side of her belt before tying the knife's sheath onto the opposite side.

She covered Luke with his blanket and searched through his belongings, where she found a smaller version of the book of faith Grady often read to her. Surprised that an assassin would carry such a thing, she stared down at the worn cover with Luke's name inscribed on it. Then she opened it to find the pages crinkled from use.

After setting the book aside, she continued her search, and in the end, she took his map and half of the food. Her saddlebag held the traveling gear she packed in Pallen, most of it still unused.

She cleaned their dishes and made sure to securely put away his food to keep animals away from the area. Then she saddled both of their riding horses. She knew Luke would come after her, and with all his special training, she worried he would be able to track her. She hoped that leaving him with two packhorses and without a saddle would slow him down.

Wanting the horses to feel refreshed for their journey, Alissia took off her gloves and held her right hand to her horse's neck before closing her eyes to concentrate. As energy began to flow from her hand, she felt a warm, unfamiliar sensation coming from her new scar. She opened her eyes to find it glowing brightly, like a star beneath her skin.

Tired and frustrated from all the mysterious changes to her body, tears filled Alissia's eyes as she stared at the glowing star. After a while, her tears stopped flowing, and a scowl spread across her face.

"You should never have gone back for your diary," she griped, wiping away the tears. "You should have stayed away from your past like you swore."

Once finished with the horses, Alissia checked Luke's pulse one last time. Her scar did not glow as she charged his heat stone to its maximum, and nothing strange happened. After setting the heat stone beside him, she dressed him in his hat and gloves. Then she tucked his blanket securely around him. She set the restraints on the ground in front of his face, hoping they would be the first thing he saw when he opened his eyes.

Staring down at Luke, guilt began to seep in, but she quickly shoved that emotion aside, reminding herself this was her only way back to the mountains. She tried to reason with him, but he would not listen.

Alissia mounted her horse and gave Luke one final look. Then she squared her shoulders and turned the two horses south. Traveling all through the night, she continuously reached out with her mind in search of wolves.

Just before dawn, she could no longer hold her eyes open, and she stopped and unsaddled the horses. Trusting them to stay close, she did not tie them to a tree.

She quickly washed her hands and face with the cleansing gel and cleaned her teeth, and with a fully charged heat stone beside her and a blanket wrapped tightly around her, she fell asleep under a tree.

A few hours later, Alissia's horse nudged her awake, and although she told the horses to wake her once they had rested, she did not want to get up. When thoughts of Luke tracking her came to mind, she immediately stood and began to load the horses.

She decided she would only stop for sleep and to relieve herself, as she could not afford to slow down for anything else. She would even have to let the horses canter occasionally. Luckily, both horses seemed to enjoy speed, although Alissia did not like bouncing for long periods of time.

She did not have to worry about wild animals, and her healing abilities kept her from getting sore from the riding. Her only concerns were getting lost and being seen by people. She pulled out the map, and as she studied it, fear and doubt crept in. X's, numbers, and lines drawn in a variety of colors filled the map, with some lines dotted and some straight.

Something within Alissia told her she would never find the Lamians. Lack of sleep and stress intensified her fear and frustration, and she soon felt tears streaming down her face.

Her mind remained busy all day, allowing her to ride until midnight without falling asleep in her saddle. Exhausted, she did not waste any time in taking care of the horses, and she soon fell asleep at the base of a tree.

Luke's horse nudged her awake early the next morning, and it did not take long for her to load the horses and begin her day of riding. She did not lead them, as they seemed to know the way.

Alissia worried about the moment they would need directions. Although she heard horses had amazing memories, she could not fathom the idea that they would remember their entire way back to Pallen.

She continued to reach out with her mind in search of a wolf, and while her thoughts were not as depressing as the day before, she longed for the distraction of a radio or cell phone. She occasionally dismounted and walked beside the horses for exercise and a mild distraction, but the silence remained. Her mind traveled to dark places, and by the time she stopped at midnight, physical and emotional exhaustion drained her.

She started her day early again the next morning, and it passed the same as before. Silence turned out to be her enemy, as ghosts from her past haunted her.

Picturing her mother and sister crying over her disappearance bothered her more than she thought it could, and thoughts of Grady, Anika, and Langley saddened her. She wondered if she would ever have a chance to make things right with them. Even if Grady was guilty, Anika and Langley deserved better from her.

She even thought about Luke, imagining wild animals attacking him while he slept, but those thoughts were immediately replaced with him waking up to kill the animals. Although hard to imagine him vulnerable, she kept remembering the fear in his voice as he told her not to leave and that she needed him. Part of her believed he did not care and just wanted to be the one to find a Lamian, yet she also believed he truly thought he was doing the right thing for her. In his mind, she needed protection, and he saw himself as her protector.

Luke made the mistake of seeing her as weak, and he tried to control her. The scar hidden beneath her tattoo continuously reminded her that she would never allow either of those things. Although she once dreamed of someone like Luke, that dream died long ago. She needed no one, and she would never be controlled by anyone again. She had never needed a man to save her, and she never would. The worst thing that could happen was death, and as a faithful believer in the Creator, she knew where she would go once her life ended.

Although she planned to find the Lamians, she would not allow herself to imagine a future with them. She learned long ago to never get her hopes up and start believing in things before they happen. She'd rather believe in nothing than to live with a shattered dream.

Thinking about the star on her hand and the strange little creature only frustrated her, so she did not allow herself to dwell on those thoughts. Instead, she tried to focus on something she had more control over, like what she needed to do to find the Lamians. Although she could not control what happened to her body, she did have control over her actions.

Late that afternoon, as Alissia rode on a narrow path surrounded by trees, she closed her eyes and reached out again with her mind. Her eyes shot open in surprise when she found two wolves at the very edge of her influence. Fearing she would lose them, she immediately called out to them with her mind, and once they began their way toward her, she stopped the horses and dismounted. She told them not to fear the wolves, and she took off her gloves and focused on calming them.

Alissia flinched when two large wolves stepped onto the trail. Although she had seen wolves at the zoo and on television, they had never looked as menacing as the ones before her.

With paws much bigger than any dog she had ever seen, these wolves had thick, grey and black fur. Although she knew they would be attracted to her, she could not help but feel somewhat nervous as she took a step toward them. She stopped abruptly when she noticed more of them stepping onto the trail, and a pack of eight fearsome wolves soon stood before her.

The pack leader stepped in front of the others, and he walked up to Alissia when she held out her hand. As she began to pet him, the bond took control, and visions filled her mind. She stayed connected to him until she could see the memory of a bloody feeding.

She bonded with each of the animals one at a time before choosing a three-year-old male. He seemed to be in the middle when it came to dominance in the pack, and she loved the personality she felt within him. It was an easy decision, as she knew immediately he was the one for her.

He gave Alissia a friendly nuzzle before their bond, and she now watched as he playfully said goodbye to his family. Once finished, he sat down in front of her, and the rest of the pack stepped back into the forest.

Alissia chuckled as she stroked his neck. "So what should I name you? Hmm? Something vicious, since you're my protector. Killer? Bandit?" Her eyes lit up. "Thor's a good one. That's a manly protector. You can be my Thor without the good looks. Although you're a handsome wolf, and all the female wolves probably think of you as a Thor-type of wolf." She frowned thoughtfully. "Maybe we should think of a nice name for you. How about Dorito or Cuddles?"

She continued to consider names while riding. The wolf disappeared on occasion to eat, and she finally decided to name him Fang.

Shortly after midnight, Alissia stopped the horses to camp under a tree. Her new companion slept beside her, keeping her warm, and she felt safe. With a renewed sense of hope, she fall asleep with a smile on her face.

Chapter 23

Alissia studied the map as she traveled the next morning. Since Luke told her the name of the last village they visited, she had an idea of her location, and she believed another village was somewhere in the area.

Knowing she should not stop anywhere near Pallen, she considered her food supply. She wished she could eat meat so that Fang could hunt for her, and if she knew how to forage for vegetation, she could live off the land.

After a lot of thought, Alissia grudgingly decided to stock up on the disgusting murdock root, and with a sigh, she put away the map. She pointed in the direction she guessed the village to be located, and she told Fang to try to find it. She also told him to find a discreet way for her to travel there, as she needed to stay off the main roads.

As he disappeared into the forest, she began to plan what she would do once at the village. Sometime during the night, he met up with her, and she followed him.

A few hours before dawn, they reached the edge of the village, and she led the horses back into the forest and unloaded them. Hoping the inn would be less crowded in the afternoon, Alissia looked forward to a long rest, and she immediately fell asleep with Fang by her side.

She awoke the next afternoon to Fang licking her face, and the two of them left the horses and walked to the edge of the forest. Her mind could not reach deep into the village, and she could only locate four dogs nearby. No one noticed as the dogs left the village, disappearing into the forest.

Alissia frowned as she stared into the eyes of two small and two medium-sized dogs. None of them looked vicious. After bonding with each of them, she sent the smaller two away. The two remaining, both females, resembled each other, with short brown and black hair. She told them what she needed, and she described the inn as a place where groups of humans slept and ate.

She watched as the two dogs entered the village. As one continued to walk toward the inn, the other stopped where Alissia could still see her. Alissia waited a few minutes before she scratched Fang behind the ear and told him to listen out for her. She checked her headscarf and the hood of her cloak one last time, and then she stepped out of the forest with her pack.

Although her dark glasses and winter headscarf looked normal while outside on a winter afternoon, she worried about being different once inside. She tried to appear casual as she walked through the village and took in her surroundings. The sound of laughter from a group of playful children and the appearance of the people gave her some reassurance. They were not as intimidating as the ones in the last village, and Alissia told herself she may be able to leave this town without trouble.

A young girl, either in her late teens or early twenties, was the only person in the dining area of the inn. She stopped sweeping and gave a friendly smile as Alissia walked over to her.

Remembering to use her fake accent, Alissia tried to sound confident as she said, "I'm in need of a hot bath and meal. Can you help me with that?"

The girl nodded and set the broom aside. "I can. Do you need a room for the night?"

Alissia shook her head. "My husband's taking care of some business in town, and I have to meet him soon. We won't be staying the night, but I do need to buy some supplies for our journey. Do you think you can gather some cleansing and food supplies for me? My mother's ill, and we're trying to get to her before she dies. We won't have time to stop again, so I was hoping to buy some murdock root and other food that will last for a while."

"I'm sorry to hear about your mother. Where are you traveling to?"

Not good with names, Alissia could not remember any of the villages she saw on the map near Pallen, and she stammered, "Uh . . . Pallen."

The girl smiled. "I'll show you to the bath and will gather your supplies. I'll have a meal ready once you come down. Will your husband need something prepared as well?"

Alissia shook her head.

"Is there anything else you require?"

"No, thank you," said Alissia, feeling a bit calmer. "That's all. I'd really just like some warm vegetables and bread if you have any."

"I can get that for you." She turned to lead Alissia up the stairs.

Alissia grinned triumphantly as soon as the bathroom door closed. She quickly threw her pack on a chair and pulled out her supplies. After rushing through a bath, she dressed and pulled her wet hair into a tight bun. She wrapped her head in a scarf and put on a pair of sunglasses before throwing everything back into her pack.

She found a seat in the back corner of the dining room so that she could watch the door, and it did not take long before the girl set a hot drink and warm plate of food on the table. Alissia's stomach growled as the girl explained she would soon have the traveling supplies ready. Although Alissia smiled politely while listening, she began to devour the food as soon as the girl turned away.

As she ate the last bit of her food, a rugged, brawny man with receding, brown hair walked in and took a seat near the door. Alissia immediately sensed trouble as he began to stare at her with a malicious grin.

The girl must have heard the bell hanging at the door, because she was soon at his table. Alissia watched them have a whispered conversation, and as the girl walked back to the kitchen, she glanced nervously at Alissia before disappearing behind the door.

Alissia was right about the inn not being busy in the afternoon, and she now found herself alone with a sinister-looking man.

Her fear grew even stronger when another man entered and sat down across from the first one. Gangly, with light brown hair, he did not look as menacing as his buddy. The two of them began a low conversation, and although Alissia desperately needed fresh supplies, it was best she make her getaway before more people joined them.

She reached beneath the table and turned so that the man watching her could not see her pull a few coins from her leather pouch. After placing the money near her plate, she looked up again.

The larger man seemed to be daring her with his expression. Alissia ignored the terror she felt, and she defiantly glared back at him while putting on her backpack.

She turned in her seat and lifted her cloak before pulling the knife from her side. Although she knew she did not have a chance against the two of them, she swore she would do as much damage as possible and would not go down without a fight.

With a tight grip on the knife, still concealed by her cloak, Alissia stood. The large man did the same, and then his lanky friend stood and turned around to face her.

Squaring her shoulders, Alissia began to walk to the door. As she went to pass them, the skinny one reached out to grab her, and her knife instantly came out, slicing through his shirt and making contact with his arm. He yelled out in alarm and stepped back.

Alissia darted to the door, but the larger man grabbed her backpack and slung her onto the table, slamming the side of her face into the wood. She tried to wield the knife behind her back, only to have it snatched away. Her attacker pulled her broken glasses from her face and then yanked her headscarf back to reveal her hair.

"It's her. Let's go," he said, lifting the hood of her cloak back over her head.

When the other man complained about his arm, her captor told him to wrap it in their room. Then he pulled her to her feet and forced her up the stairs. As soon as they entered the room, he shoved her onto a bed and held her down.

"Get the rope," he ordered.

Although Alissia did not make it easy for them, she soon found herself sitting on the bed with her hands tied securely behind her back and a dirty cloth stuffed into her mouth. She watched as they bandaged the man's arm, taking pleasure in seeing a deep cut that needed stitches.

While rushing through their packing, a knock came at the door, and the lanky man slowly opened it before letting the young woman into the room. Avoiding Alissia's eyes, she walked to the other bed and set a bag down.

"Thank you, Tella. You're the best," replied the gangly man. He grinned and gave a wink. "Once this is over, I'm going to have to come see you again."

"I'll be waiting," Tella crooned. She glanced at Alissia, and her brows furrowed. "Will she be hurt?"

The man chucked, shaking his head. "No, we'll take her back to Pallen, where she belongs, and once I get the reward money, I'll come back to you." He took her hand and added, "But you have to promise me that you won't tell anyone about this. Others are looking for her, and they don't need to know anything."

She nodded.

He grinned and gave Tella a peck on the cheek before dropping her hand. "Good! We have to leave before someone sees us. Can we go through the kitchen?"

"Let me distract my parents first. It won't take long."

He gave her a quick kiss on the mouth and handed her some money. Then he led her to the door. Once she left, he turned to his buddy with a triumphant grin.

The larger man snickered. "I guess you won't be coming back."

"You should take lessons," the skinny one responded.

"I like my way better."

The large man pulled a knife from a leather sheath at his side and walked over to Alissia. As he pressed the side of the blade to her cheek, a jolt of uncontrollable terror went through her, and memories of the night her father stabbed her flashed through her mind.

She closed her eyes and held her breath as he leaned down and warned, "We're going to walk to the stables, and I'm going to keep this close. If you make any sound, I'll slice you. No, I won't kill you, but I promise you'll want death by the time I'm finished with you."

When he pulled the knife from her face, both relief and shame filled Alissia. It did not matter that her body would heal itself. Her memories made her powerless when it came to a knife. She believed a gun held to her head would not cause as much fear as a knife.

"Do you have another pair of glasses?" he asked roughly.

She nodded, and he began to search through her pack. After putting another pair of glasses on her face, he turned to the other man. "Emmett, go see if the kitchen is empty."

The lanky man put on his backpack and grabbed the bag from the other bed before leaving the room. Alissia's aggressor put on his pack and roughly pulled her to her feet. After taking the cloth from her mouth, he pulled out his knife and rubbed the side of the blade along her neck. An evil grin filled his face.

Terror slammed into Alissia, and it took all her strength not to cry out or flinch. Refusing to be bullied, she forced a defiant look onto her face and met his gaze.

Emmett burst into the room. "Let's go."

The large man sheathed his knife and picked up his cloak. He put it around Alissia before buttoning it at her neck. Even with her backpack on, the cloak still touched the floor, but it served its purpose and hid the knife at her back as they walked down the stairs, through the kitchen, and out the back door.

As they walked the short distance to the stables, Alissia wanted to reach out with her mind to the dogs, but fear of the knife paralyzed her.

Two saddled horses and one packhorse awaited them at the stables. Emmett gave a coin to the young stable boy and told him that Tella needed him inside. After the boy left, Alissia's captor removed his cloak from her body. He swiftly picked her up and set her in the saddle. As he put on his cloak, Alissia reached out to the two dogs and told them where to find her, but by the time they arrived, both men were in their saddles, with the larger one seated behind her.

She mentally commanded the dogs to follow her from a distance, and once they knew which direction she traveled, they needed to find Fang and lead him toward her.

Alissia cringed as the man behind her put his arm around her waist and pulled her close. With her hands tied behind her back—in a very bad place—she felt his hot breath on her ear as he laughed. She tried to wiggle away, but he responded by tightening his embrace to where she could barely breathe. She stopped struggling and reminded herself that Fang would find her. She just needed to be patient.

Not even out of the village, his hands began to explore her body, and she immediately guessed his intentions. She struggled again in his arms, and he laughed and nipped her ear as he held her tightly in a painful grip. She relaxed her body and reminded herself to be patient. She needed to be far from the village so that Fang's attack would not be noticed.

Emmett followed in silence as they rode along a path outside the village, and Alissia's aggressor continued to move his hands to forbidden places on her body. She could feel his excitement grow, and her disgust and displeasure grew with it. He fumbled with the layers of her clothing before she felt his calloused hands on her bare skin. She began to struggle again, but she soon realized he enjoyed her body writhing against his. She stopped moving and reached out with her mind in search of Fang, but she could not find him. Fear rose within her, as she worried her plan would not work.

His fingers began to trace the handprints on her abdomen, and memories of being raped as a teen came to mind. Feelings of shame and powerlessness filled her. Even as she told herself it was not her fault, she could not push back the disgust she always felt toward herself for allowing it to happen. Numbness began to take over, and Alissia stared at the horse's right ear. She tried to focus on it and ignore her thoughts of blame and guilt. A tear slid down her face as something from within told her she deserved everything that happened to her. Her mind could be cruel, and harsh words from her father began to remind her of her worth.

As his fingers found her scar, Alissia's eyes widened, and fury instantly slammed into her. The only time she had ever allowed anyone to explore it was the day she got the tattoo, and the man that had given her the tattoo had been smart enough not to ask any questions.

Her captor had no right to touch what she protected for so many years. Without caring about the consequences, Alissia viciously grabbed, squeezed, and twisted his manhood beneath her hands. He responded by giving her a forceful shove, and as she fell from the horse, she desperately screamed Fang's name.

Pain shot through her right shoulder as she hit the ground, and within seconds, her attacker leapt on top of her. He yelled foreign obscenities while punching her repeatedly. Confusion abruptly filled his face, and his fist stopped in midair.

"She has purple blood."

Emmett walked over and stared down at her. "They mentioned she wasn't human. This must be why they want her. Why else would they want her so—"

Alissia shrieked as a large and powerful mass of fur tore into her abuser's neck, slamming both men to the ground. The horses bolted in a state of terror, and she closed her eyes and reached out to them. Distracted by fear, they could not hear her, and just as they got to the edge of her consciousness, she mentally screamed in desperation for them to stop.

Relief filled Alissia when the horses finally obeyed her command. She coaxed them into turning around and continued to soothe them as they walked toward her. Once she could hear them nearby, she opened her eyes and slowly and painfully sat up. She turned her attention to Fang, and reality instantly slammed into her.

Blood seemed to be everywhere and still oozed from the gaping holes in both men's necks. Bite marks covered their hands.

Fang sat beside the two bodies, staring at her, while his tongue licked the fur around his mouth. Blood covered his face and spotted other parts of his body.

Alissia tried to smile as she called to him, but a sharp pain in her lip stopped her. The blood in her mouth tasted similar, yet sweeter than human blood.

Fang walked over and licked her face, and she drew back from his wet tongue. Although she felt as if in the middle of a horror movie, his protectiveness lifted her spirit.

"Good boy. You saved me. Can you get this rope off me?"

His sharp teeth found her skin now and then as he tore away at the rope. As she endured the pain at her wrists, she felt her face healing.

The pain in her shoulder also weakened, and she knew she did not have to worry about scarring.

Once free, she removed the extra rope at her wrists, and her survival mode immediately set in. Worried that someone would soon come along, she told Fang to drag the two bodies into the woods, and she told the horses to follow him while she tried to hide as much of the blood as possible. Luckily, it would soon be dark, which would help to conceal any blood left behind.

She followed the animals into the forest and pulled another pair of sunglasses from her pack. Only two remained, and she hoped they would be enough.

Alissia assessed the situation before letting out a long sigh. She told the three horses to wait beside the bodies until she returned, and then she ran behind Fang through the forest. The running felt good after what just happened, and it helped to clear her mind. By the time she reached her and Luke's horses and saddled them, she had a plan in place.

Too consumed with the task at hand, she did not have time to get emotional. When she returned to the bodies, she forced her will onto the insects that had found them, and she ordered them away. With shaky hands, she searched the bodies and combined their moneybags into one. Then she hid it in one of her packs.

Since someone saw her leave the village with the two men, Alissia needed to make sure their bodies would never be found. Ignoring her dread, she turned back to them with a strong sense of determination.

Not wanting a trail of clothing left behind, Alissia stripped the bodies of everything but their pants and socks. She wrapped their clothing inside their cloaks before tying them to their saddles. She then tied the men's feet to ropes connected to their saddles, and she mounted her horse. Turning to Fang, she told him to lead the way back to the road and to alert her of any people in the area.

The loud sound of the bodies dragging along the forest floor caused her to cringe the entire ride back to the main path. Now dark, she hoped to see no other travelers on a cold, winter night.

She closed her eyes and reached out to the nocturnal animals starting to move within the forest. She told them to walk behind the horses to pick up anything left behind from the bodies. She did not demand they leave their territory, and each animal retreated before that happened.

After an hour of traveling this way, Fang ran back to her, and she quickly led the horses into the forest. She listened as a group of people passed, and then she waited a long while before going back onto the road.

She eventually stopped the horses and walked up to what remained of the bodies, now covered in manure and even gorier than before. Alissia ran to the edge of the forest and lost everything in her stomach. She held her breath and avoided looking at the bodies as she cut them loose from the saddles. She told Fang to drag each one deep into the forest, and she pulled out the map before mounting her horse.

As she continued to travel, she studied the map in search of a private path. Frustrated and confused, she put away the map and told herself that Fang would be able to locate another trail the next day.

Without anything to distract her, it did not take long before she began to think about the two men. Although Fang actually killed them, she knew she was the one responsible for their deaths. She had always known she was a cold person, but she never would have believed herself to be capable of stripping bodies and dragging them behind horses. Her father had been right about her. She was heartless.

Alissia began to fall asleep in her saddle a few hours before dawn, so she led the horses into the forest. Barely able to keep her eyes open, she unpacked the horses and set everything in a large pile on the ground.

She then charged the heat stone and wrapped her cloak and blanket around her. With Fang at her side, she soon fell into a deep sleep.

Chapter 24

Alissia moaned as a growling sound entered her awareness. The events of the night before began to play through her mind, and she dreaded facing another day. The growling intensified, becoming fierce, and her eyes shot open to find Fang about to attack.

"No, Fang! Stop!" she called out, sitting up.

Her protector immediately stilled, but he continued to stare menacingly at the intruder. Luke lowered his sword and eyed Alissia for a moment. "Hello, Pixet. I see you've been busy."

Her gaze went to the pile of saddles—specifically the two men's saddles—and she forced back tears as her heart rate settled back down. Although happy to see Luke, as she did not want to be alone for a while, her pride demanded she not show any emotion. She picked up her dark glasses and put them on before turning back to Luke.

"Two men kidnapped me."

He glanced at the extra horses. "I noticed, and I'm guessing your new friend took care of the problem for you. How did you meet your little friend?"

Alissia shrugged. "He was alone and without a pack when I found him, and he likes me."

"That's strange," replied Luke, looking at her thoughtfully. "From what I saw, it looked like he had a pack with him when you found him. In fact, I clearly heard some of his family as I traveled through their territory."

She frowned. "I'm too tired to fight with you, Luke, and I don't feel like talking about some things."

"Tell your friend to go play while we talk," he instructed, eyeing Fang.

Although she usually hated Luke telling her what to do, she now wanted him near her. She gave a curt nod to Fang as she mentally told him to go for a hunt, and once gone, Luke walked over and sat down beside her.

"You really do look horrible right now," he said, smiling. He set his sword down beside him.

Alissia let out a small laugh. "Only you would tell me that."

"Do you realize how uncomfortable it is to ride a horse bareback?"

She smiled, imagining his discomfort.

"You're the most difficult person I've ever met," Luke teased, "and I still remember the night I first saw you at the ball. You didn't talk much, and you looked shy and innocent. That was an act, wasn't it?"

Alissia leaned into him and put her cheek and hand on his chest, suddenly not trusting herself to speak. Her emotions battled within, and she just wanted to find comfort—even if a lie and only for a moment.

Luke pulled her blanket over her shoulder before putting his arms around her, and she closed her eyes and fought against the threatening tears. She told herself to stay strong, but part of her was too tired to continue fighting.

After a while, she decided she needed his help. She had tried everything with him, except the truth. Maybe if he knew why she could not go to the North, he would help her get near the mountains. She could give him enough information without telling him where the Lamians were.

"I can't go with you to the North," she said weakly, breaking the silence between them.

Luke let out a sigh. "I can protect you there, Alissia."

"But you don't know the truth." She sat up and looked him in the eyes. "I'm not really a Lamian. This time last year, I had green eyes and dark brown hair."

Knowing he did not believe her, Alissia slowly stood and pulled back her cloak before lifting the layers of her shirts. With his face eye-level to her stomach, he could see the handprints clearly.

"The Lamians did this to me to save my life. They changed me, and I can't remember any of it. The only proof I have are these handprints and all the changes to my body."

She closed her eyes as his fingers began to trace the handprints on her stomach. Memories of being touched by her aggressor filled her mind, and the sound of Luke saying her name pulled her back into reality. She opened her eyes to find him staring up at her.

"Sorry, I guess I'm still tired," she said, forcing a smile.

"I'm guessing this hidden scar isn't from the Lamians."

She pulled her shirts back down. "No, that's mine." She sat down facing him. "When I went to the ball that night, I didn't know the Lamians were a people in hiding. Grady and I were searching the library's historical records, and we couldn't find anything about them. I still can't believe others knew about it when we searched so hard."

"Where did this happen to you?" Luke asked.

"Now that I know how much they risked saving my life, I can't repay them by leading anyone to them." She added firmly, "I'll guard that secret with my life."

He nodded, as if he understood her reasoning. "You crossed the mountains to get to Pallen, and now you want to go back over them. Why?"

She considered how much to tell him before answering, "Because I had another problem to worry about at that time, and I needed more answers."

"What answers?" At her hesitation, he warned, "I can't help you if you don't tell me everything. I can't do this blindly."

Alissia chewed on her bottom lip as she looked down at her hands. Seeing the dried blood on them, she quickly looked back up. After letting out a sigh, she said, "Because I'm not even from this reality. My name's Alissia Roswell, and I'm from the United States of America. I'm used to electricity, cars, and phones. Everything in this reality is new to me."

He studied her face for a moment with a mix of shock and disbelief. "How'd you get here?"

"That's why I went to Pallen. I wanted to find the person responsible for pulling me into this reality and nearly killing me in the process. He lives there, but he can't help me get back home." She let out a sarcastic laugh. "In fact, I'm stuck here for the rest of my life. The only people I know in this reality are Anika, Langley, and Grady. Now, they're gone, and you expect me to go to the North. If I do that, I'll never know what's happening to my body." She lifted her filthy hands. "I even have purple blood now."

Luke reached out and turned her face to the side, examining it intently. "Did one of them beat you?"

Alissia lifted her hand and felt the dry, crusty blood that seemed to be everywhere on her face. As she nodded, she thought she saw a flash of anger in his eyes, but it did not last long.

He picked up her hands and examined them. "So, where are your bruises and cuts?"

"They're healed."

Confusion filled his face, and she leaned toward him, her eyes pleading. "Luke, I don't even know if I'm human anymore. I don't know what I am, and if you take me to the North, I'll never know. I'll spend the rest of my life not knowing what I am, and I don't even know how long I'm supposed to live."

His face hardened, and he let go of her hands. "Why should I believe you? You've proven that you're capable of lying."

"And what would you have done in my situation?" she challenged. "You've made it clear that all you want to do is get me to your people so that no one else can have me."

Ignoring her question, he asked, "How do you expect to travel in the South when a bounty's on you? And the Eldership probably knows about you now. They'll have everyone looking for you."

Alissia's gaze went to the large tree Luke leaned against. While chewing on her bottom lip, her face twisted in thought. After a while, her eyes lit up, and she grinned.

"I have a plan."

His eyes narrowed. "So far, your schemes have never ended well for me."

"Yes, but they've worked for me most of the time. And I promise I'm not planning anything evil toward you."

Luke let out a sigh. "All right, Pixet, what has your devious little mind thought of now?"

"Well, now that I have Fang, I can remain outside a village when we need something, and you can go in alone. Even if a storm comes, I'll have to stay away from villages. We could travel south, and I could stay safely hidden in the forest with Fang's protection."

"And how do I know you won't just try to kill me and take my horse?"

"You didn't leave me any other choice." Alissia's scowl turned into a smug grin. "Besides, I didn't try to kill you. I only did to you what you did to me."

"So, it's my fault you drugged me and took my horse?"

Alissia stared back at him as if the answer was obvious. "Yeah," she said slowly, "because you were trying to force me to do something I didn't want to do. And remember how many times you tied me to a bed?" She crossed her arms. "Now we're even."

Luke laughed. "Let me think about it today, but first, you need to tell me about last night so that I can see what needs to be done."

The smile left Alissia's face, and she uncrossed her arms. "There's nothing to be done."

"From what I've seen," he said, staring intently into her eyes, "I'm guessing your wolf killed two men, and the horses dragged their bodies along the road."

"I had to, because someone saw me leave with them," she explained, forcing herself not to turn from his gaze. "If I left the bodies, they would have been found, and it would have brought too much attention to me." She gave a half shrug. "I did what needed to be done. Now, they're unrecognizable, and Fang dragged what's left of them deep into the woods."

"All right, why don't you tell me what happened?"

Alissia looked down at her hands and sighed. Then she began to divulge the events of the night before. Luke silently listened as she spoke without any emotion in her voice.

Once finished, he smiled and said softly, "Sometimes, you sound as if you're from another world, but I guess I know why now. I'm still trying to get a grasp on some of your words."

After a comfortable silence between them, she asked, "Luke, why do people want me so badly?"

He picked up a twig and absentmindedly began to strip the bark from it. "There are different stories about the Lamians, and they usually involve wealth, power, and good health. If they saved your life, that proves they have special abilities. They were tortured long ago, because people wanted to control and use them."

He tossed the twig and wiped his hands on his pants. "There are also the scrolls at the Eldership. Those are considered historical, not mythical, and if they prove the Lamians helped to conquer an entire land, the Eldership won't stop until they find you. They'll use the league to search for you, and if I do decide to help you, I'll be outnumbered. I'm mostly on my own in the South, and my contacts are in the North." His brows lifted, and he stared intently into her eyes. "Do you see why traveling near Pallen isn't a good idea?"

"But, do you see why I have to? Luke, I can't live like this," she pressed.

"Let me think about things." He stood and held out his hand. "Come on."

"Where are we going?"

He grinned down at her. "There should be a stream not too far from here where we can camp for the night. I don't know if you realize this, but you *really* need a bath, and we can wash our clothes, too." Pulling her to her feet, he added, "You smell like a wolf, among other things."

She looked down at her filthy hands, with dried blood and dirt caked under her nails. She could only imagine what her face looked like.

Alissia grinned as she rubbed her body against his. "Now you stink, too."

Luke began to saddle the horses, while Alissia located some water and soap. After scrubbing her hands, she found some fresh pastries in the bag Tella packed for the two men. As she finished her breakfast, she unintentionally met Luke's eyes as he cut the remnants of rope from one of the two saddles. She quickly turned away and busied herself by cleaning her teeth. She was grateful he did not ask questions as he picked up the dead men's belongings and loaded them onto the horses.

After mounting his horse, Luke made comments about riding in a saddle again, and it did not take long before they joined the two horses he left near the edge of the forest. They crossed the public road and entered the forest on the other side, and Alissia followed as he used a compass to lead the way. Although tempted to ask how he knew where to go, she did not like the idea of letting him know how lost she would have been without him.

Fang followed from a distance as all seven horses traveled deep into the forest, where they eventually came to a stream. Luke helped her unload the horses before he disappeared in search of a wild, purifying flower. While gone, she gathered wood and began to set up camp. It did not take long before he returned with more than one flower, and he set up the bathing container near the stream.

Together, they washed their laundry in the container with the help of the botch stone and a lot of detergent. Although uncomfortable at first with Luke so close to her intimate clothing, Alissia soon got over it.

Once finished, clothes hanging from ropes filled the trees, while the clothes they planned to wear that evening surrounded the fire.

Luke dumped the container and filled it with fresh water, and then he hung a blanket between the fire and the bath for privacy. As she bathed, she could hear him cooking, and she grinned mischievously.

"Need any help with dinner?" she called out.

"Hah! I'll never trust you with food again!"

Alissia laughed heartily. She scrubbed every part of her body while the purifying flower absorbed all the blood from her face.

She quickly dried off, and Luke handed her a blanket warmed by the fire. She wrapped in the blanket and sat down by the fire to wait for her clothes to finish drying. A hot bowl of vegetable soup and some water was ready for her, and she eagerly devoured it. When she finished eating, she lowered her body to the ground and fell asleep.

When she woke, Luke stared at her from his seat by the fire. He appeared deep in thought, and although she knew it was late, she wondered how long she had slept. As she slowly began to sit up, her lack of clothing made her self-conscious. Luke must have noticed, because he stood and swiftly gathered her clothing. He dropped them into her lap and walked over to the horses.

She dressed in the tent, and when she came back out, she found Luke sitting by the fire. The filthy clothes she wore that day now hung in place of the blanket. Luke even washed her heavy cloak, and she wondered how it could possibly dry before morning.

"Thank you," she said, eyeing the cloak.

"You're welcome."

She turned to face him. "Why are you doing this?"

"Doing what?"

"Why are you being so nice to me? I mean, I drugged you and ran away, and you know what I did to those two men. I didn't just kill them. I completely mutilated them. Why aren't you mad or even scared of me?"

He chuckled lightly. "I'm not scared of you, Alissia, or your new pet. And I still have those restraints you so kindly left for me to find."

Remembering Fang, she reached out with her mind to find him not too far away.

"I now understand why you're so desperate to go back," Luke said, "and I'd feel the same if I were you. As for what happened with those men, I believe it was in self-defense, and you did what you thought needed to be done. I know you didn't enjoy any of it. In fact, I'm quite amazed you were able to do it. I still remember the first time I had to kill and dispose of a body." He looked hard into her eyes. "It comes with consequences, and I don't wish that on anyone."

Alissia sat down by the fire. "How many people have you killed?"

"That's not important. What is important is how many lives I've saved."

"Will you help me with my life?" she implored. "Will you help me cross back over the mountains?"

Luke sighed before nodding. "I'll help you."

"You will?" Alissia asked, her eyes wide with excitement.

"I will."

Alissia grinned elatedly. She clasped her hands together and brought them to her lips, her excitement spilling out of her. Then a confused expression came over her, and she set her hands in her lap.

"But why?" she asked, not hiding her distrust.

"Because you told me the truth."

"What?" She frowned. "You mean, if I would have told you the truth in the beginning, you would have never forced me to travel to the North? All I had to do was tell you the truth?"

He thought for a moment before shaking his head. "That's not what I said."

"So, you still would have kidnapped me?"

"I didn't kidnap you. I was protecting you," he said calmly, "and yes, I probably would have still taken you to the North."

Alissia's face twisted in confusion. "So, why are you going to help me now?"

"Why do you have to ask so many questions?" he asked, with an edge in his voice. "Can't you just be happy?"

Seeing that her question made him uncomfortable, a fearful thought came to mind. "Is it because you want to find the Lamians for yourself?"

Luke frowned. "No, Alissia, I'm not doing this for myself." He stood and leaned down to pick up a plate with two pastries on it. "Here, you need to eat before a breeze will be able to knock you from your horse."

Once she took the plate, he walked away and prepared for bed.

A couple hours later, Alissia tossed restlessly in her blanket as memories of torn flesh and pieces of bone haunted her. Having a knife held to her face reminded her of the night her father tried to kill her.

Eventually, she gave up on pushing back the memories, and they flooded through her mind as if a dam had been broken. Silent tears rolled down her face as her father's words began to rip at her heart. Deep down, she knew better than to believe any of the stifling words, but the two men's reaction to her purple blood and the other men saying she was not a human brought about the same feelings.

Although it had only been a few months ago, it felt like years since she had been a successful young woman living in New Jersey. Now, everything was different. She was even different. With an uncertain future, she felt as though she could barely hang on.

Alissia finally fell asleep, only to awake shortly thereafter with a scream. She hoped Luke did not hear her as she sat up and looked down at him. Even though his eyes remained closed, she remembered the night he pretended to sleep while she tried to escape.

She flopped back down and closed her eyes, but seeing the walking corpses of the two men in her nightmare left her unsettled. At some point, her exhausted body won over her mind, allowing her to fall asleep.

Chapter 25

Alissia awoke alone in the tent late the next morning, and she wondered why Luke did not wake her at dawn. After getting dressed, she walked out to find him packing. He explained that their clothes were just now dry enough to be put away, and the two of them would be leaving soon.

She ate the breakfast waiting for her, and then she helped him load all of the horses. She did not see the two men's packs and clothing, but she decided against asking about it. Luke took care of the details, which was fine with her.

As they rode together, she described her old reality. He listened intently and seemed interested in everything she said. After dinner, he asked her to join him for a self-defense lesson, and she made sure to explain to Fang that she and Luke were about to play rough. Luke asked her to describe how the two men captured her, and then he spent the next hour showing her what to do if ever in that situation again. His training seemed more intense than usual, and she found herself slammed to the ground more than once. Her pride kept her from crying out, and she calmed Fang each time he began to growl.

They went to bed early, and once again, her mind proved to be an enemy. She slept restlessly and suffered another gory nightmare. Luke was right about there being consequences, as she was certain the images of the two bodies would haunt her for the rest of her life.

They got up at dawn the next morning, with Alissia eager to leave now that they traveled toward the mountains. She helped with the chores, and as they rode together, she told him about the creature that gave her the scar. Since he did not know about all her abilities, she did not mention how the scar glowed while healing the horses.

At first, Luke was bothered with her for not telling him as soon as it happened, and she patiently listened while he vented. He told her she was lucky she was not dead or her hand had not fallen off, but once his anger subsided, he began to ponder various legends.

The only magical creature he knew about that resembled what she described was called a talor. Although they did not glow or fly in any of the stories, they were tiny and known for being mischievous. They were not poisonous, but their pranks sometimes caused great suffering and even death in the stories involving them. Luke concluded that she probably met one, and it bit her for fun.

Since they could hear other wolves in the area, Alissia told Fang not to leave the campsite that night, and she went to bed after another strenuous self-defense lesson. Exhausted, it did not take long for her to fall asleep. Shortly thereafter, she awoke to the sound of deep growling and yelping. She jumped up and ran outside to find Fang desperately trying to defend himself against a larger wolf, while two others attacked his legs and back.

Luke stood defensively against three other growling wolves, holding a glow stone in his left hand and his sword in the other.

Alissia immediately closed her eyes and mentally screamed for the animals to stop, but they were too distracted with their fighting. She tried to yell at them, but Luke was the only one to glance her way. He ordered her to go back inside.

By now, blood covered Fang's face as he and the large wolf bit at each other. No match for three wolves, he let out a loud yelp, and Alissia ran over to protect him. Without hesitating, she kicked the wolf biting his back leg, and pain immediately shot through her bare foot, causing her to cry out in alarm.

"Go back inside the tent!" Luke demanded.

Ignoring him, she willed the wolf she had just kicked to submit. Relief filled her when the wolf obeyed, and then she kicked the other smaller one before commanding him to leave the fight as well.

The fiercest wolf viciously attacked Fang's neck, and her kick to his side did not distract him. Fang's wounds greatly worried Alissia, and he needed her help.

Although busy with the other wolves, Luke continuously yelled for her to go back inside, and she dodged him when he went to grab her. She called out to Fang, and when he glanced her way, she took the opportunity to mentally command him to stop fighting. She only thought of protecting Fang when she reached out with her hand to the attacking wolf and screamed for him to stop.

The massive wolf lunged at her, and pain shot through her arm and hand as his sharp teeth ripped through her flesh. Just as she made eye contact with the wolf and yelled again, Luke moved in and dropped him with one great swing of his sword.

As the other wolves went to attack Luke, she screamed for them to stop, and she mentally demanded they submit. Each of them immediately took on a submissive posture of lowering their bodies to the ground or lowering their heads and looking away. Some even whimpered.

Alissia ignored Luke's angry glare as she looked around. Out of the six wolves in the pack, he had killed one and severely wounded the alpha and another. She could sense their suffering, and something within her yearned to ease their pain. Ignoring the large amount of blood flowing down her own hand, she sat down beside the alpha to begin the healing process. The scar glowed brightly beneath her skin as she pushed power into the alpha, and it happened again as she healed the other wolf.

After sending the pack away with the body of their dead, she sat down beside Fang and gently put his head in her lap. She looked up at Luke to find him silently watching her with fury in his eyes.

Fang's whimpering made her look down, and she placed her hand on his chest and began to send power from her body. Her wounded arm throbbed, but she dared not look at it, knowing Luke would say something.

Alissia soon began to feel lightheaded, but she continued to heal Fang. She was aware of Luke speaking, but his words sounded distant. The pain in her arm intensified, and she tried to ignore it. Then darkness suddenly overtook her.

When she opened her eyes sometime later, she found herself tucked in her blanket with her shirtsleeve pulled up on her left arm. Luke sat beside her in his undershirt while he wrapped a bandage around her wound. She turned to see his outer shirt in a wad beside him, covered in purple blood.

"What were you thinking?" he asked in a tight voice.

Once the confusion left her, she silently chided herself for fainting in front of Luke. Her arm throbbed, but she refused to show any sign of discomfort.

"What do you mean?"

"Don't even act as if you don't know what you did," he snapped. "I told you to go back inside the tent."

"So, you're mad because I didn't obey you?" She tried to tug her arm from him.

"You never listen to me!" He pinned the top of her arm down with his knee, causing her to flinch. As he continued to bandage her wound, he ranted, "And what were you thinking when you placed yourself in front of an attacking wolf? You could have gotten yourself killed. Luckily, I was expecting you to do something daft, and I was able to get to you before he could rip you apart."

He finished with her arm, and as soon as he released her, Alissia sat up, fuming.

"I had a plan, and I had everything under control." She poked Luke's chest with her finger. "In fact, if you didn't stab him, he would have stopped anyways. I had his attention and was about to make him submit." She lifted her arm and added smugly, "And my arm will heal. That was part of my plan, too. Fang was about to get killed, and I didn't have time to do anything else. I did what I had to do."

Luke went to his side of the tent and washed her blood from his hands with the cleansing gel. Sitting on his blanket, he put on another shirt before looking back at her. He ran his hand through his hair and let out a sigh. In a resigned voice, he said, "If you had told me about whatever it is you can do with animals, I could have helped you accomplish your goal without you getting hurt."

"You're the one that said I shouldn't trust anyone."

A muscle in his jaw twitched. "Alissia," he said tightly, "how am I supposed to help you if you don't tell me everything?"

Although his mood had softened, the pain in her arm and his comment about her doing something daft bothered her.

"Maybe it's because when you found me, you planned to drag me to your Eldership against my will," she accused. "Oh, and don't forget. You told me I didn't have to like you, because you planned to dump me at the Eldership so that I wouldn't be your problem anymore. Do you remember that or did you forget?"

He got under his blanket. "We'll finish this conversation in the morning. We have all day tomorrow for you to tell me everything."

She began to move toward the door of the tent.

"Where do you think you're going?" he asked warningly.

"I need to check on Fang. I don't think I finished healing him."

"Fang is well enough. You need to heal yourself before you do any-thing else. You fainted, and that proves you have limits."

The look in his eyes told her she would have to fight him to get out of the tent. She scowled and got back under her blanket. Then she rolled over, and he covered the glow stone.

"Are you sure Fang is all right?" Alissia asked softly.

"Yes. It'll soon be daylight, and you can see him then. He's sleeping now."

Chapter 26

Luke woke Alissia shortly after dawn, and even her eagerness to get back to the South was not enough to wake her without a struggle. When he reminded her of Fang, she pulled herself from the blanket and rushed to get dressed.

Fang nearly knocked her down as she stepped out of the tent, causing her to laugh at his liveliness. She found a few wounds that needed some healing, and she quickly finished the job she started the night before. Once finished, she noticed Luke watching her while saddling one of the horses. She gave him a quick smile before walking to the fire to eat breakfast. As soon as they started riding, he casually asked, "What changes have you noticed since your encounter with the Lamians?"

"I'll talk to you about it after you cut off this itchy bandage," she said, holding out her arm. Noticing the hesitant look on his face, she added, "I bet it's completely healed by now."

Luke reached for a knife, and Alissia pulled up her sleeve. He leaned toward her and swiftly cut through the stained cloth, and after she removed the bandage, she held it out to him. He took it from her, and she rubbed her fingers along her soft skin.

"I told you it would heal," she boasted, holding out her arm.

He nodded. "Now, what other changes have you noticed since encountering the Lamians?"

While pulling down her sleeve, she made the decision not to mention her night vision or anything else he did not already know about.

"Well, my hair used to be dark brown, and my eyes were once green. Now, I have purple blood, and I heal, which makes me wonder if I'm even human anymore. My eyes burn in the sun. I can't eat meat. Even a strong smell of meat will make me sick, but I can eat things made with milk and eggs—although, the milk in this reality tastes gross."

She smiled thoughtfully. "Maybe that's why animals love me so much now. They know I won't eat them, and I can heal them. They listen to me and do what I want.

"My nails are purple, sparkly, and long. My hair's the healthiest it's ever been, and I've also noticed my muscles getting firmer. If I were still in my reality, I wouldn't stand out as much. People would think I colored my nails and hair to look like this, and we have things called contacts instead of glasses that could change the color of my eyes." Alissia frowned. "Apparently, I look like a freak here."

"I don't know what a freak is, but I do know that different isn't always a bad thing. Have you always been so tiny, or is that new?"

"Oh, for goodness sake! I'm *petite*. I've always been petite, and it's never gotten me into trouble until now. Lots of people are small."

Luke laughed, and her scowl deepened. Once he was serious again, he said, "Tell me how you got into this reality."

Alissia's eyes clouded with sadness, and she looked down at the reins in her hand. "I left my childhood home over ten years ago but came back for my dad's funeral. After the funeral, I went to a place I spent a lot of time as a teenager." She turned back to Luke. "It was at an oak tree by a pond."

With a dismissive wave of her hand, she said, "Anyways, I had an old diary hidden in the base of the tree, and I pulled it out. Apparently, someone had set up a window there and watched me when I was younger. This person became obsessed with getting into my reality and started doing experiments. The only thing he could do was put a small tear in the window, and he sent a link to my diary. His plan was to pull me through the window, hoping my body would make the hole bigger."

Noticing a look of anger on Luke's face, Alissia stopped talking.

"And what happened to you when you were pulled through the window?" he prodded, in a controlled voice.

"Well, the hole didn't get any bigger, because I squeezed through it. I don't remember anything but the pain—a *lot* of pain. I think I remember when the Lamians healed me, or at least, I remember them speaking a foreign language over me." She gave a half shrug. "They ran away when they heard someone coming. I was found covered in blood and unconscious. When I woke up, I was fine, except for the new handprints that were itchy at the time. I didn't notice the other changes until a couple days later."

"Who pulled you through the window?"

Alissia shook her head. "I can't say."

"You want to protect him?" he asked, bothered.

She thought for a moment. "I was furious at first, and even when I met him, I wasn't nice. But, it happened over ten years ago, and he's not the same person he was back then. What he did was completely wrong, and I don't want to be friends with him or even see him again. But, I forgive him. Even though I didn't do something as bad as him,

I'm not the same person I was ten years ago. No one should be judged by their past."

He did not respond, and they rode in silence until they stopped for lunch. During their afternoon ride, they talked about self-defense, and he spent most of his time emphasizing how she needed to stop and think before reacting. He continuously stressed that she always remain logical, not emotional.

That evening, he gave her another lesson that ended with her chiding herself for her body's reaction to his touch. She also woke from another nightmare during the night.

They continued this routine for more than a week, and he did not ask any more personal questions. Each night, Alissia found herself stuck between exhaustion and restless sleep. Their conversations usually involved Luke describing certain scenarios where he'd ask how she should respond. He said he was trying to get her into the habit of planning, or at least thinking about, situations.

If other wolves were in the area at night, Luke and Alissia would leave some glow stones outside. They would keep the fire burning and have Fang sleep in the tent with them—his massive size leaving them cramped.

Luke decided to go to a village after she promised she and Fang would stay hidden where he left them. Not only did he plan to buy more food, but he also planned to sell the extra horses. He returned shortly after dark, and once they finished their dinner by the fire, he surprised Alissia with fresh sticky buns.

He silently watched as she slowly ate one of the buns, savoring each bite. When she bit into a second one, she met his gaze, expecting him to tease her.

"Tell me about the scar hidden beneath the butterfly."

Alissia almost choked on her dessert. As she reached for her drink, he said, "How about this? We take turns asking each other questions. I'll answer anything you ask if you do the same for me."

She took a few sips of her drink and wiped the corners of her mouth before turning to him with narrowed eyes. "And why would I do this?"

"You're not the only one with secrets," Luke replied, "and if you ask the right questions, you might be surprised by the answers."

Alissia set down her drink, suddenly losing interest in her food. She stared back at him for a moment. "All right, but you can't ask anything about the Lamains, because those aren't my secrets to tell." Lifting her finger into the air, she added, "And I get to ask the first question."

Luke's calculating smile made her nervous. She expected that he would ask uncomfortable questions, and she wanted to do the same for him. She stared thoughtfully at him for a moment.

"I thought you were going to ask the first question," he teased.

"I am. You had time to think about your questions, but I haven't." She thought for a bit longer before saying, "All right, you said you didn't have parents, so I'm thinking you were orphaned. How did that happen?"

He shrugged. "I was left on the steps of an orphanage when I was a baby, so I never had parents." With an eager grin, he clapped his hands together. "Now, my turn. Tell me about your scar."

"That's cheating," Alissia answered. "You didn't ask a question, and I'm not just going to tell you about it."

He laughed and gave a nod. "All right, what happened?"

"A knife hit me. Now my turn—"

"That's not an answer," he interjected, shaking his head. "A knife can't hit anyone."

Alissia grinned, knowing he caught her trying to be sneaky. "Okay, someone was holding the knife as it hit me. So, you don't know anything about your parents?"

"No. Who was holding the knife?"

"My father," she replied, taking satisfaction in seeing the surprise in his eyes. She quickly continued, "You said you've killed people. Why did you kill them?"

"Because it's my job to protect the innocent and enforce the laws of the Eldership. I did what had to be done. Why did your father cut you with a knife?"

Alissia shrugged. "He was drunk, and I was there. Will you show me your tattoo?"

He pulled back his cloak and unbuttoned his outer shirt before lifting his undershirt. She stood from her spot by the fire and sat down next to him.

"What does the writing mean?" she asked, her fingertips touching the writing beneath the side view of a grim reaper.

He shook his head, chuckling. "It's my turn. Do you miss anyone from your old reality?"

"No. Now, what does the writing mean?" She pulled her hand from his chest.

"The writing's what makes the tattoo official. It identifies where my training took place and which division I'm a member of. Why did you choose a butterfly to hide your scar?"

"It represents change and new beginnings." She looked into his eyes. "Have you ever killed an innocent person?"

"No," he said, lowering his undershirt, "I'm not a murderer, and death is always the last option. I protect the innocent. What change and new beginning does the tattoo represent for you?"

Alissia turned her gaze to the fire. "It's when I left my hometown and worked my way into a new life. What do you like most about your job?"

She watched him consider her question for a moment. "Travel, money, and respect." He looked down and buttoned his outer shirt. Looking back up, his eyes locked with hers. "Do you love Grady?"

She hoped he did not notice the effect his question had on her. "That's a question I can't answer until I tell him first. He should be the first person to know how I feel about him."

"You never told him?"

She shook her head before remembering it was her turn. "I get two questions now. Have you ever been in love?"

"No."

"Have you ever been close to falling in love?"

"Some people weren't made for love," he answered. "Why didn't you tell him?"

His statement took her by surprise, as it was the same thing she often told herself. It had been her motto since her childhood.

At her silence, Luke asked again, "Why didn't you tell him?"

"I just didn't."

"That's not an answer."

Alissia frowned. "Why are you asking me this?"

"Because you agreed to answer my questions, and I agreed to answer any of yours. Now, why didn't you ever tell him?"

She let out a frustrated sigh. "Because I never felt like it. In fact, my last words before I slapped him were that I never loved him." She stood. "Are you happy now? I'm done. No more questions."

She left him by the fire and prepared for bed. When he entered the tent, she pretended to be asleep with her back facing him. Thoughts of Grady confused her and filled her with guilt. It felt like years since she had last seen him, and so much had happened since then. Gory images of death consumed her dreams, and survival and getting back to the Lamians controlled her thoughts each day.

Alissia often wondered if Grady missed her and if he worried about her. Maybe he hated her for telling him she never loved him.

Luke did not mention their conversation again, and they resumed their routine for the next few days. One morning, they awoke to drizzly weather, and after spending the day traveling in the wet cold, a dreary mood claimed her. Just as she began to feel sorry for herself, a small cabin came into view.

"Why didn't you tell me?" she asked, suddenly excited.

"Tell you what?"

She groaned loudly before asking, "Is it safe?"

He nodded. "No one will be looking for you here."

Alissia nudged her horse into a canter, and by the time Luke reached the cabin, she was already on the porch. He laughed at her excitement as he dismounted, and she hastily began to help him unpack.

"Why don't you go in and get a hot bath?" he asked, holding out her packs. "I'll finish all this."

Her brows lifted. "You sure? You don't mind?"

"No, I know you're going to take a long one, and I'd like one also, so you might as well start yours while I get the horses settled."

She grinned and grabbed her bags. He unlocked the door to the cabin, and once inside, she immediately felt relief from the wet and cold, winter air. She went straight to the bathroom.

Alissia scrubbed her body and used the hair removing cream. She rubbed scented lotion into her skin and dressed in her cleanest clothing. Once finished with all the pampering, she smiled at her reflection. She felt clean, refreshed, and warm, and she looked forward to sleeping in the soft bed.

As she put her bags in the bedroom, her stomach growled at the smell of food, and she joined Luke in the kitchen. She ladled a bowl of soup and poured herself a mug of hot chet before sitting down across from him.

"Feel better?" He picked up his empty bowl and stood.

"You have no idea."

He laughed and set his dishes on the counter. "I'll admit that I'm ready to get these wet clothes off and enjoy a dip in the warm pool." Rubbing his hands along his scraggly beard, he asked, "Think I should keep this?"

Alissia shook her head, eyeing his muddy clothing. "You look beastly."

He roared with laughter and left the room.

Once finished eating, she cleaned the kitchen and made herself comfortable on the sofa with a blanket over her. Luke stepped out of the bathroom, and a fresh, woodsy scent filled the air as he strolled to the sofa. He sat down on the opposite end and lifted the blanket as he pulled his legs up beside hers. The light and warmth coming from the heat stones and fireplace soothed Alissia, and she soon fell asleep.

When she woke, she slowly sat up, careful not to wake Luke. Then she gently slid to his end of the sofa. Staring down at the peaceful expression on his face, she felt an urge to move a strip of hair from his eyes. She pulled her bottom lip between her teeth and slowly lifted her fingers to his face. The moment they touched his hair, his hand flew up, grabbing her wrist, as his eyes shot open.

Alissia held her breath as he peered searchingly into her face. Without warning, he pulled her onto his chest and rolled on top of her. Chills went through her entire body as she looked up to find his eyes suddenly burning with desire.

Luke slowly lowered his head, and she lifted hers to meet him halfway. When their lips met, heat filled her veins. His hand went to her hair, while the other went to her back, pulling her into him. Both of Alissia's hands dug into his hair as she kissed him hungrily.

When he broke the kiss, she lowered her head onto the sofa. With ragged breaths, they stared into each other's eyes. She tenderly stroked the side of his face with her fingertips, and he closed his eyes and turned to kiss the inside of her hand. She smiled up at him and ran her fingers through his hair before he opened his eyes again.

A sudden image of Grady flashed through Alissia's mind, and Luke's body stiffened above her. His expression turned guarded, and he pulled away and stood.

"I'm going to check on the horses for the night," he said gruffly. "You should go to bed. I know you're tired from all the traveling."

Before she could respond, he grabbed his boots and cloak and went outside, leaving her dazed and confused.

She remained on the sofa for a while before getting ready for bed. Luke was still outside by the time she came out of the bathroom and went to her bedroom for the night. After a lot of tossing and turning, she finally fell asleep, but she soon awoke with a scream from one of her nightmares. This one involved Luke, Grady, and the dead men.

She sat up, completely awake and restless. After a while, she let out a frustrated sigh and got up from the bed.

Luke appeared to be asleep as she crept to the bathroom and shut the door. Once finished, she carefully opened the door and walked into the sitting room.

Seeing him asleep on the sofa reminded her of their kiss, and a sudden thrill went through her body. She closed her eyes and mentally scolded herself before slowly making her way to the fireplace. She cautiously picked up her warmed boots and cloak, and she began to tiptoe toward the door.

"You know I'm awake, don't you?"

Alissia cringed and turned around. "I'm not running away, and you can go back to sleep. I just want to go outside, because I can't sleep."

"And you know I'm not going to do that."

Alissia frowned. "You still don't trust me? Where would I even go?"

When Luke did not respond, she began to put on her boots, and he sat up.

"Why don't you read a book?"

"What book?"

He picked a book off the floor and held it out to her, and she took it from him. After reading the title, she looked up in exasperation.

"*The Battle of Loreck*? You've got to be kidding me. Why would I want to read this?"

"You might like it, and if you don't, you'll fall back to sleep within the first few pages."

She groaned and plopped down in the chair across from him. "You have no Internet," she complained, taking off her boots. "You have no TV. Not even a phone. Right now, I'm beginning to think this reality isn't all that great compared to mine."

Luke laughed. "So, you'd rather destroy what the Creator gave us and kill animals so that you can have something to do in the middle of the night?"

She answered him with a dirty look.

"Alissia, we do have fun things in this reality, but tonight, you're stuck in a small cabin. If it weren't so cold and wet outside, I'd show you what we do on sleepless nights. You haven't had a chance to see anything, and you haven't truly experienced our reality. There's a reason why our people cherish what we're given."

She pulled her feet into the chair and gave a sarcastic laugh. "I've never seen you do anything for fun, except torture me, and the only time you laugh is when you're doing something to make me miserable."

"You get angry so easily," he said, grinning. He added softly, "Besides, I've been too busy trying to keep you safe and haven't had time to show you anything. Tonight, if it weren't so wet outside, I'd build a fire, and we'd look up at the stars. I'd show you some of our constellations and teach you how to travel by the stars so that you'd never get lost."

She gave him a doubtful look. "We've spent many nights by the fire under the stars, but you've never done anything like that."

"We've been too busy, and you've had other things on your mind."

She wondered if he meant Grady. "Why are you helping me?" she asked, cocking her head. She studied his face.

"Because I don't want the southern Eldership to find you."

"That didn't answer my question," she persisted. "If you didn't want the southern Eldership to find me, you could try to force me to go to the North. My question is why did you change your mind and decide to help me find the Lamians?"

"Because I agree that you need to know what's happening to you."

"So, you're doing it for me?"

Luke nodded. "It appears that way."

"What does that mean?" she questioned. "Either you are, or you aren't."

"I guess I am."

"So, when will we be able to go to the mountains?"

Alissia then remembered she never told him she only needed to go to the mountains. She told him she needed to go farther than Allure, which meant he was willing to travel a long way with her.

"Luke," she asked softly, "what will you do if we find the Lamians?"

"What do you mean?"

"I mean, you'd know where they are. Who would you have to tell?"

He frowned. "I don't have to tell anyone. Being a member of the Eldership doesn't mean I don't make decisions for myself. My job and training within the Eldership is for the protection of the people. The Lamians have been hiding for over a thousand years, and I'm not going to be the person responsible for changing that." He looked hard into her eyes. "I may not be as nice as some people, but I'm not that bad, Alissia. I have a conscience, and I do the right thing."

"I didn't mean it like that." Her eyes pleaded for him to understand. "This isn't my secret to tell, and it involves an entire race of people. I can't go around telling everyone."

"You know where they are, don't you?" he asked knowingly.

"Well," she said hesitantly, "I kinda know where they are. I mean, I don't know exactly where they are. I just know where I need to go, but I don't know what will happen when I get there."

Luke frowned. "Alissia, where do I need to take you?"

She stared down at her hands and began to chew on her bottom lip. After a while, she looked back up. "Can I trust you?"

"I give you my word I'll guard their secret with my life."

She stared into his eyes for a moment before letting out a resigned sigh. "The mountains."

"Where in the mountains?"

"I don't really know." She shrugged. "They found me on Allure's side, but I have this feeling I don't have to go to that exact location. I think I just need to get to the mountains, and they'll help with the rest."

"What do you mean by feeling?" His eyes narrowed. "Alissia, what else are you not telling me?"

Trying to sound innocent, she answered, "I just have a feeling."

He shook his head. "No, you're not telling me everything. What do you mean you just know?"

"Are you calling me a liar?" she challenged.

Luke frowned. "No, I'm not calling you a liar, but I've learned when you're trying to avoid my questions—which is all the time." Ignoring her dirty look, he added, "Alissia, you're expecting me to help you with this, but you're keeping a lot of important secrets from me. I'm not the bad person here."

"You mean, 'bad guy'."

"What?" he asked in confusion. He shook his head and waved his hand dismissively. "Never mind. Don't answer that. You're just trying to change the subject again." His eyes locked with hers. "Alissia, how much do you trust me?"

"You're the one who told me not to trust anyone. Remember?"

He silently stared at her, his dark, penetrating eyes making her uncomfortable. She looked down and began to fiddle with the wedding ring on her finger.

"I think the Lamians get into my head while I'm sleeping, and they know what's happening to me," she divulged. She looked up at him. "They'll know when I'm in the mountains, and now that there's a threat, I think they'll find me. I don't think they want me to get caught or kidnapped again."

"I never kidnapped you," he said gently. "What else have you not told me that might help?"

"I can't think of anything else you should know."

"But I'm sure you thought of things I shouldn't know," he grumbled.

Alissia pretended to look offended. "You don't trust me, do you?"

"No, I don't. Now, can we go back to sleep? Take the book. The writer was very descriptive."

Luke caught the book before it made contact with his head.

"I'll go to bed," she said, "but I'm not reading a book about a war unless it involves elves or dragons."

Chapter 27

Sleep came faster than expected, and once Alissia woke, she continued to enjoy the soft bed for another hour before crawling out from under the covers. After a visit to the bathroom, she went to the kitchen and grabbed a bag of seeds. She took Luke's blanket from the sofa and went outside to find him doing one of his sword routines.

Wrapping herself in the blanket, she sat down on the porch and watched him while she ate the seeds. Sweaty and breathing heavily, he did not seem to notice her until he finished. He smiled, and she smiled back before going inside.

She found something else to eat and sat at the table. Still shirtless, Luke walked into the kitchen, and she caught herself staring and looked down at her food. After gulping down a glass of water, he sat down across from her and grinned.

"I thought you'd sleep all day. You do realize how late it is, don't you?"

While outside, Alissia guessed it to be around noon, and she told herself she deserved a day of rest. Ignoring his question, she crinkled her nose and teased, "You smell like sweat."

Luke stood and wiped his wet arm across her face, and she shouted at his back as he darted out of the room. While he bathed, she cleaned the kitchen and changed clothes. Then she swept the floor of the small sitting room and cleared a space. Just as she started to do yoga, he walked out of the bathroom.

He sat down on the sofa and began to watch her. Within seconds, his gaze made her uncomfortable, but she refused to let him know. Instead, she closed her eyes and lengthened her stretch. The sound of furniture dragging along the floor caused her to open them again, and she found Luke clearing the middle of the room. He then stood in front of her, imitating her pose.

"What are you doing?" Alissia asked, coming out of her stretch.

Luke grinned. "I'm learning your yoga."

"And why are you doing that?"

"Because I'll teach you how to throw a knife today if you teach me yoga."

His cheery attitude reminded her of when she first met him, and it made her nervous. Not used to seeing him in such a good mood, she thought of how attractive he looked when he smiled. She immediately chided herself for her thoughts and asked, "Why do you want me to teach you yoga?"

He shrugged. "Why not?"

Alissia rolled her eyes and sat down to do some floor stretches, and Luke followed along. At the end of the warmup, he laughed. "This isn't so bad."

Smiling to herself, she began to plan the hardest yoga routine she could handle. She had been going to the gym almost daily for more than seven years and had been in the advanced classes of yoga and Pilates. She also enjoyed kickboxing, and although she could not swing a sword, she knew she could twist her body in places he could not.

She first showed him how to do the forearm stand, and he surprised her when he got his feet into the air. She then demonstrated a version of the firefly position, and as he lifted his body with his hands, she began to worry he would be able to do all her poses. Obviously, he had arm strength and balance, but she wondered if he could do intense stretching.

A difficult pose came to mind, and Alissia sat down and looked at Luke with an innocent smile. She lifted her left leg behind her head and grabbed her toes with both hands. With her elbows in the air and foot behind her head, she drew her head back to touch her foot, doing a deep backbend.

"I'm done," he announced, not even attempting the pose.

She laughed and released her foot.

"You're supposed to start slowly when teaching someone," said Luke, "and I'm thinking that wasn't for beginners."

Grinning, Alissia began to show him easier positions, and the two of them did yoga for the next hour. Then they washed their laundry and ate before going outside for a knife-throwing lesson.

As he set up a target in the clearing in front of the small cabin, she played with Fang near the porch. Once he finished with the preparations, she joined him.

"There are many ways to throw a knife," he explained, "but I want you to learn how to throw from the handle without a spin. You'll need to learn aim and power, which will take many hours of practice. I've been practicing since I was a child, so I don't expect you to catch up to me; however, I do expect you to learn to pull a knife quickly and hit your target with a powerful throw."

He bent down and picked up one of the knives from the pile at his feet. "I'll throw some first. Pay close attention to my hand and the position of my feet."

Luke showed her his grip on the handle before throwing the first knife in slow motion. He continued with the other knives until only two were left. Alissia watched as he threw a fast overhand. Then he did a powerful side-handed throw at an amazing speed. He collected the knives from the target and piled them at her feet.

"Your turn," he said, handing her a knife.

She positioned her feet and looked at the target before pulling back her hand.

"No, you're not watching your grip," he said, grabbing her hand.

As he positioned her fingers where they needed to be, her pulse quickened, and she recalled their kiss. She could barely concentrate on his words, too busy trying to appear calm.

The lesson continued until it began to get dark, and it ended with Alissia feeling flustered from Luke's touch. She never achieved a successful throw.

Once inside, she quickly gathered her clothing and went to the privacy of the bathroom. While bathing, she continuously reminded herself of how annoying, controlling, and difficult Luke was. She vowed she would not allow herself to surrender to her body's desire.

Luke sat at the table eating when she entered the kitchen. He smiled and said, "Tomorrow I'll try to get something different for dinner."

"What are the plans for tomorrow?" she asked, ladling some of the soup into a bowl.

"I haven't decided yet."

"What do you mean?"

"I need to go to Pallen to see what the Eldership knows about you. So far, we know there's a bounty, but that's nothing compared to the Eldership. If they're searching for you, it's going to be hard to get to the mountains. However, if I go to Pallen tomorrow and the

Eldership notices me, they'll easily remember I left at the same time you disappeared."

"What if they don't know about me?" Alissia asked, sitting down across from him.

"If they aren't searching for you, then we can go straight to the mountains without any problems."

She took a few bites of her soup before asking hesitantly, "Luke, is there any way I can see Grady? I mean. . . could he come out here so that I could talk to him and find out what really happened that night?"

He shook his head. "Even if the Eldership isn't searching for you, Grady's being watched, and it's too much of a risk for him to come near you."

Alissia continued to think about Grady as she ate her food. Then she pushed her bowl aside and took a few sips of her water.

"Could you talk to Grady or give him a note from me?" she asked.

He stared back into her pleading eyes for a moment. "I won't carry a note that can be read by others, and I don't know if going to Grady would be such a good idea. That would get me noticed."

"Luke, I have to know the truth about that night," she implored. "My last words to him were that I never loved him, and I slapped him. If he was innocent, he didn't deserve it, and I was cruel."

He cocked his head, eyeing her intently. "So, you feel guilt?"

"Yes, I feel a lot of guilt."

"Why do you want to see him the most?" Luke placed his elbows on the table and leaned closer. "Is it love or guilt?"

Alissia stood and set her dishes on the counter. "I'm not going to answer that question."

He left his chair to stand in front of her. "Do you love him?" he asked determinedly. She tried to walk around him, but Luke grabbed her wrist and pulled her into him. With his face inches from hers, he breathed, "Why did you kiss me last night?"

"It was an accident," she answered, struggling against her sudden desire. She tried to pull away.

He shook his head. "It wasn't an accident, and neither is this."

Although she told herself to fight, her body melted in his embrace. When his mouth came down on hers, she eagerly responded with the same amount of passion.

His hands traveled through her hair and down her back as his lips explored her mouth and neck, leaving Alissia breathless. When he finally pulled away, she felt weak in his arms.

Luke grinned. "That answered my question."

"What do you mean?"

"You don't love Grady as much as you think you do," he said smugly.

Alissia stiffened and pulled away, glaring at him. "There's a difference between love and lust, Luke."

"There's also a difference between love and guilt."

She immediately charged past him and darted into the bedroom, closing the door behind her.

Alissia spent the rest of the night locked away in her room and only came out to go to the bathroom. Sleep did not come easy, and when she woke from a nightmare, she did not get out of bed. She found a note on the kitchen table the following morning that read:

Pixet:

I have gone to Pallen in hopes of learning more about your situation and will return later today. I left some knives for you to practice throwing and hate that I won't be here to teach you more moves.

Try not to miss me too much,

Luke

Frustrated by his egotistical sarcasm, Alissia read the note more than once. She ate breakfast before doing Pilates and then went outside to play with Fang. After lunch, she practiced throwing knives.

While eating a small dinner, she decided to practice her abilities with the animals. She wrapped Luke's blanket around her and went outside to sit on the porch. With a lot of concentration, she achieved a small success of reaching a greater distance with her mind.

She took an evening nap on the sofa and then ate a snack. As she put more logs on the fire, her mind began to wander, and she worried for Luke.

Once ready for bed, she curled up on the sofa in Luke's blanket, hugging his pillow. Desperate for a distraction, she picked up his book and began to read. The first two chapters bored her, and she soon fell asleep. Shortly thereafter, she woke with a scream, the image of Luke lying in a puddle of his own blood still fresh in her mind.

Chapter 28

"*I* see you missed me."

Alissia's eyes shot open at the sound of Luke's voice. He and Grady stood in the sitting room, both dressed in fine clothing instead of traveling clothes. They each held a bundle, and while Grady appeared apprehensive, Luke stared down at her with his usual, overconfident smile.

"I knew she'd still be asleep," said Luke, to Grady. He turned back to Alissia. "You're not dreaming, and we brought you breakfast."

Grady gave a weak smile. "Alissia, can we talk in the kitchen?"

She could barely breathe as she nodded and allowed him to help her to her feet. She cleared her throat and excused herself. Once alone in the bathroom, she rushed to freshen up. Staring at her reflection, she took a shaky breath and told herself to calm down. Then she walked back into the sitting room.

Grady followed her into the kitchen, and she closed the door. He set his bundle on the table and pulled her into his arms.

"I've been so worried and wasn't sure I'd ever see you again," he said, his voice cracking.

His body trembled with emotion, and Alissia found herself unable to speak. He pulled away and held her at arms' length, his pleading eyes locking with hers.

"Alissia, I was drugged and nothing happened that night. Holt found me at the library and told me Nevara had translated some things in the scrolls that resembled you, but she had not yet given any of the information to the Eldership. I followed him to their house to meet with her, and the last thing I remember was sitting at the kitchen table with a drink in my hand. I then woke up to find you staring down at me with Nevara wearing my shirt. When I woke again the next morning, I was alone in their house."

Pulling her back into his arms, he continued, "Nevara came to me later that day, because she had nowhere else to go. Holt was dead, and you were missing. The only thing the lady at the inn could tell me is that you ran outside sick, and Holt followed you. Then, another man came in and collected your belongings, and shortly after that, another set of men came in asking if anyone had seen you." He squeezed her tightly. "You completely disappeared, and I didn't know if I'd ever be able to find you."

Alissia put her arms around him. "I'm sorry. I should have let you talk that night. I didn't even give you a chance." Her face twisted in confusion. "How did Holt die? Who killed him?"

"Luke seems to think it was the men who showed up at the inn." He kissed the top of her head before pulling away. "You should eat. We have a lot to discuss before we leave."

She sat down in the chair he pulled out. "Are we going to the mountains today?" she asked, not hiding her confusion.

He opened the bag and pulled out some freshly baked bread and pastries, along with a small container of juice. "It's not going to be that easy," he answered, sitting down across from her, "and things are more difficult than we thought."

"What do you mean?" she asked, ignoring the food.

He rested his arms on the table and clasped his hands. "Alissia, the day you disappeared Nevara told us the Eldership in Pallen would learn about you within the week, so Anika, Langley, and I decided upon a plan. I went to the Eldership and told them you'd been kidnapped. I admitted you were a Lamian and said that someone brought you to me. I also told them you had no memory. The only name you could remember was Pallen, and I took you there, hoping to learn more about you. But, after searching the library, we found nothing about your people.

"That's when I tried to talk you into going to the Eldership, but you were too scared. I took you to the ball so that I could introduce you to some of the people and let you see there was nothing to be afraid of. You were just starting to consider going to them when you were kidnapped, and I lost you."

Grady opened the container of juice and pushed it toward her. "Because I knew you personally, the Eldership put me in charge of finding you. I moved into the castle and resumed fulltime duties there, but I soon began to notice things that made me uncomfortable."

He picked up a muffin and held it out, and as she took it from him, he caught her by the hand. "Luke told me about this," he mumbled thoughtfully, rubbing his thumb across the star-shaped scar. He inspected it for a moment before letting go, setting his hand on the table.

"The Eldership hired Langley to manage the stables," he continued, "and they wanted him Tiand Anika to move into the castle. That seemed odd, because someone in that position doesn't normally live at the Eldership. The only reason they'd want him and Anika to move there would be to watch them. I told him to take the job, because I was afraid of what would happen if he didn't."

Grady frowned, and Alissia thought she noticed worry in his eyes. "A lot of procedures are being broken, which could get them into serious trouble with the elders in Allure, yet they continue to break the rules in front of me." He looked intently into her eyes. "That leads me to believe they don't expect me to make it back to Allure. The same goes for Anika and Langley. I think they want me to know if I don't follow along with them, things will be different."

He paused, giving her a questioning look, and she nodded to let him know she understood.

"Because they're blatantly breaking the rules," he continued, "it means they either want to take control or become independent from us." He leaned back in his chair. "Luke agrees, and he confirmed what I've been expecting. I think Alrik Durst is taking control of the Eldership here, and since he has a bounty on you, that could only mean he wants your help."

Alissia nearly choked on her muffin, and she quickly swallowed. "How am I supposed to help him?"

"Alrik is a powerful and wealthy man and is known to be somewhat ruthless in the business world. He's worked his way up from nothing and now controls most of the trade routes between the major cities."

Grady leaned on the table and let out a sigh. "If he thinks you can offer him more wealth and power, he'll want you. And if he thinks the king was able to take over the entire land because of the Lamians, he may think you can help him break away from the Eldership."

Worry lines creased his forehead as he frowned. "I've already noticed how much control Alirik has in Pallen, and he's not even a member of the Eldership. He's been living in the castle for over a year as a guest, and I think he's controlling the assembly. I've checked into Pallen's military, and there seems to be a lot of recruiting going on—more than the Eldership can afford or is legally allowed."

"What is the assembly?" Alissia asked, selecting a fresh pastry.

"There's only one group of elders, and they're based in Allure. Each city has a group of assembly members that report to the elders, so the assembly is the highest form of government within a city."

Alissia wiped the honey from the corners of her mouth and swallowed her bite. "So, I'm going to the Eldership where Alrik is. And what am I supposed to do there?"

Grady stood and walked around the table to sit down beside her. Pulling her into his lap, he kissed her forehead. "He doesn't know we know about the bounty, so he'll want you to trust him. He'll probably try to buy your friendship, and all you have to do is smile and act timid until we find a way out of this."

"Why don't we just go to the mountains now?" she asked hopefully, setting her unfinished pastry on a cloth napkin. Remembering Anika and Langley, she frowned, knowing she could not leave them behind.

He sighed. "I wish we could, but you haven't looked outside. A band of soldiers and two of their league members accompanied Luke and me 'for our protection.' I'm sure you'll be given your own personal group of bodyguards once we get to the castle, and a handmaiden will follow you around, as well. Our biggest challenge is that you'll be heavily guarded at all times."

He paused before adding, "It also means moments like this won't be possible. I've told them we were never engaged, and my only concern for you was to introduce you to the Eldership. I did this so they'd trust me with more information when it comes to you."

Grady moved Alissia's hair from her face, and his fingers began to caress her neck. "If they knew my true feelings, they would never tell me anything. As far as they know, you bonded with Anika. I was concerned about your memory loss and wanted to introduce you to the Eldership, and Luke was traveling home when he saved you from some kidnappers in one of the villages. His only concern was to get you back to Pallen, where you want to be."

He lifted her head and looked into her eyes. "Alissia, no matter how distant and unemotional I appear in front of the Eldership, never forget that I love you, and I won't leave you. We'll find a way out of this, and I'll take you to the Lamians." His eyes searched hers as he asked, "You haven't forgotten that I love you, have you?"

She shook her head, and he leaned down to give her a long, tender kiss.

"What's wrong?" he whispered, pulling away. His fingers caressed her neck as he stared down at her questioningly.

Guilt filled Alissia as she stared up at Grady. Not wanting to hurt him more than she already had, she struggled for the right way to tell him about Luke.

She heard the sadness in his voice as he said, "I know you thought I hurt you, and you've been traveling alone with Luke. You're beautiful and easy to fall in love with. Has something happened between the two of you?"

Alissia's brows furrowed. "We've kissed twice this week," she admitted softly.

He did not seem surprised, and he asked, "Do you still have feelings for me?"

She nodded.

"Do you have feelings for him?"

Alissia's eyes went to Grady's shirt collar as she thought about Luke. She told herself she was only physically attracted to him, but something within her disagreed. Only the night before, fear and worry consumed her, and she fell asleep missing him.

"I don't know," she confessed, looking back at Grady. "I mean, I walked away from him both times thinking about you. I've thought of you every day, and I've missed you ever since I left Pallen. Once I began to realize you were innocent, I hated myself for what I did. I didn't like being around Luke in the beginning, and I even drugged him and ran away."

Grady smiled slightly. "He told me everything last night. He said you could make a man miserable if you really wanted to, and he warned me to never eat anything you cook." He paused before adding somberly, "He also told me about how you escaped your kidnappers, and I'm sure something like that isn't going to be easy to forget."

Alissia rested her head against his shoulder as he held her in his arms, and they sat in silence for a moment.

"I love you, Alissia. I'm going to do everything I can to get you back to the mountains, and then I want to spend the rest of my life with you. That's what I want you to think about every night when you rest your head on your pillow, and that's what I want you to dream about."

"What about Nevara?" she asked, wishing she could find comfort in his arms. "Where is she?"

"She was terrified and left Pallen immediately after telling me about Holt's death, but I thought Anika was going to kill her before she left. I don't think I've ever seen her that angry."

Regret filled Alissia. "I didn't even tell Anika and Langley goodbye. Are they mad at me?"

"No, they understand. They've been very worried, and they're eager to see you. Anika needs you right now. She hates living at the Eldership, and she's miserable." He lifted Alissia's face to look into her eyes. "Which means you should start getting ready. She's waiting for you."

Grady leaned down, and they shared a kiss. Then he let out a sigh and nudged her from his lap. They walked into the sitting room to find Luke on the sofa.

Noticing them, Luke set his book aside and stood. Although he glanced at Grady's hand holding hers, he did not seem bothered. Instead, he smiled and said, "Why don't you get dressed before we leave? You look as though you were up all night."

Alissia smiled back at him, hiding the hurt and rejection she felt. As she turned to go to the bedroom, he said, "Oh, there's a package for you on the chair."

She picked up the bundle, and once alone in the bedroom, she opened the package to find a new riding outfit with matching boots and underclothing. Knowing how much Anika loved to shop, Alissia laughed out loud as she grabbed her pack before making her way to the bathroom.

As she put on the black, lacy undergarments, she remembered Anika insisting she buy something similar to go beneath her dress for the ball. Her new, black riding boots matched her pants that fit like leggings. Her grey undershirt felt soft against her skin and matched the long, grey shirt made of a warm, thick material. A small pair of gold earrings shaped like hearts and a pair of black sunglasses finished the outfit, along with a grey headscarf made in a soft and thick material.

Alissia smiled at her reflection in the mirror. The new clothing boosted her confidence, and it warmed her heart to know Anika picked them out for her. After collecting her clothing, she walked into the sitting room to find both men on the sofa.

"I see Anika spent more of your money," she teased, rubbing her hand along the front of her shirt. "I love it!"

Grady gave a tight smile. "No, Alissia, I believe it's a gift from Luke."

The assassin sat with his hands behind his head and his legs stretched out in front of him, crossed at the ankles. Staring at her with a broad grin on his face, he winked.

Heat rushed across Alissia's cheeks, and she tried to appear calm as she walked the short distance to the bedroom. Once alone, she slumped against the closed door.

Chapter 29

The sound of low, angry voices soon caught her attention, and she opened the door to find Grady and Luke standing in front of the sofa, glaring at each other. Noticing her, they both smiled.

She tried to think of something to say, but she found herself completely speechless.

"Alissia, I need to talk to you before we leave," said Luke.

She nodded and looked expectantly at Grady. He walked toward her with an unreadable expression on his face.

"You'll need to pack everything," he said, meeting her at the door of the bedroom, "and I forgot to tell you to use your fake accent. Some of the words you use can be recognized by a Watcher."

She nodded, and he bent down and kissed her tenderly on the lips. Then he turned and walked out of the cabin.

As soon as the door closed, Luke said roguishly, "You look tempting today."

Alissia's face twisted into a scowl. "What are you doing? Are you trying to hurt Grady even more?"

He held up his hands, as if to surrender. "I bought those before I knew he was coming. In fact," he added, dropping his hands, "I did something nice for you, and now you're angry with me. I'm beginning to get confused. Am I supposed to be mean to you?"

Her face softened, and she let out a frustrated sigh. "Thank you for the new outfit. I just wish it had happened differently. That's all."

"So, you want me to continue to be nice to you?" Luke asked, wearing a lop-sided grin.

"Not if it's going to hurt Grady."

The smile left his face. "Did you tell him?"

"Tell him what?"

"You finally had the chance to tell Grady that you love him."

Alissia stared at Luke in disbelief. "And when was I supposed to do that? After asking for his forgiveness for leaving, or after telling him about kissing you?" She laughed bitterly, throwing her hands into the air. "Or maybe it was after he explained how I'm about to be dragged to the Eldership by an army that thinks I'm a Lamian!"

Luke grinned. "You told him about us?"

"I'm not going to lie to him. And what 'us', Luke? There is no 'us'. You didn't seem too bothered when I held his hand or kissed him. You didn't even notice." She let out a harsh breath. Then her eyes locked with his. "This isn't a game, and you're hurting Grady. I'm beginning to think you enjoy it."

He shot across the room. With his eyes boring into hers, he said heatedly, "You really want to know the truth? I noticed every look and touch you gave him, and that was after I had to sit out here while the two of you had your private reunion in the kitchen! You have no idea what it feels like to have to sit and watch you with him!"

Alissia took a step back, shocked. Shaking her head, she uttered, "This is just a physical attraction, and we'll get over it."

"Is that what you're telling yourself?" Luke's face softened, along with his voice. "Do you know you talk in your sleep? At first, you would mumble Grady's name, but that changed. You now call out my name before you wake each night. It's different than how you mumbled Grady's. When you call out mine, you sound as though you need me—you want me."

His dark eyes suddenly blazed with emotion. "I did the right thing, Alissia! I didn't pursue you—no matter how badly I wanted to. I held back, but you came to me. I woke to you staring down at me."

Alissia could barely breathe as Luke paused, watching her. She felt herself swallow, and he smiled slightly. "The look on your face said everything that night," he said softly. "You wanted me just as much as I wanted you."

She shook her head. "I was just curious and was only going to touch your hair," she said weakly. "I wasn't going to kiss you."

"But, you did kiss me," he asserted, "and it wasn't a small one, either. The only thing that's keeping you from me is the guilt you feel for hurting Grady, and you've never even told him how you feel." Luke took a step toward her. "Why didn't you tell him when you had the chance?"

Alissia took a step back.

His lips curled into a smile, and he took another step. When she tried to back away, he gently grabbed her wrist and pulled her into his arms.

"It's just physical," she breathed.

He shook his head and began to brush his lips along the side of her face. "You were worried about me last night, weren't you?" he whispered, his warm breath caressing her neck. "You missed me just as much as I missed you."

Chills went throughout her entire body as his lips slowly traveled to her mouth, teasing her along the way. "Stop fighting me, Alissia," he said firmly, yet tenderly.

Although she told herself to pull away, her lips parted, welcoming his tongue. One of his hands cupped the back of her head, while the other one pulled her into him. Losing herself in the tender kiss, Alissia clung to his shirt. Her body melted in his embrace.

After a while, Luke broke the kiss. With his dark, intense eyes staring into hers, he asked, "Do you really want me to leave you alone?"

Yes! Yes! Yes! Tell him to leave you alone! her mind screamed. However, the unguarded, questioning look on his face only strengthened the battle raging within her.

His fingers burned into her tingling skin as he pushed her hair back. His mouth went to her neck, and she closed her eyes, his touch intoxicating. He lifted his lips to her ear and whispered, "Tell me, Alissia. Do you really want me to stop pursuing you?"

She squeezed her eyes shut, reminding herself of Grady.

Luke traced his fingertips down her face and along her neck, and she opened her eyes to meet his gaze.

"If you truly want me to stop, I'll leave you alone," he promised. His eyes searched her face, studying her intently. "Do you want me to stop?"

Alissia closed her eyes, hating herself for being weak. "No," she conceded, her voice barely audible.

Luke's mouth came down hard on hers, and he lifted her into his arms. His touch took a passionate turn, as if he had been holding back until that moment.

Alissia's arms curled around his neck, and her fingers dug into his hair. No longer fighting with herself, she freely gave in to her desire.

After a while, Luke broke the kiss and stared into her eyes, their ragged breathing the only sound to be heard. With a determined look on his face, he vowed, "I *will* find a way to get you out of this, and you *will* be mine one day."

Barely able to breathe, she followed him to the sofa, where they both sat down and turned to each other.

"I need to tell you what to do while in Pallen," he said, in a serious tone. He took her by the hand. "I'll have to appear distant, and I don't know when we'll have another moment alone, as you'll be watched and guarded at all times."

"Why does everyone have to act that way toward me?"

"Not everyone. You'll have Anika and Langley as friends, but if Grady or I show our true feelings, we won't be able to do as much for you. They wouldn't trust us." He frowned and gave a shrug. "Although, I doubt they will anyway. I have a better chance with them than Grady does, though."

"Why do you say that?"

"If they're planning a war with Pallen, they'll want other cities to join them. I'm from the North, and I'm sure they'll want us as allies. However, Grady isn't just from Allure. He's a high official from Allure. We both believe they don't want him dead, and they may want to use him in the future."

Staring hard into her eyes, he added, "But, they'll kill him if necessary. Grady needs to stay as far away from you as possible, because they aren't going to want you to be close to a high official from Allure." He paused, and she nodded in understanding. "Anika and Langley aren't as important, and they're safe as long as they keep you happy and don't cause any trouble.

"Grady did the right thing by telling them his main goal was to get you to trust the Eldership and that you got close to Anika during your time together. Now, they believe he's given you positive thoughts toward them, and you're not in love with someone from Allure. Anika will be used as a way to keep you happy as you transition into your new life at the Eldership."

He frowned, furrowing his brows. "Alissia, the Eldership in Pallen would never have let them return to Allure, because they know too much about you. If Grady had not gone to them with his story, the three of them would have become a target. His story most likely saved their lives."

Alissia looked down at her lap and closed her eyes. After taking a deep breath, she met Luke's gaze again. "Am I going to cause a war?"

"No," he answered, shaking his head. "Alrik's been living at the Eldership for a year. He was making preparations long before you came along. Even if Pallen doesn't start a war, other cities aren't happy with Allure."

He pulled her into his arms. "We'll find a way out of this. I'll act loyal to their cause and earn their trust. I've already sent for my people, and we won't be alone."

Alissia put her hand against his chest, taking comfort in his confidence and strength. "What about Grady, Anika, and Langley? I won't leave them behind."

Luke sighed. "Somehow, I knew you'd feel that way."

She pulled out of his embrace. "You're not going to kidnap me again 'for my own safety,' are you?"

"No, Alissia. You would never forgive me for that," he assured. Shaking his head, he added, "You're the most stubborn person I know, and you never make things easy for me."

She crossed her arms. "Is this your way of pursuing me?"

"No, this is." He stood and picked up a bundle from the floor. Then he pulled her to her feet and set the bag on the sofa. "I have some accessories for your new clothing," he said, untying the bundle. He moved aside so Alissia could see the contents, and she laughed, staring down at a pile of small daggers.

"Luke, do you know anything about women?"

"One day, you'll thank me," he said confidently. He picked up a dagger and held it up. "Jewelry won't save your life, but these will."

He squatted and slid the knife into her left boot. After grabbing another one, he did the same to her right boot. Although Alissia noticed the sheaths inside the boots while dressing, she did not realize they actually served a purpose.

Without warning, Luke lifted the left side of her shirt and under-shirt, and he placed a dagger in another sheath attached at her waist, on the inside of her pants. As he repeated the process on the other side, she began to feel hot and flustered, aware of his hands touching her bare skin. He looked up with a knowing grin.

"Having fun?" she asked sarcastically.

He chuckled. "Yes, I am." He stood and picked up the last dagger, situated in a leather sheath with straps dangling from it. "Shall I put this on you now?"

She stared at the dagger in confusion. "Where does it go?"

"It's a shoulder strap that goes under your shirt."

Alissia snatched the dagger and sheath from his hand. "I'll figure it out on my own later."

Luke laughed heartily before saying, "This will give you five hidden daggers. I could have chosen a loose pair of pants with extra pockets, and you would have been able to hide more."

"Why didn't you?"

His gaze went to her legs. "I like these much better."

"Luke, did anyone help you go shopping?" she asked, her eyes narrowed.

"No."

"Not even the undergarments?"

The corners of his mouth turned up. "Not even the undergarments. I had to do a lot of visualizing in that store, and I even had a discussion about you with the wonderful ladies that worked there."

Shaking his head, he added, "And can you believe they said most men aren't comfortable shopping in their little store? I learned a lot, though, and I think we should go there together sometime, if we ever get the chance."

"And when did you find the time to go shopping?" she asked, refusing to give him the satisfaction of seeing her flustered.

"I got to Pallen just as the shops opened, and I went to the same ones I go to for my clothing and weapons. It didn't take long to pick them out." As if proud of himself, he added, "The other items were a bit harder, but I managed it all in less than two hours."

"How did you get caught?"

The humor left his face, and he ran his hand through his hair. "I didn't. I got noticed, and I knew I couldn't come back without being watched."

"Do you really think we'll be able to get away?" she asked, not hiding her worry.

He surprised her with a kiss that left her breathless. "We'll figure something out," he said, still holding her in his arms. "And you never know. Once they see how much trouble you are, they may even throw you out of the city."

She rolled her eyes, and he let go of her and began to walk toward the kitchen. "You should go pack while I put things away." He stopped and turned around. "Oh, I need your ring back."

She took off the wedding ring and held it out. "What will Pallen be like?"

Luke took her hand as he accepted the ring. "It'll be beautiful," he said soothingly. "There'll be extravagant parties. You'll be given the finest clothing, and you'll live in a castle. All women want that. Remember?"

Alissia tried to smile. "And I'll be a prisoner."

"There's that, too, but they prefer to call it 'special guest.' Just act timid and remember you don't have any memories. You're scared and alone."

He squeezed her hand and grinned. "I remember the first time I saw you at the ball. You looked uncomfortable and shy. You fooled me, and I was surprised by your fiery personality the first night I met you." He chuckled. "I think that's why I put you to sleep that night. I knew you were trouble the moment you assaulted me."

"You told me to think of you as my knight in shining armor," she said wryly.

He gave her a quick kiss on the cheek. "And that's what I am." Dropping her hand, he said, "Now, get packed. There are a lot of men outside waiting for you, and you're already playing the part of royalty by having them wait so long."

Alissia went into the bedroom and threw her belongings into her packs. Then she put on her cloak and gloves.

"What about Fang?" she asked, rejoining Luke in the sitting room.

He thought for a moment. "Can you get him to follow you to the city without being seen? Then, he can travel along the city walls and stay in the forest between the castle and the mountains."

"I can."

"Anything else?" he asked.

"No."

He shook his head. "You forgot something."

"What?"

He took her in his arms and gave her a long, heated kiss. Pulling away, he groaned in frustration. "Our last kiss for a long time. Now, are you ready?"

Alissia took a deep breath before nodding.

Luke put his hand on the door handle. "Remember," he said firmly, "you're shy, scared, and timid. So, don't go out there looking as if you want to kill everyone."

She gave him a dirty look. "I'm not mean."

"Just remember. You're a lost and lonely, little Lamian. Not a feisty, stubborn, little pixet that'll poison you the first opportunity she gets."

Before Alissia could ask what he meant by pixet, he opened the door. She took a deep breath and walked past him, ready to confront her future.

Unexpected Entrapment

Alissia Roswell: Book Two

Chapter 1

Alissia Roswell stood on the porch of the cabin and stared at the large group of men before her. She quickly estimated there to be about twenty of them sitting on horses in perfect form. Almost all of them were wearing maroon uniforms trimmed with gold, and they each wore a sword at their side. Some also carried bows and arrows. They were sitting straight in their saddles, at attention. Two men wearing black were at the back of the line, and she guessed them to be the two members of the league.

Her first instinct was to stand tall and stare back at them defiantly, but she immediately remembered what Luke had just told her. She was to act shy and timid, which was the complete opposite of how she felt now—cornered and forced to go somewhere against her will.

If she could not fight her way out of the situation, she should at least be able to get some gratification by causing trouble.

She then noticed Grady and another man in uniform walking towards her, and she quickly looked down, cringing to herself. As her thoughts went to what had just happened in the cabin, blood rushed to her face. Not only had she betrayed Grady by giving in to Luke's advances, but she had also told Luke she did not want him to leave her alone.

"Lady Alissia, this is Captain Bayard. He will be leading your escort today to the castle," Grady said.

She looked up and politely nodded as the captain gave a short bow. "It is an honor to meet you, Lady Alissia. Are you ready to begin the short journey?"

"I am," she answered softly, with a smile.

She followed the captain to a horse in the middle of the group, and then she smiled at the young, uniformed man holding his hands together for her to step onto. Once on the horse, she watched Luke and Grady follow the captain to the front of the procession.

She looked down and closed her eyes as she began to search for Fang with her mind, and she was surprised when she found him frantically pacing near the edge of the tree line. He was confused, panting wildly, and did not know what he should do to protect her. She felt his urge to bellow a long, deep howl, but she immediately began to soothe him.

As her horse began to move, she completely focused on soothing the agitated wolf with her mind, and it was not long before he stopped pacing. She continued to comfort him as he secretly began to follow the group of horses.

After a while, her mind drifted to what all she had learned from Grady and Luke that morning. Her fix-it personality continuously tried to think of a solution to their situation, but her frustration quickly grew strong as she realized there was nothing she could do. She would have to rely upon Grady and Luke, and Grady seemed powerless at this point. Luke would have to find a way for them to get out of the city, but how could he save them all?

She could not help but feel responsible for Grady, Anika, and Langley. If they had never met her and tried to help her, their lives would not be in danger. In a way, this was her fault. They were in Pallen because of her.

Guilt consumed her as she thought over what had happened back at the cabin. Although she had kissed men before, she had never gone further with them, except for the night she had been raped while on what seemed at first like a teenage date. This morning she had passionately kissed two men within the same hour. Although she had heard stories from her friends and had never judged them, her actions went beyond who she was.

She had never really believed in love or getting close to anyone, yet she had been drawn to both Grady and Luke back at the cabin. It frustrated her how she had completely lost herself in Luke's kiss, as if he were an intoxicating drug she was addicted to.

Once she could see the massive gates to the city of Pallen, her focus went back to Fang. Although he was much calmer than before, his fur was still standing straight up on his massive, tense body. She hated what she was about to do. Wolves were pack animals, and he had left the safety of his pack to be with her.

She scanned the area with her mind to check for other wolves and was relieved at the lack of their presence. She had already learned what a pack of wolves would do to a lone wolf found in their territory, and the idea of Fang being killed because of her filled her with fear.

She looked down and closed her eyes again, in an attempt to hide her own emotions.

"Fang, my dear protector, you cannot follow me once I get to the city. I want you to follow the wall of the city, and it will lead you towards the mountains." A sudden thought came to mind, and she added, hopefully, *"I have friends in the mountains, similar to me. If you find them, they will give you rest and shelter until I can meet you there."*

She felt his emotions surge, and she immediately began to soothe him. As the trail left the thick forest, she warned Fang to stop at the tree line. She had to push aside her own feelings of loss, as she commanded with authority, "*Stop, Fang! Follow the wall and go to the mountains.*" In an attempt to soothe his pain, she added, "*You are my protector, Fang. Be strong for me.*"

The large wolf sat down at the edge of the forest and began to whimper. Once again, she reminded him to be strong, and he sat up tall and proud for her. Although she soon lost her mental connection with him, she knew the wolf's eyes were staring directly at her, and they would continue to do so until she was no longer in sight.

Her group stopped at the gates to the city, and she watched as the captain handed something to one of the guards before they continued. As she passed through the gates, she noticed the same guard handling a bird and guessed he was sending a message to someone at the castle about her arrival. She took a deep breath and tried to calm herself.

Her anxiety grew even more as everyone around them turned to stare at her, the lone woman surrounded by guards traveling through the city. She pulled the hood of her cape lower over her head and was thankful for her dark glasses.

After traveling through the city, they moved along a private path surrounded by bright and bushy evergreen trees. The procession stopped near the edge of the trees, and Alissia heard the captain give orders before the men in front of her moved aside and motioned her forward.

She gave a confused look to the captain, Luke, and Grady as they smiled back at her. She then nudged her horse to move on and soon caught her breath as the castle came into her line of vision.

"Lady Alissia, welcome to your new home," Grady said as she stopped between him and the captain.

Alissia was speechless as she stared out in front of her. Her new home was a massive castle that circled endless gardens filled with gazebos, paths, statues, small ponds, and fountains. The garden alone was big enough that she could get lost in it for days, but the castle itself was something she could see herself never finding her way out of.

The castle was made of stone, and she guessed it to be bella flowers that covered most of the walls, even at the top. She immediately thought of how cold it had to be and wondered how hardy the bella flowers were to survive such frosty weather.

After a moment, Grady asked, "Is it as beautiful as I described?"

An ache caught in her throat as she realized he was putting on a show for the captain. "Yes, you were right. I will love it here," she responded politely.

He grinned and replied, "Welcome to the Eldership, Lady Alissia. I'm sure you will love it here."

So this is how it was to be? Yes, she had known how they would act towards each other while at the Eldership, but she had not anticipated the ache in her heart she would experience by acting so distant towards someone she loved.

As they began to move again, she looked down and thought about how hard this truly had to be for Grady. She knew he had been a wreck while she was missing; yet he had acted professional and personally uncommitted the entire time, even with his own life in danger. A new sense of respect filled her as she realized how strong Grady truly was.

The sound of horses' hooves on stone made her look up, and once again, she found herself in awe of her surroundings. They were now traveling on a stone path surrounded by an arched-canopy, covered in white bella flowers.

She stared at the backs of the three men traveling in front of her. Both Luke and Grady sat straight in their saddles, so unlike the casual way she was used to seeing them.

When she glanced at the soldier riding on her right side, he acknowledged her with a smile, and she looked down at her saddle.

It was not long before the covered path ended, and they were in a clearing near one of the entrances of the castle. They rode around a large, three-tiered fountain before stopping, and the two soldiers that had been riding at each of her sides dismounted. One of the men took the reins from her, while the other lifted her from the horse and set her down.

She then followed Captain Bayard, Grady, and Luke to a group of older men standing on the stairs to the castle entrance. The moment she recognized Alrik Durst as one of the men in the group, she had to look down to gather her emotions. She was thankful for her dark glasses, because she knew her anger would easily show through her glaring eyes.

Grady introduced Alissia to the five assembly members, but she quickly lost track of their names. She did not pay much attention to their polite welcome speeches either. She did, however, study Alrik's every word.

"My dear girl, we have been worried about you, and I am told we can thank Luke for your rescue and safety."

His overly kind tone with the same accent as Luke made her cringe, but she forced a polite smile onto her face and answered, "Yes, I am most grateful to him for bringing me back to Pallen, and I'm sorry to have caused everyone so much worry."

He picked up her hand and hooked it onto one of his arms as he began to lead her up the stairs. "You have nothing to apologize for," he said, patting her hand. "We're all glad you are safe, and everyone is excited to have you here as an ambassador for the Lamians. I do hope you can join my wife and me for dinner once you are settled in. I would love to hear more and want to help you in any way I can. Grady tells us you have suffered some memory loss."

If she had actually had memory loss and did not know he had put a bounty on her, she would have thought he was the kindest man she had ever met. His smile, touch, and voice truly appeared genuine. However, Alissia knew the truth--that he had slithered into Pallen, wrapped his coils around the city, and was constricting it to do his bidding--and she saw him for the foul and evil snake that he was.

At that moment, she was grateful she had been instructed to act shy and timid. She kept her head down as she forced a smile onto her face and answered, "Yes, I have lost a lot of my memories. As for dinner, maybe later." She looked up at him and added, "I am quite weary from all the traveling I've done. Although I am very grateful to Luke for his rescue, he was extremely determined to get me back to Pallen in a timely manner. He woke me before dawn each morning, and we traveled our entire days on horseback. I look forward to a comfortable bed, warmth on my skin, and some real food."

She hoped her words would buy her a few days of solitude.

He stopped walking and took her hand from his arm as he turned to face her. "Of course, you need plenty of rest. I can only imagine how difficult things have been for you." He squeezed her hand and added, "Say no more. I will let the assembly know you need rest. Do you require the service of one of our fine doctors?"

"No, thank you."

"Then I will leave you now in the hands of Odell. She is to be your lady's maid and will show you to your chambers. She will provide you with all your needs, and all you have to do is ask. Remember, this is your home now, and you are safe." He motioned towards the two guards standing off to the side and added, "The assembly has appointed guards to stand watch at all times over you. They will be posted outside your door, and the Eldership guarantees your safety. We will try our best to provide you with anything you require, so please don't be afraid to ask. We all want to help you."

Alissia nodded as he let go of her hand, and then she turned to face the long, grey-haired woman. Odell bowed her head politely, and the sound of Alrik's footsteps as he walked away helped to ease some of the tension Alissia had felt during his presence.

"Lady Alissia, it is an honor to meet you and be in your service. Shall I take you to your chambers now?"

"Yes, please."

Alissia followed the woman through the massive doors of the castle and stepped into a large foyer with a high, floral-painted ceiling. Bright sunlight came down from the large windows situated above the entrance doors. Thick, burgundy curtains hung down at each side of the windows, and a beautiful, enormous chandelier with polished glow stones hung in the center of the room. The floor was shiny and resembled white marble and had variously-colored glow stones assembled in place like tiles. The glow stones were arranged so that their natural light made an intricate floral pattern. Each of the walls held paintings and was decorated with detailed carvings. Large, handcrafted chairs, benches, and tables were positioned throughout the room with fresh flowers situated in various places.

Alissia did not realize she had stopped following Odell until the woman got her attention by saying, "It's amazing, isn't it?"

"Very," Alissia answered, in awe.

"Although the castle was originally built well over a thousand years ago, it is always under reconstruction, but the Eldership tries to keep things as they were."

Alissia nodded and started walking, but as soon as they went through another door, she became distracted again. Every room and hallway they entered while on the way to her chambers was filled with intricate designs and amazing art like nothing she had ever seen before.

Although she knew Pallen was a place known for its art and had seen a lot while walking through the city, nothing had compared to what she now saw in the castle. She imagined someone could spend years in the massive, city-like structure and still find new and amazing things to look at every day.

As they took an elegant elevator up to the third floor, she silently wondered what was the source of its power without electricity. In the end, she gave up on her curious thoughts and reminded herself she did not think like an engineer. She was sure she would still not understand, even if someone explained it to her, but this was a feeling she had grown quite accustomed to since being torn from her reality and dropped into this one.

Dear reader,

Thank you for joining Alissia on her adventure. Her journey continues in *Unexpected Entrapment,* where she's forced to reign in her fiery personality and pretend to be someone she's not.

The third book, *Unexpected Peril,* dives deeper into the fantasy realm and takes a darker turn. With new creatures and settings, it's a wild ride you don't want to miss.

Unexpected Beginning, the fourth book in the series, is set for release in the spring of 2016. With more intriguing creatures in a world full of imagery, Alissia's journey seemingly comes to an end.

But wait! It's not over! You'll soon learn this author is full of surprises. In the spring of 2017, be sure to look for *Unexpected Legends,* the fifth and final book in the series. After reading the last words of Alissia's story, you'll hug the book to your chest. With glistening eyes, you won't know whether to smile or cry.

I enjoy hearing from my readers and am greatly honored by the kind words and support I've received. Writing a novel is a passion that takes an immense amount of time and effort. I ask that you please leave an honest review on Goodreads or Amazon for the books in this series. It's the best way to show your support, especially for a new author such as myself.

You can receive the latest updates on my current projects by going to my website and subscribing to my newsletter. I can be found at the following locations:

www.tiannaholley.com
https://www.facebook.com/authortiannaholley
https://www.google.com/+TiannaHolley
https://twitter.com/holley_tianna
https://instagram.com/tiannaholley/
http://tiannaholley.tumblr.com
https://www.goodreads.com/author/show/7140745.Tianna_Holley

Thank you for your support,

Tianna Holley
Writer of passionate fantasy romance without the guilt.